WATTERS · LEYH · SOTUYO · LAIHO

LUMBERJANES™

PARENTS' DAY

BOOM!
BOX™

BOOM! BOX™

LUMBERJANES Volume Ten, December 2018. Published by BOOM! Box, a division of Boom Entertainment, Inc. Lumberjanes is ™ & © 2018 Shannon Watters, Grace Ellis, Noelle Stevenson & Brooklyn Allen. Originally published in single magazine form as LUMBERJANES No. 37-40. ™ & © 2016-2017 Shannon Watters, Grace Ellis, Noelle Stevenson & Brooklyn Allen. All rights reserved. BOOM! Box™ and the BOOM! Box logo are trademarks of Boom Entertainment, Inc., registered in various countries and categories. All characters, events, and institutions depicted herein are fictional. Any similarity between any of the names, characters, persons, events, and/or institutions in this publication to actual names, characters, and persons, whether living or dead, events, and/or institutions is unintended and purely coincidental. BOOM! Box does not read or accept unsolicited submissions of ideas, stories, or artwork.

For information regarding the CSPIA on this printed material, call: (203) 595-3636 and provide reference #RICH - 807194

BOOM! Studios, 5670 Wilshire Boulevard, Suite 400, Los Angeles, CA 90036-5679. Printed in USA. First Printing.

ISBN: 978-1-68415-278-0, eISBN: 978-1-64144-140-7

THIS LUMBERJANES FIELD MANUAL BELONGS TO:

NAME:_____

TROOP:_____

DATE INVESTED:_____

FIELD MANUAL TABLE OF CONTENTS

A Message from the Lumberjanes High Council.............................**4**

The Lumberjanes Pledge..**4**

Counselor Credits..**5**

LUMBERJANES PROGRAM FIELDS

Chapter Thirty-Seven...**6**

Chapter Thirty-Eight..**30**

Chapter Thirty-Nine...**54**

Chapter Forty..**78**

Cover Gallery: Let's Be Prank...**102**

LUMBERJANES FIELD MANUAL

For the Intermediate Program

Tenth Edition • October 1984

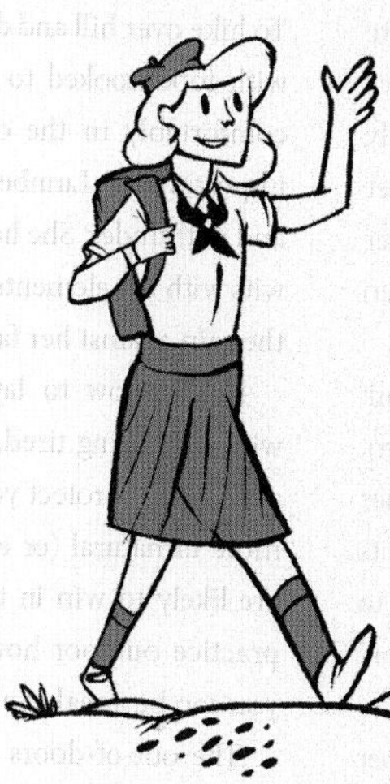

Prepared for the

Miss Qiunzella Thiskwin Penniquiqul Thistle Crumpet's

CAMP FOR [redacted] HARDCORE LADY-TYPES

"Friendship to the Max!"

A MESSAGE FROM THE LUMBERJANES HIGH COUNCIL

miss
Qiunzella Thiskwin
Penniquiqul Thistle Crumpet's
Camp for
HARDCORE LADY TYPES
FRIENDSHIP to the MAX!

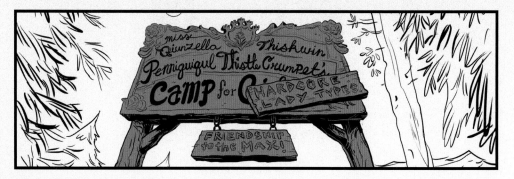

In our Lumberjanes Pledge, we ask so much of you scouts. And each and every child who dons a Lumberjanes sash or vest will excel in some of these areas and struggle in others. Some may eagerly rush to help or protect their friends, but have a harder time with being truthful, or compassionate, for example. This will vary greatly, and it is important to always recall that no two scouts — no two people — are the same.

Even if you find that respecting nature does not come naturally to you, or if you must fight against fear and anxiety in order to be brave and strong, always remember this: of all the things we ask of you, the most important Lumberjanes value is to do your best, every day, and in all you do. You will go through periods of difficulty and frustration — everyone does — but what matters most is not that you be perfect, or even that you always achieve and maintain your own perfect, but rather that you don't stop trying. Your ability to be a good friend, a good citizen, and a good scout is still developing, and the road will not always be perfectly smooth.

Like climbing a mountain, there will be be points at which you forge ahead tirelessly, and feel as if you've made more progress in the past few weeks than you had made in all the months before. But there will also be times when you seem to hit a plateau, and making progress seems impossibly difficult. There will even be times when you lose your foothold, and backslide into old mistakes or habits you thought you'd conquered.

There are many important things to remember, in this case. Firstly: you are newly, acutely aware of errors you've made before, or are making now, precisely because you have come so far and improved so much. Secondly: the most important thing is that you still continue to climb, because you will move forward...even if it takes longer than you might hope. Don't beat yourself up excessively, but do try to pick yourself up and continue onward. And lastly, and most importantly: this is exactly why the belay system exists. In mountain or rock climbing, belay refers to a system of ropes and pulleys, which are designed to keep you safe as you climb. In the Lumberjane scouts, think of your belay system as your friends, your family, and your counselors: the loving support system that surrounds you and catches you when you stumble or fall. They help you to right yourself again, to brush yourself off, to take a break and catch your breath, so that when you are ready, you can safely and happily continue your climb.

THE LUMBERJANES PLEDGE

I solemnly swear to do my best
Every day, and in all that I do,
To be brave and strong,
To be truthful and compassionate,
To be interesting and interested,
To pay attention and question
The world around me,
To think of others first,
To always help and protect my friends,
[redacted]
And to make the world a better place
For Lumberjane scouts
And for everyone else.

THEN THERE'S A LINE ABOUT GOD, OR WHATEVER

LUMBERJANES™

PARENTS' DAY

Written by
Shannon Watters
& Kat Leyh

Illustrated by
Ayme Sotuyo

Colors by
Maarta Laiho

Letters by
Aubrey Aiese

Cover by
Kat Leyh

Badge Design & Designer
Kara Leopard
Assistant Editor
Sophie Philips-Roberts
Series Editor
Dafna Pleban
Collection Editor
Jeanine Schaefer
Special thanks to **Kelsey Pate** for giving the Lumberjanes their name.

Created by **Shannon Watters, Grace Ellis, Noelle Stevenson & Brooklyn Allen**

LUMBERJANES FIELD MANUAL

CHAPTER THIRTY-SEVEN

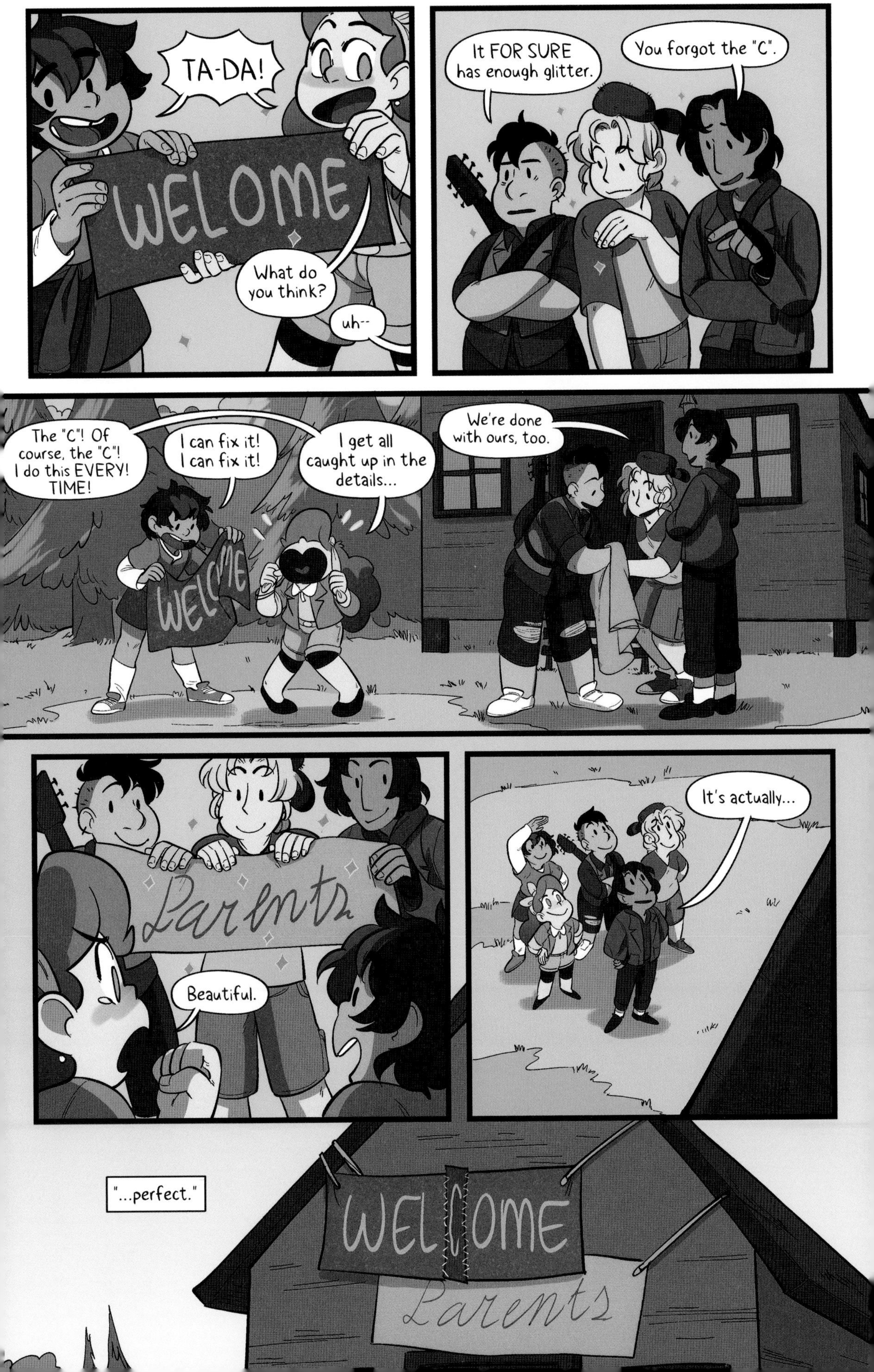
TA-DA!
WELOME
What do you think?
uh--
It FOR SURE has enough glitter.
You forgot the "C".
The "C"! Of course, the "C"! I do this EVERY! TIME!
I can fix it! I can fix it!
I get all caught up in the details...
We're done with ours, too.
Parents
Beautiful.
It's actually...
"...perfect."
WELCOME
Parents

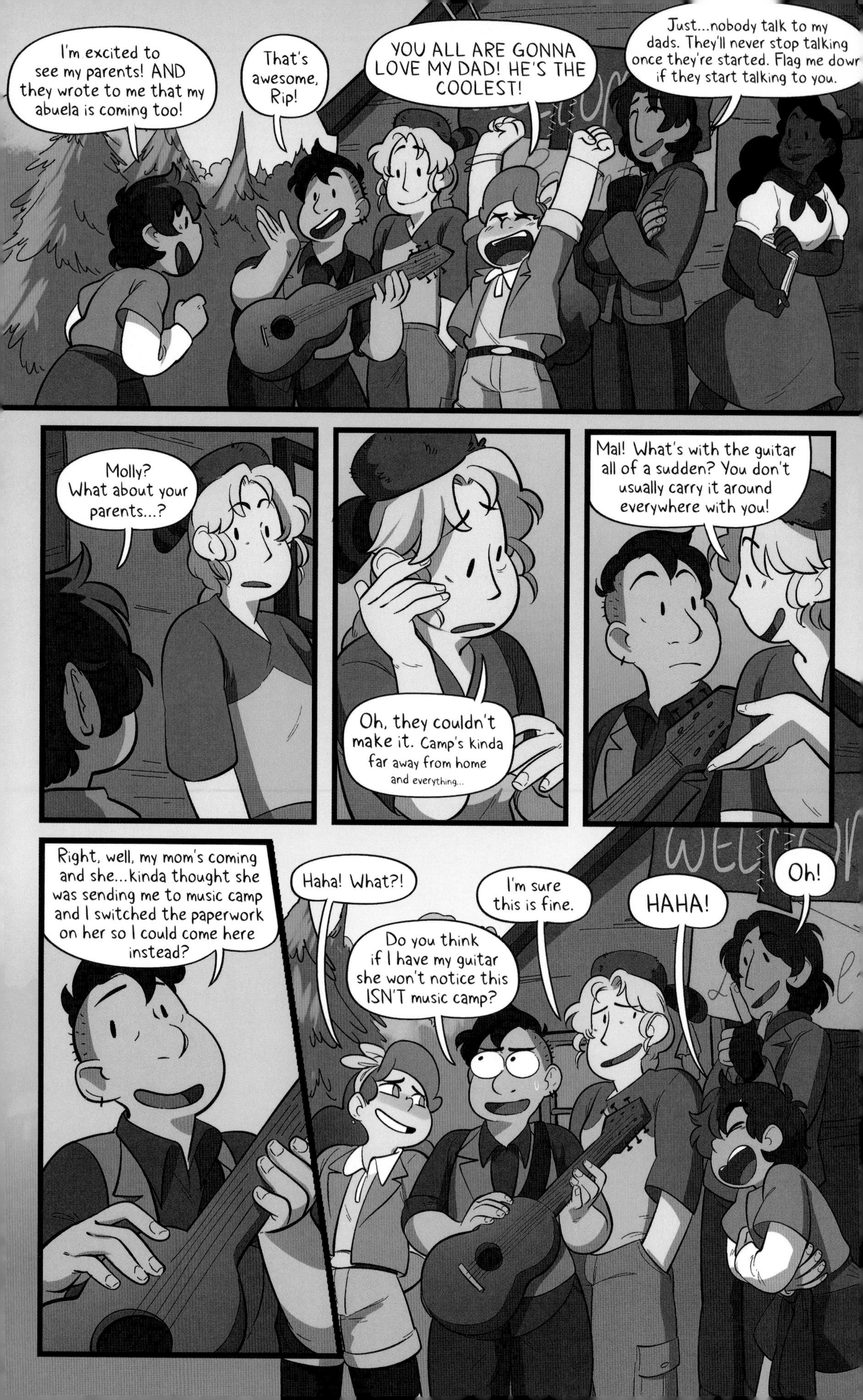

I'm excited to see my parents! AND they wrote to me that my abuela is coming too!
That's awesome, Rip!
YOU ALL ARE GONNA LOVE MY DAD! HE'S THE COOLEST!
Just...nobody talk to my dads. They'll never stop talking once they're started. Flag me dowr if they start talking to you.
Molly? What about your parents...?
Oh, they couldn't make it. Camp's kinda far away from home and everything...
Mal! What's with the guitar all of a sudden? You don't usually carry it around everywhere with you!
Right, well, my mom's coming and she...kinda thought she was sending me to music camp and I switched the paperwork on her so I could come here instead?
Haha! What?!
Do you think if I have my guitar she won't notice this ISN'T music camp?
I'm sure this is fine.
HAHA!
Oh!

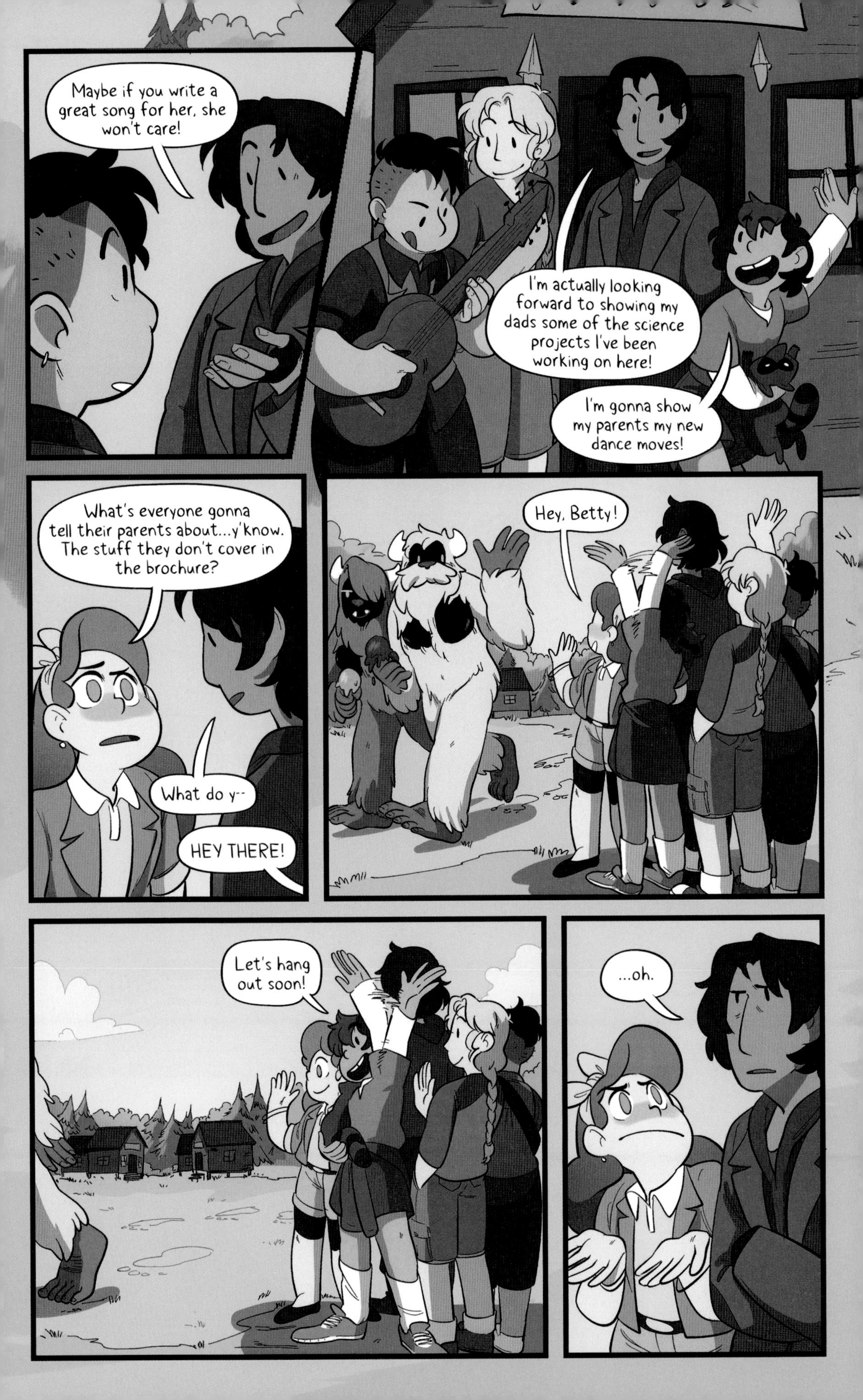
Maybe if you write a great song for her, she won't care!
I'm actually looking forward to showing my dads some of the science projects I've been working on here!
I'm gonna show my parents my new dance moves!
What's everyone gonna tell their parents about...y'know. The stuff they don't cover in the brochure?
What do y--
HEY THERE!
Hey, Betty!
Let's hang out soon!
...oh.

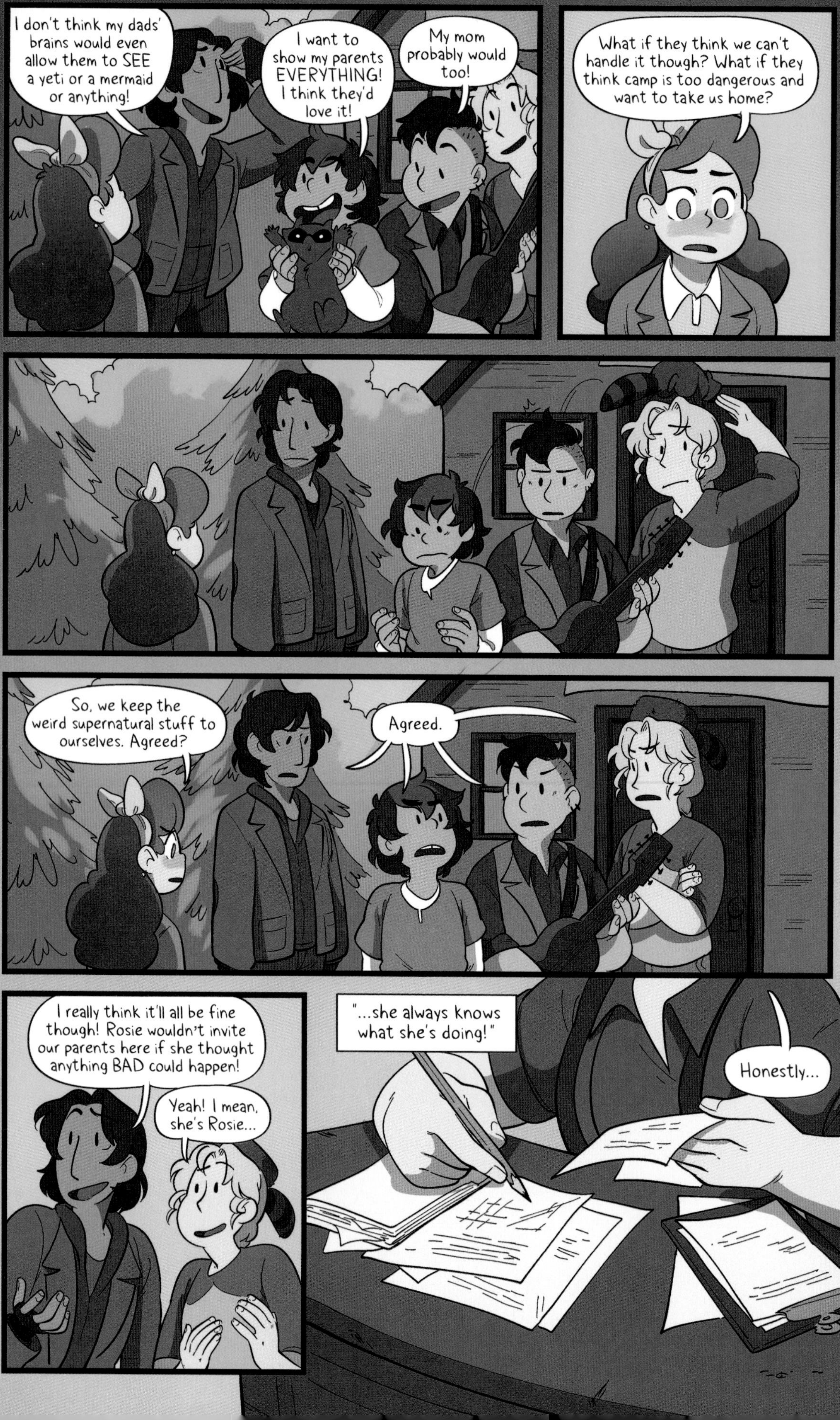
I don't think my dads' brains would even allow them to SEE a yeti or a mermaid or anything!
I want to show my parents EVERYTHING! I think they'd love it!
My mom probably would too!
What if they think we can't handle it though? What if they think camp is too dangerous and want to take us home?
So, we keep the weird supernatural stuff to ourselves. Agreed?
Agreed.
I really think it'll all be fine though! Rosie wouldn't invite our parents here if she thought anything BAD could happen!
Yeah! I mean, she's Rosie...
"...she always knows what she's doing!"
Honestly...

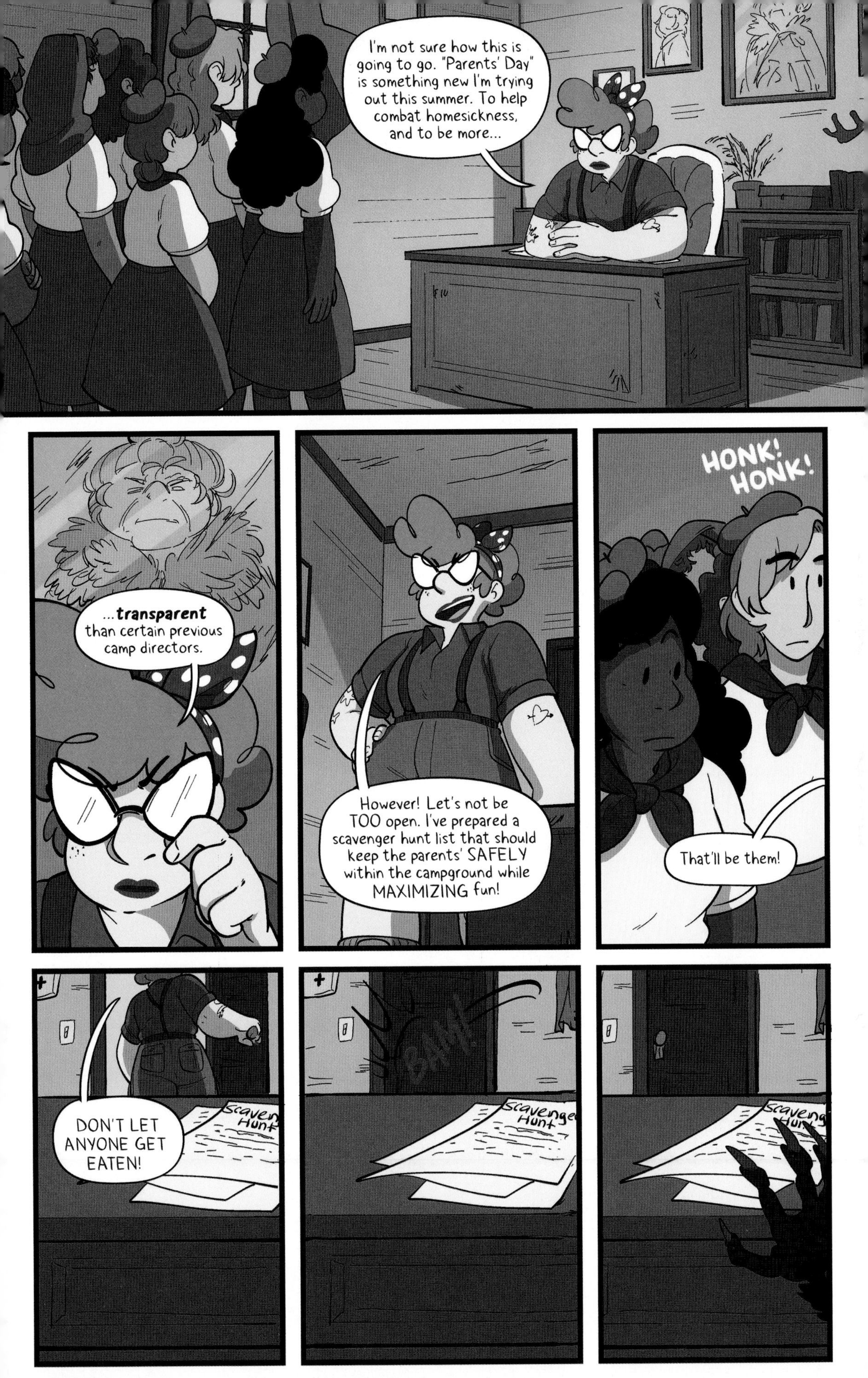
I'm not sure how this is going to go. "Parents' Day" is something new I'm trying out this summer. To help combat homesickness, and to be more...
...**transparent** than certain previous camp directors.
However! Let's not be TOO open. I've prepared a scavenger hunt list that should keep the parents' SAFELY within the campground while MAXIMIZING fun!
HONK! HONK!
That'll be them!
DON'T LET ANYONE GET EATEN!
Scavenger Hunt
BAM!
Scavenger Hunt
Scavenger Hunt

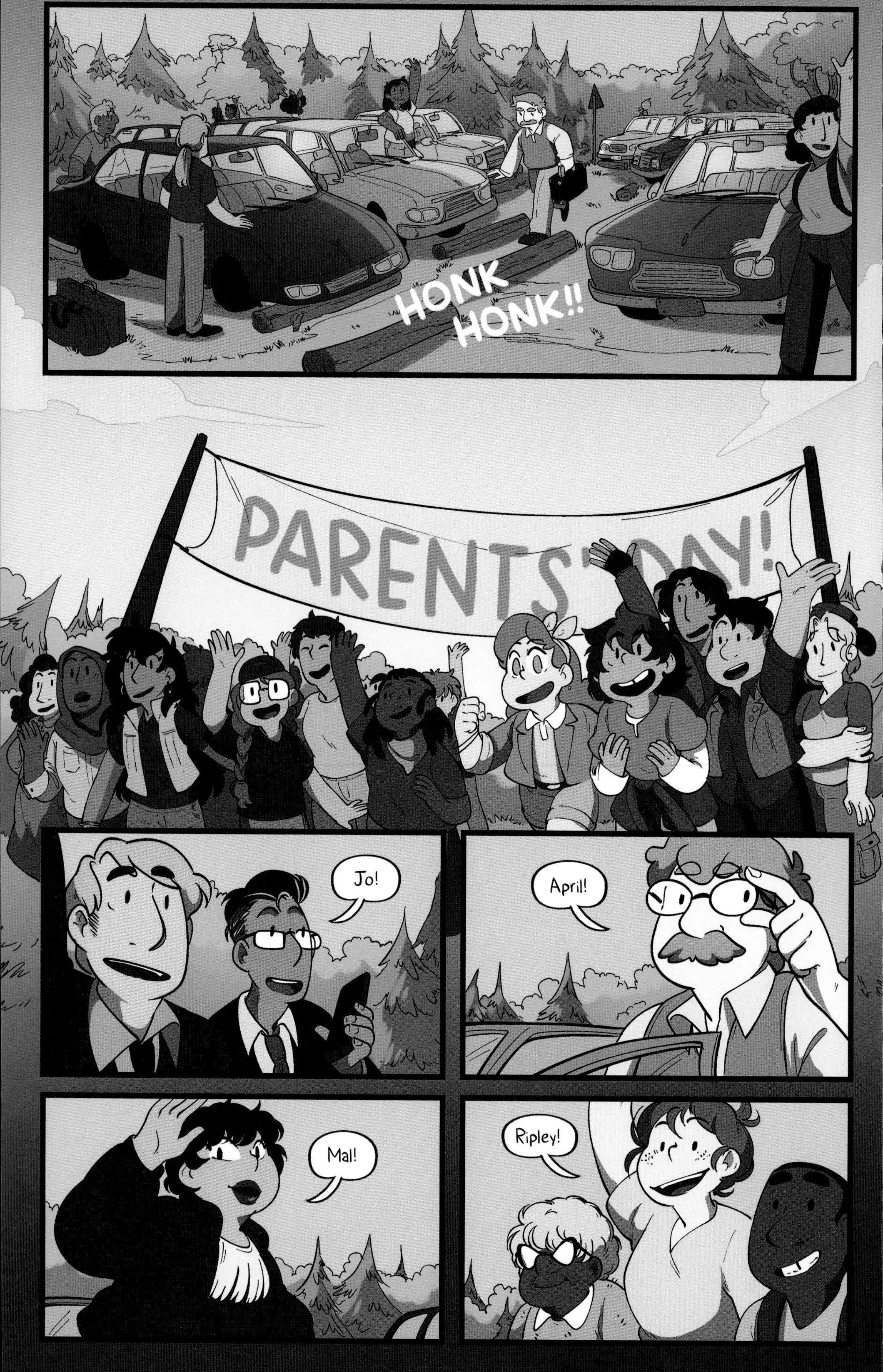
HONK
HONK!!
PARENTS' DAY!
Jo!
April!
Mal!
Ripley!

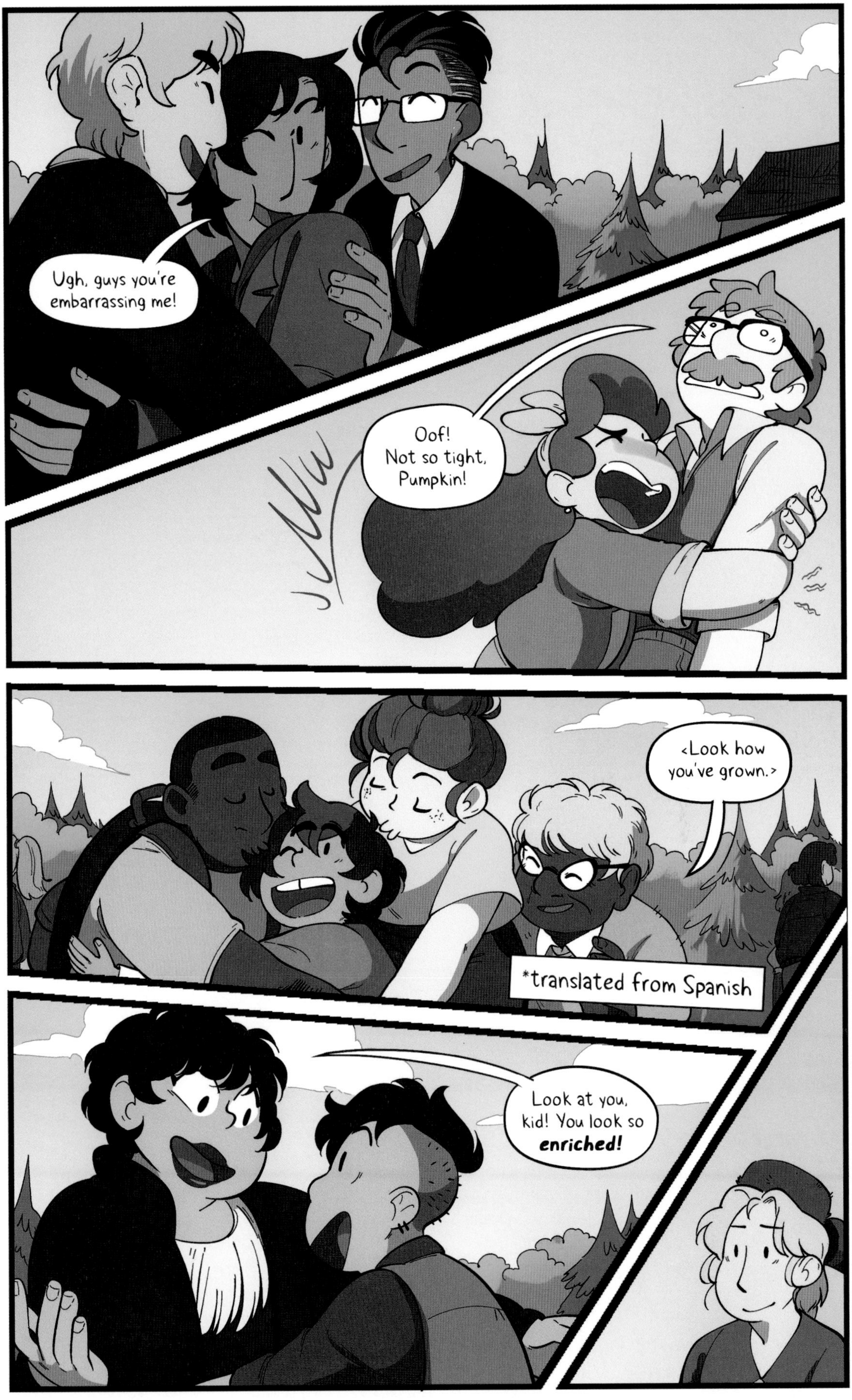
Ugh, guys you're embarrassing me!
Oof! Not so tight, Pumpkin!
<Look how you've grown.>
*translated from Spanish
Look at you, kid! You look so enriched!

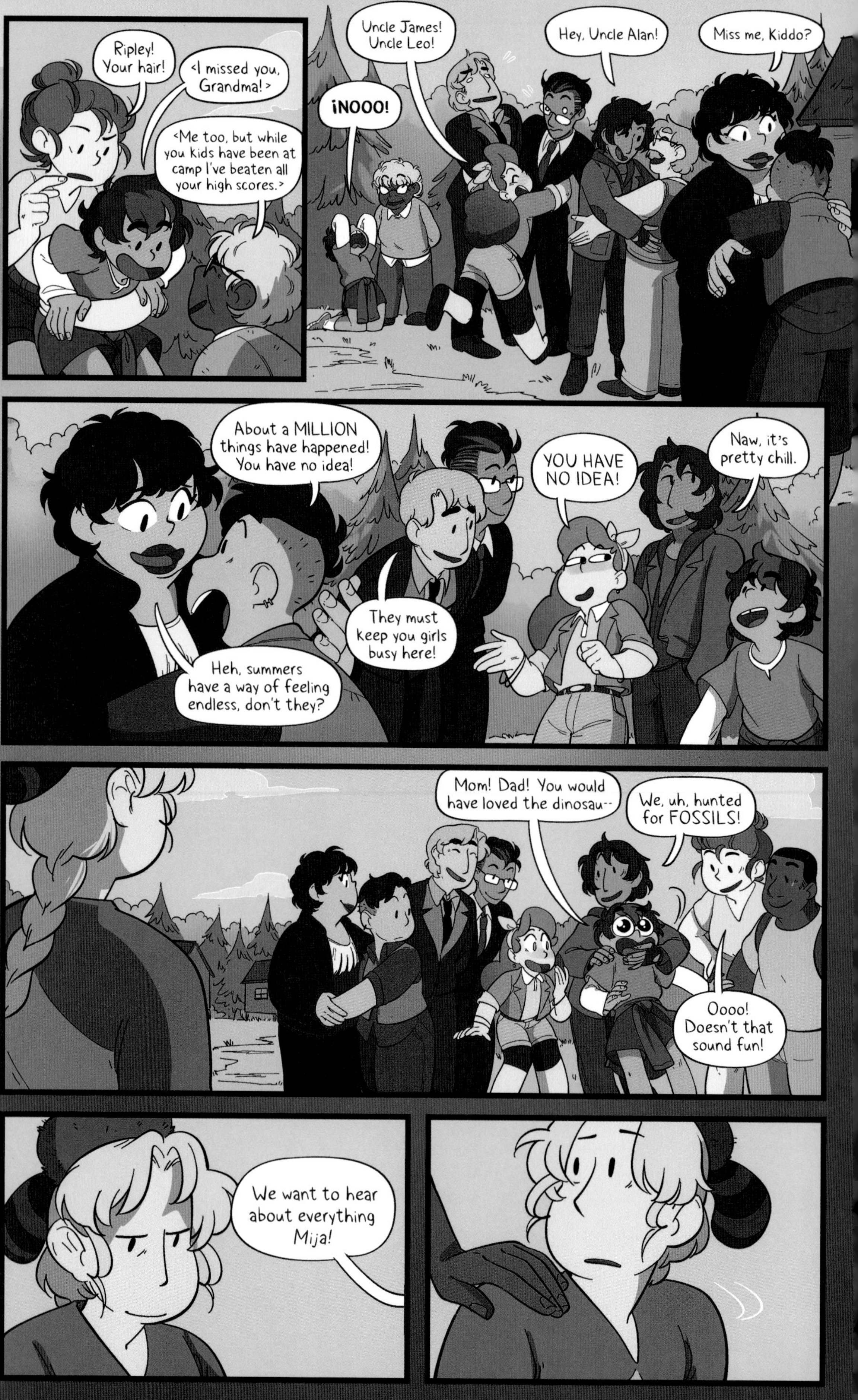
Ripley! Your hair!
<I missed you, Grandma!>
<Me too, but while you kids have been at camp I've beaten all your high scores.>
Uncle James! Uncle Leo!
¡NOOO!
Hey, Uncle Alan!
Miss me, Kiddo?
About a MILLION things have happened! You have no idea!
Heh, summers have a way of feeling endless, don't they?
They must keep you girls busy here!
YOU HAVE NO IDEA!
Naw, it's pretty chill.
Mom! Dad! You would have loved the dinosau--
We, uh, hunted for FOSSILS!
Oooo! Doesn't that sound fun!
We want to hear about everything Mija!

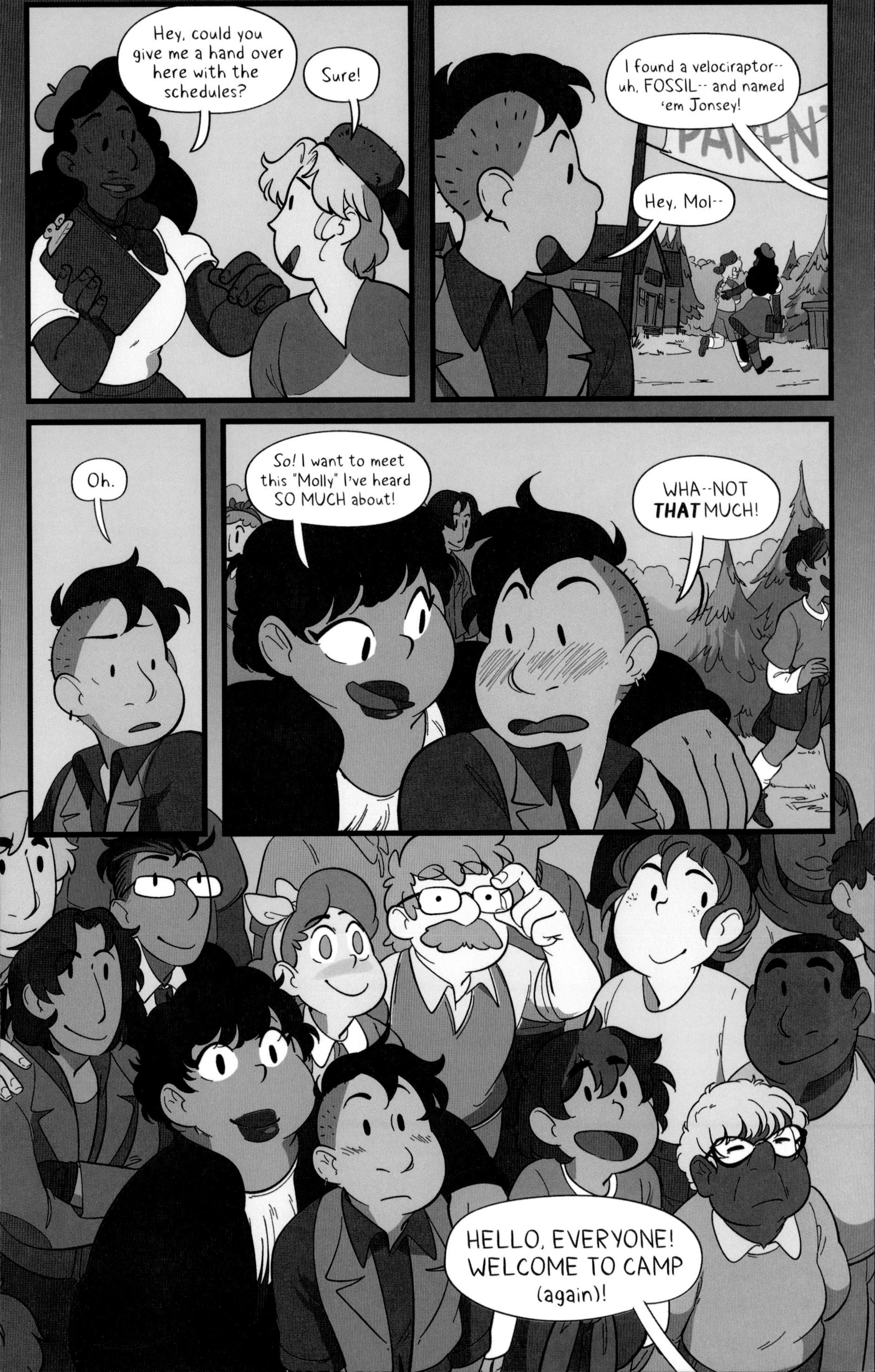
Hey, could you give me a hand over here with the schedules?
Sure!
I found a velociraptor-- uh, FOSSIL-- and named 'em Jonsey!
PAREN
Hey, Mol--
Oh.
So! I want to meet this "Molly" I've heard SO MUCH about!
WHA--NOT THAT MUCH!
HELLO, EVERYONE! WELCOME TO CAMP (again)!

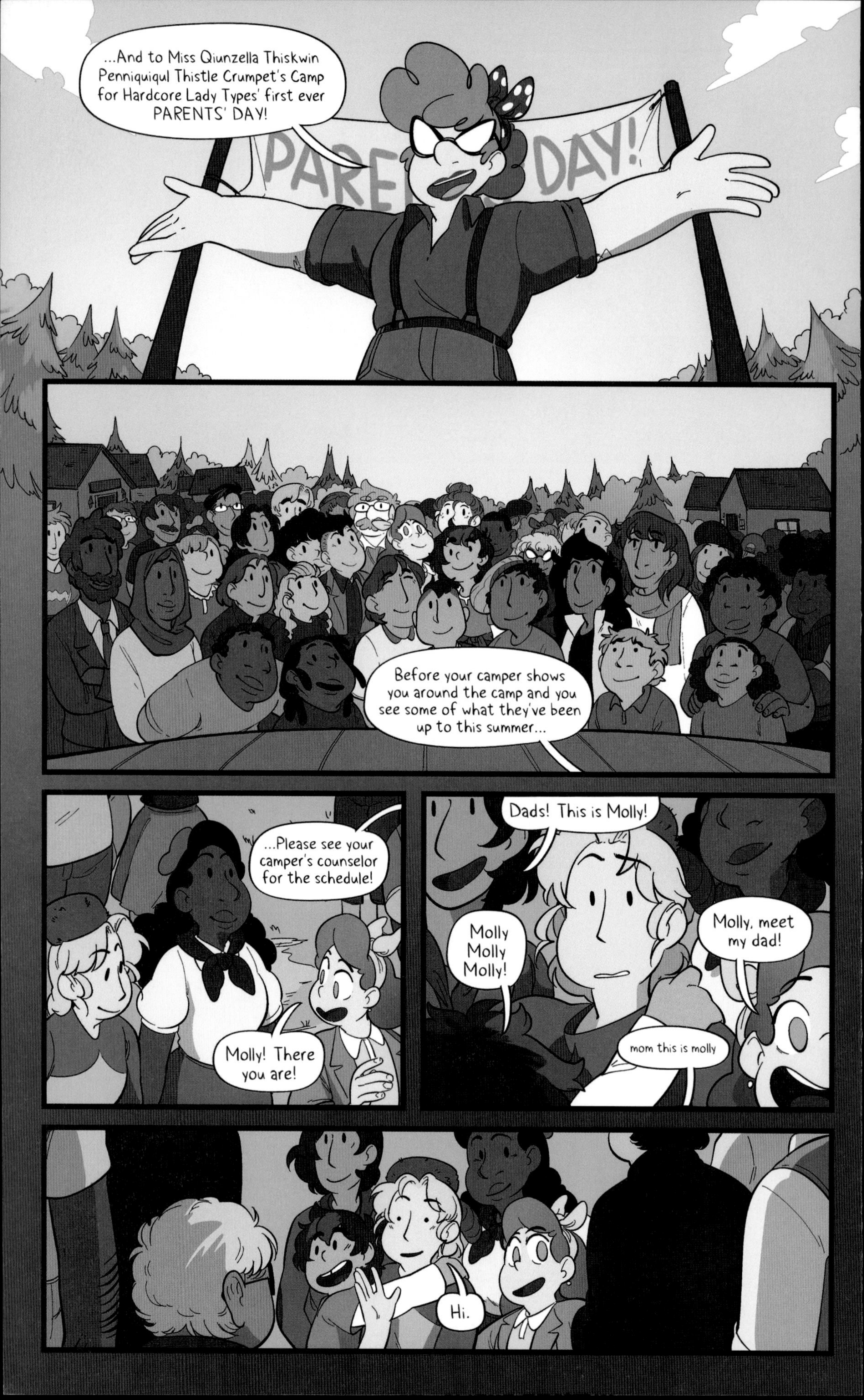
...And to Miss Qiunzella Thiskwin Penniquiqul Thistle Crumpet's Camp for Hardcore Lady Types' first ever PARENTS' DAY!
Before your camper shows you around the camp and you see some of what they've been up to this summer...
...Please see your camper's counselor for the schedule!
Molly! There you are!
Dads! This is Molly!
Molly Molly Molly!
Molly, meet my dad!
mom this is molly
Hi.

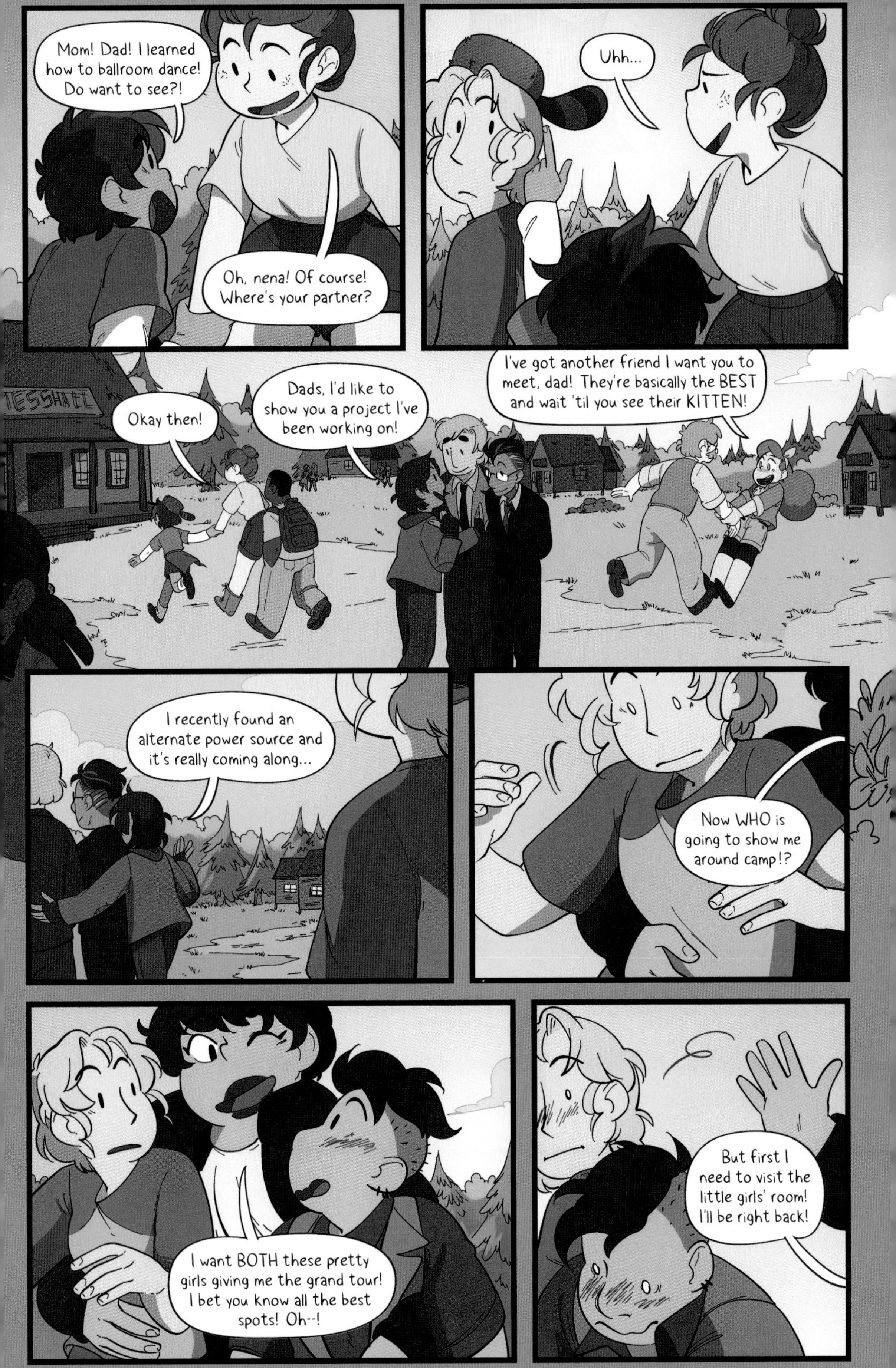
Mom! Dad! I learned how to ballroom dance! Do want to see?!
Oh, nena! Of course! Where's your partner?
Uhh...
Okay then!
Dads, I'd like to show you a project I've been working on!
I've got another friend I want you to meet, dad! They're basically the BEST and wait 'til you see their KITTEN!
I recently found an alternate power source and it's really coming along...
Now WHO is going to show me around camp!?
I want BOTH these pretty girls giving me the grand tour! I bet you know all the best spots! Oh--!
But first I need to visit the little girls' room! I'll be right back!

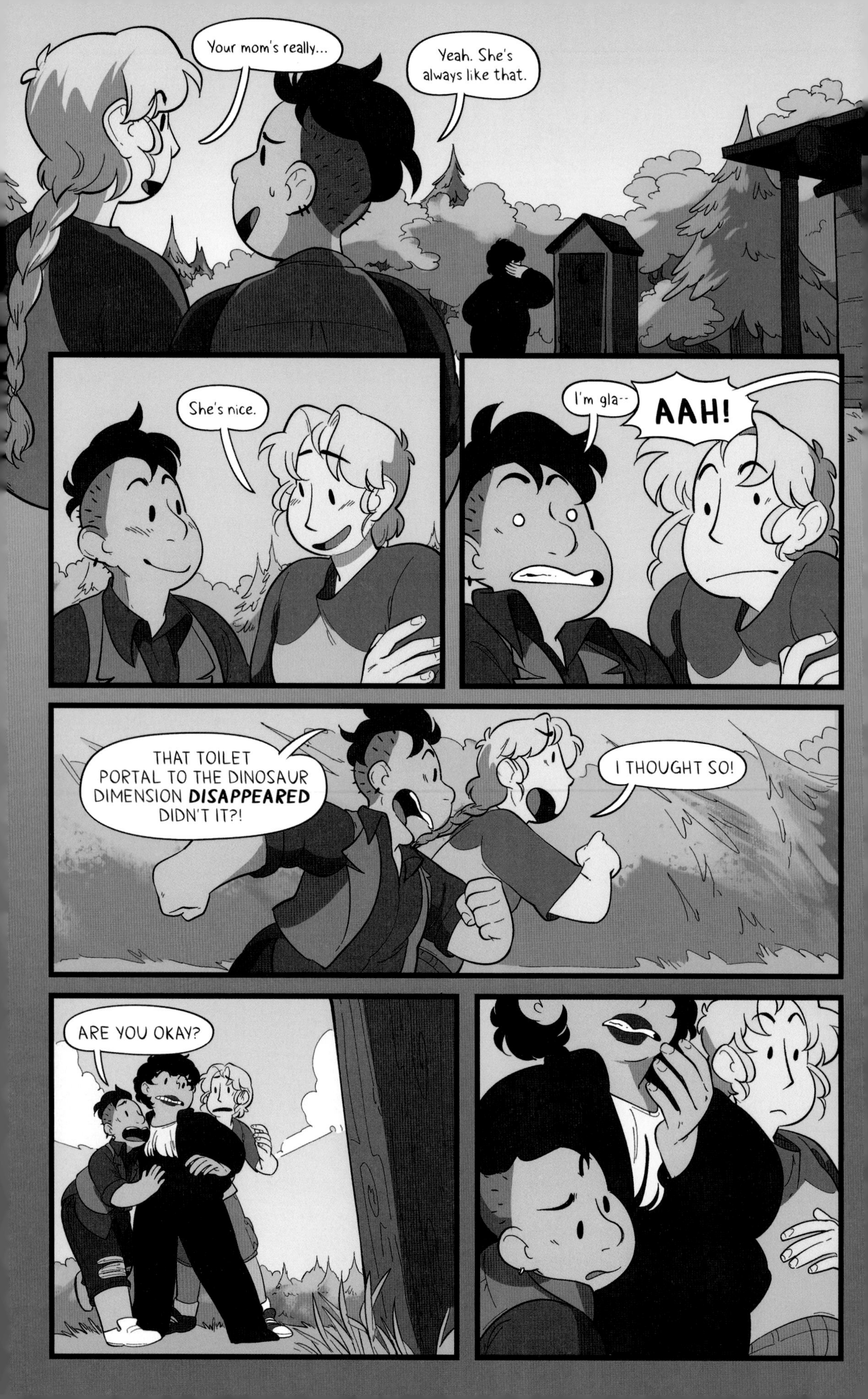
Your mom's really...
Yeah. She's always like that.
She's nice.
I'm gla--
AAH!
THAT TOILET PORTAL TO THE DINOSAUR DIMENSION **DISAPPEARED** DIDN'T IT?!
I THOUGHT SO!
ARE YOU OKAY?

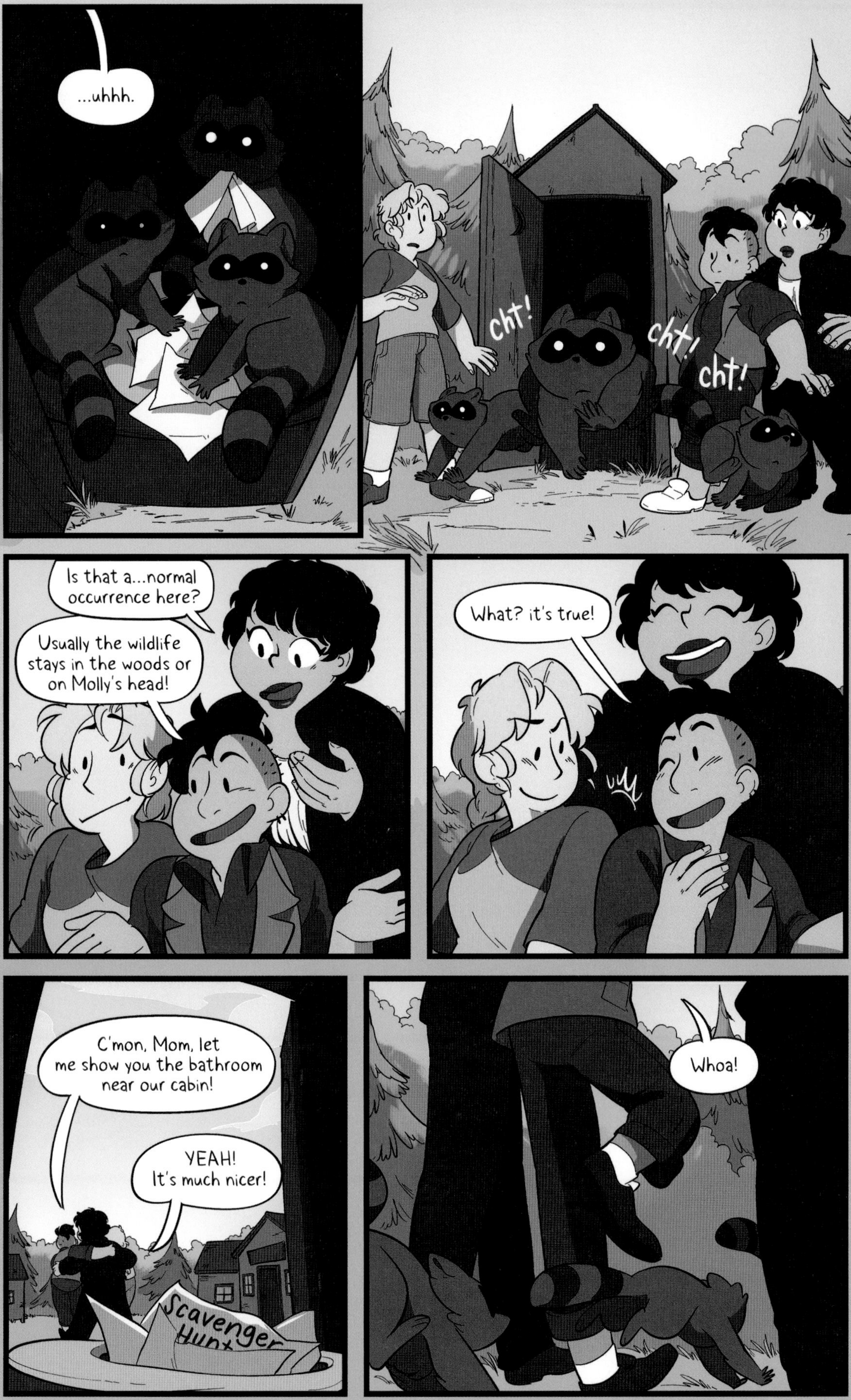
...uhhh.
cht!
cht!
cht!
Is that a...normal occurrence here?
Usually the wildlife stays in the woods or on Molly's head!
What? it's true!
C'mon, Mom, let me show you the bathroom near our cabin!
YEAH! It's much nicer!
Whoa!

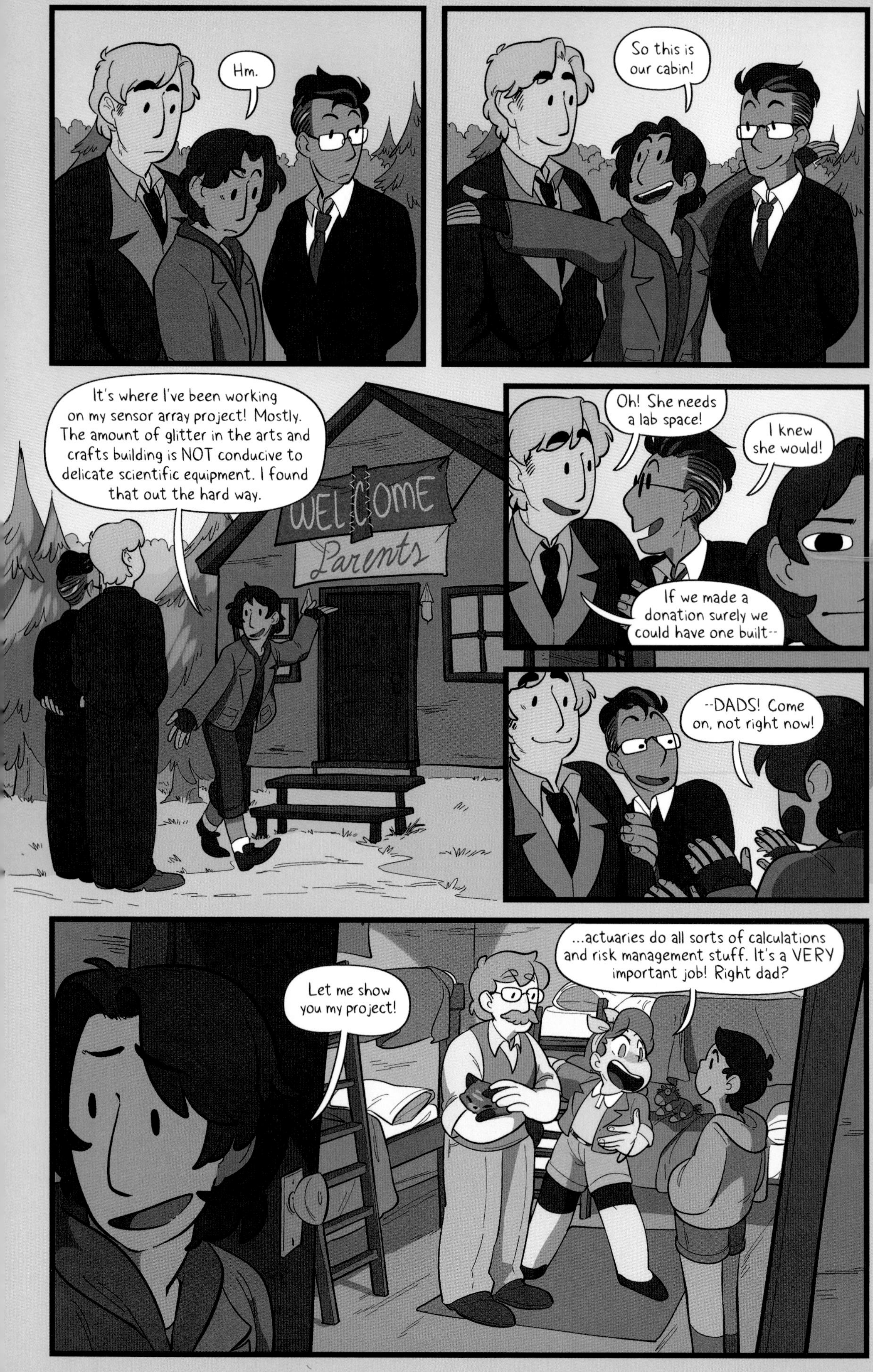
Hm.
So this is our cabin!
It's where I've been working on my sensor array project! Mostly. The amount of glitter in the arts and crafts building is NOT conducive to delicate scientific equipment. I found that out the hard way.
WELCOME
Parents
Oh! She needs a lab space!
I knew she would!
If we made a donation surely we could have one built--
--DADS! Come on, not right now!
Let me show you my project!
...actuaries do all sorts of calculations and risk management stuff. It's a VERY important job! Right dad?

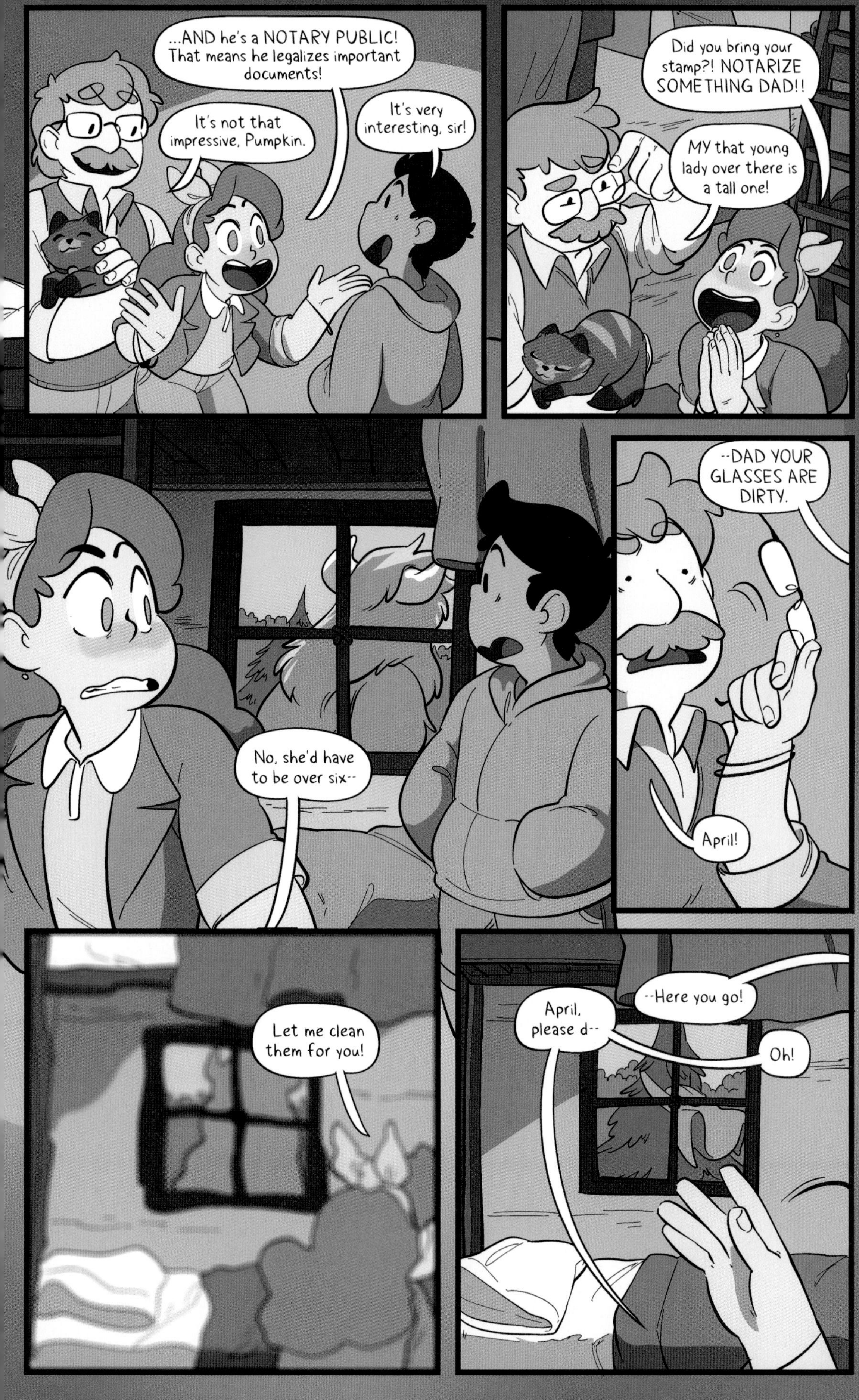
...AND he's a NOTARY PUBLIC! That means he legalizes important documents!
It's not that impressive, Pumpkin.
It's very interesting, sir!
Did you bring your stamp?! NOTARIZE SOMETHING DAD!!
MY that young lady over there is a tall one!
--DAD YOUR GLASSES ARE DIRTY.
No, she'd have to be over six--
April!
Let me clean them for you!
April, please d--
--Here you go!
Oh!

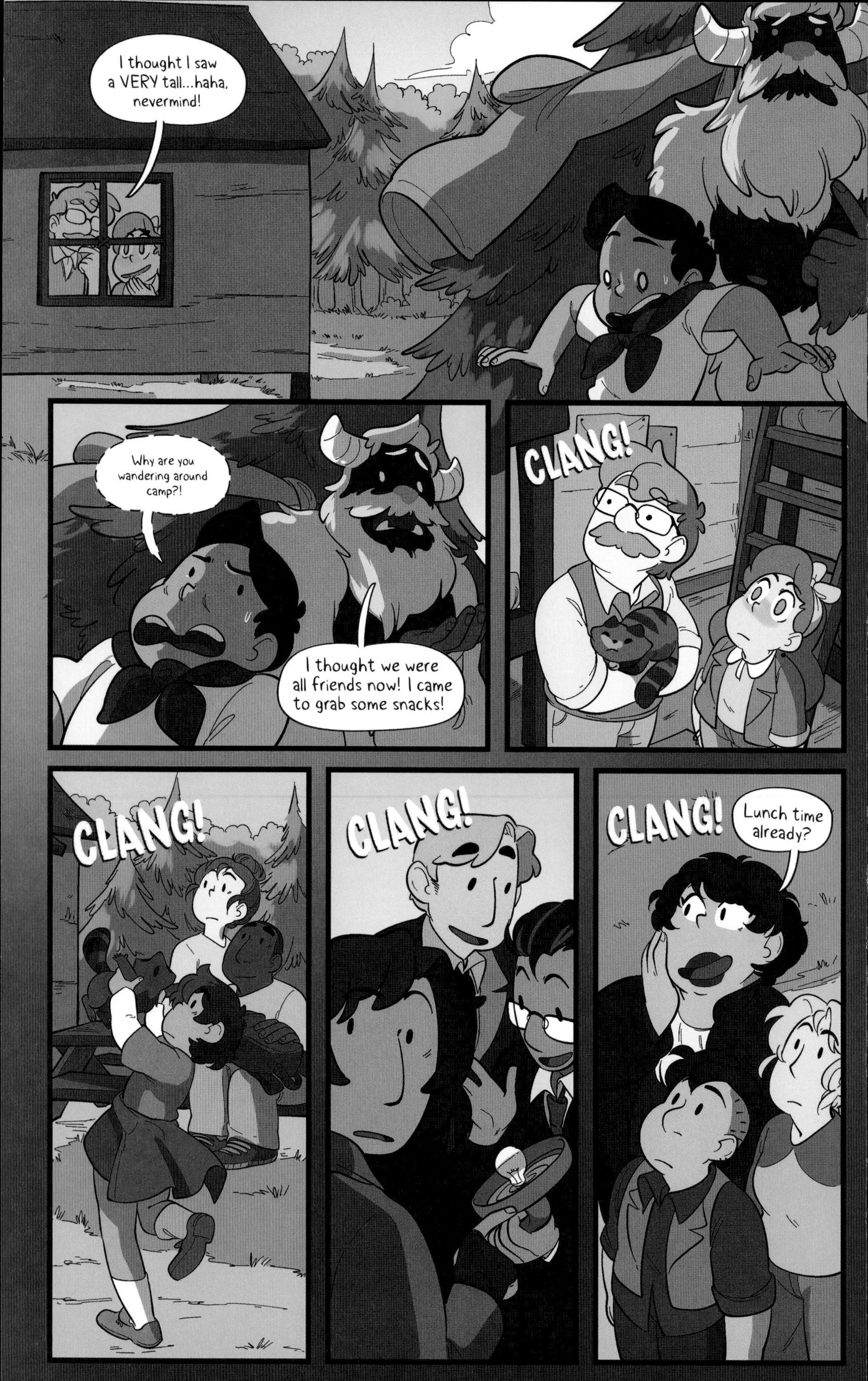
I thought I saw a VERY tall...haha, nevermind!
Why are you wandering around camp?!
I thought we were all friends now! I came to grab some snacks!
CLANG!
CLANG!
CLANG!
CLANG!
Lunch time already?

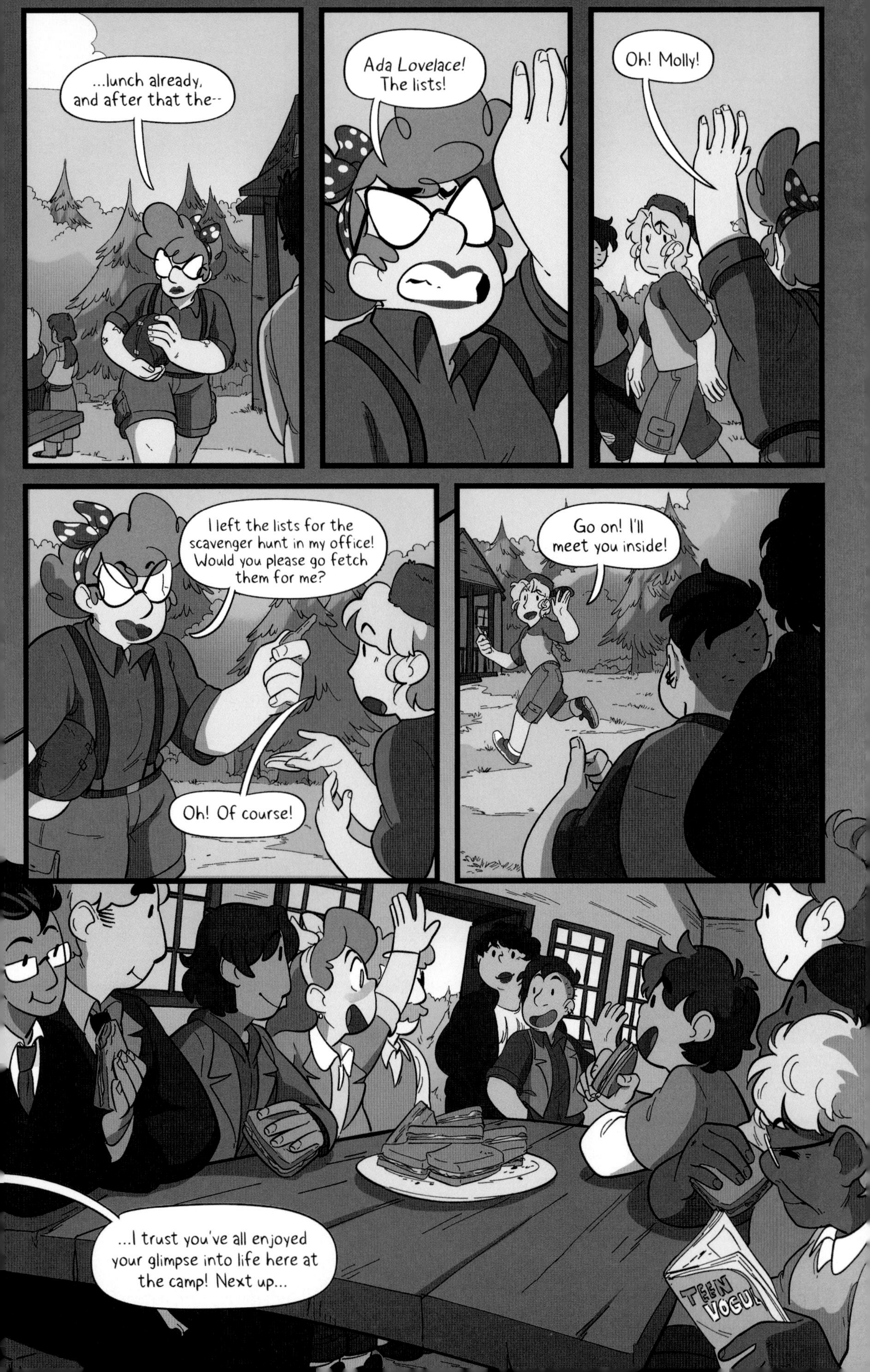
...lunch already, and after that the--
Ada Lovelace! The lists!
Oh! Molly!
I left the lists for the scavenger hunt in my office! Would you please go fetch them for me?
Oh! Of course!
Go on! I'll meet you inside!
...I trust you've all enjoyed your glimpse into life here at the camp! Next up...
TEEN VOGUE

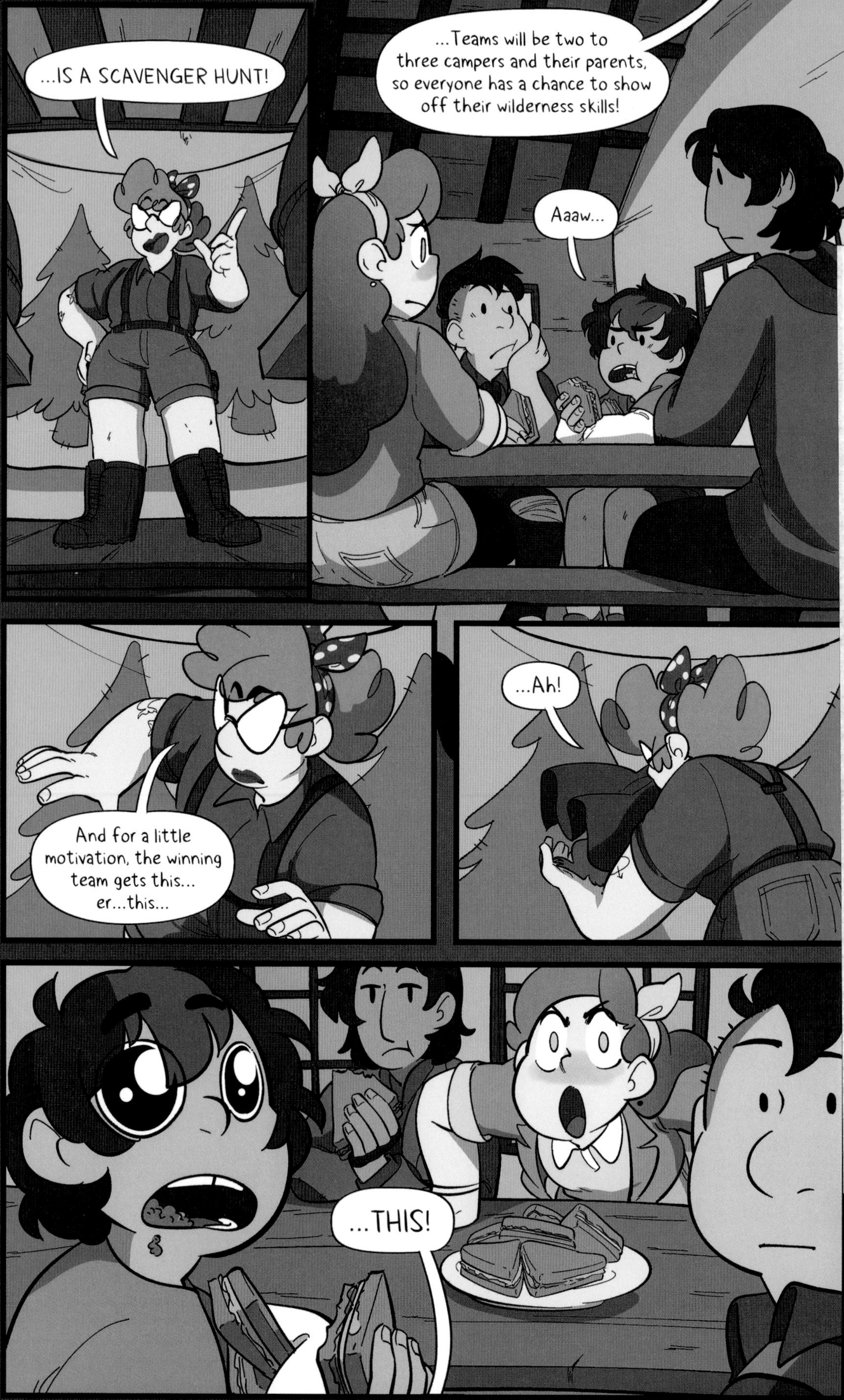
...IS A SCAVENGER HUNT!
...Teams will be two to three campers and their parents, so everyone has a chance to show off their wilderness skills!
Aaaw...
And for a little motivation, the winning team gets this... er...this...
...Ah!
...THIS!

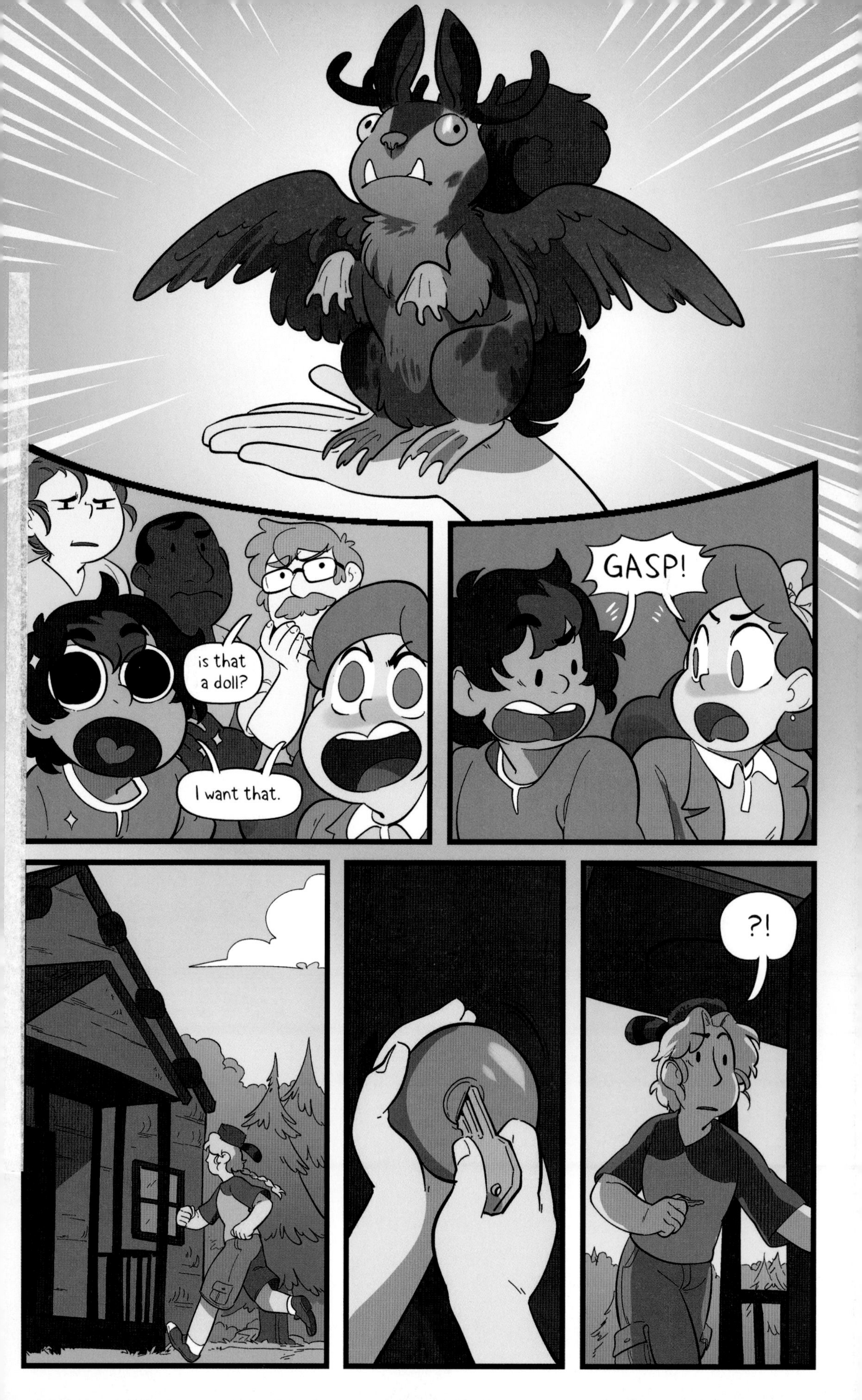
is that a doll?
I want that.
GASP!
?!

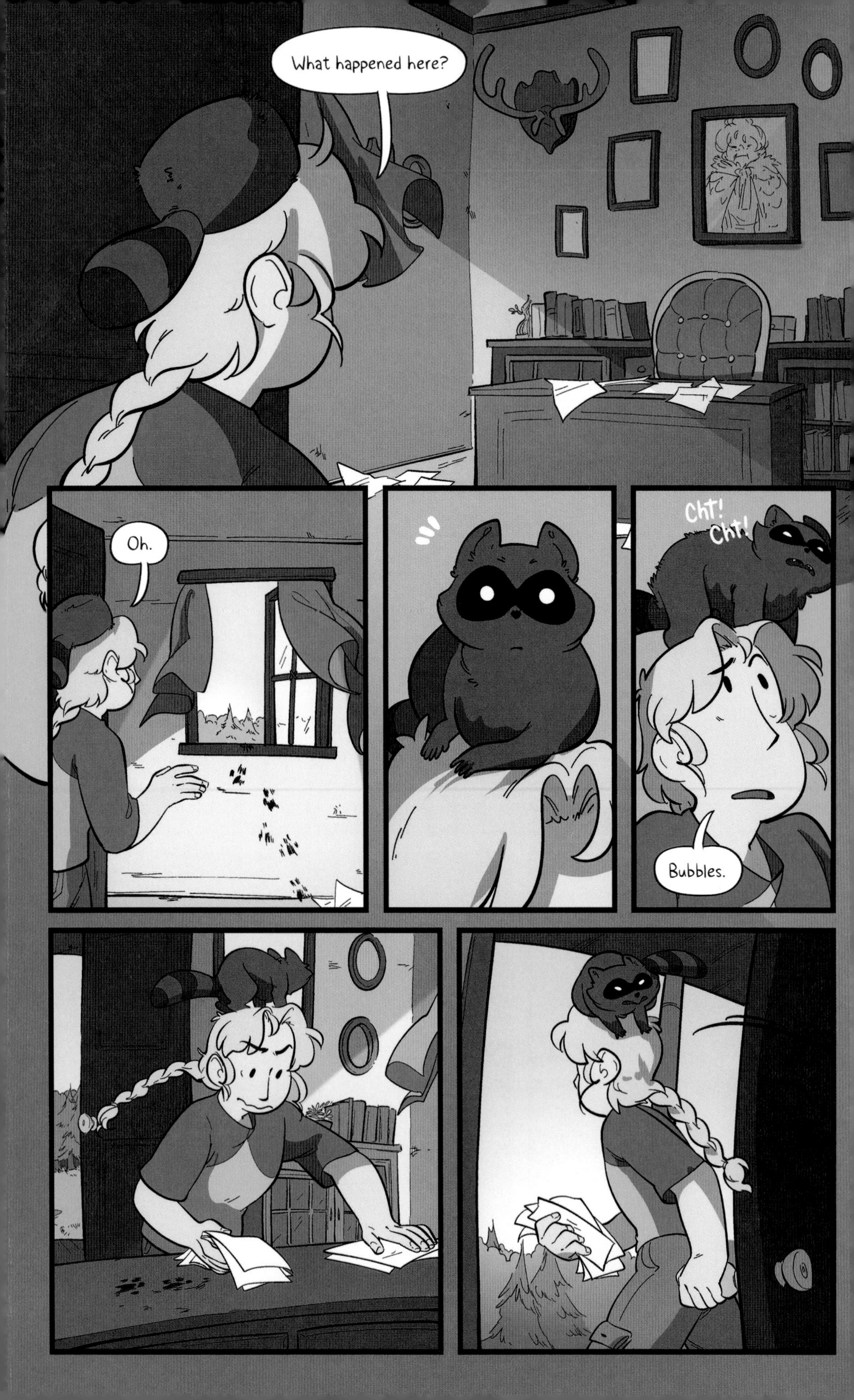
What happened here?
Oh.
Cht! Cht!
Bubbles.

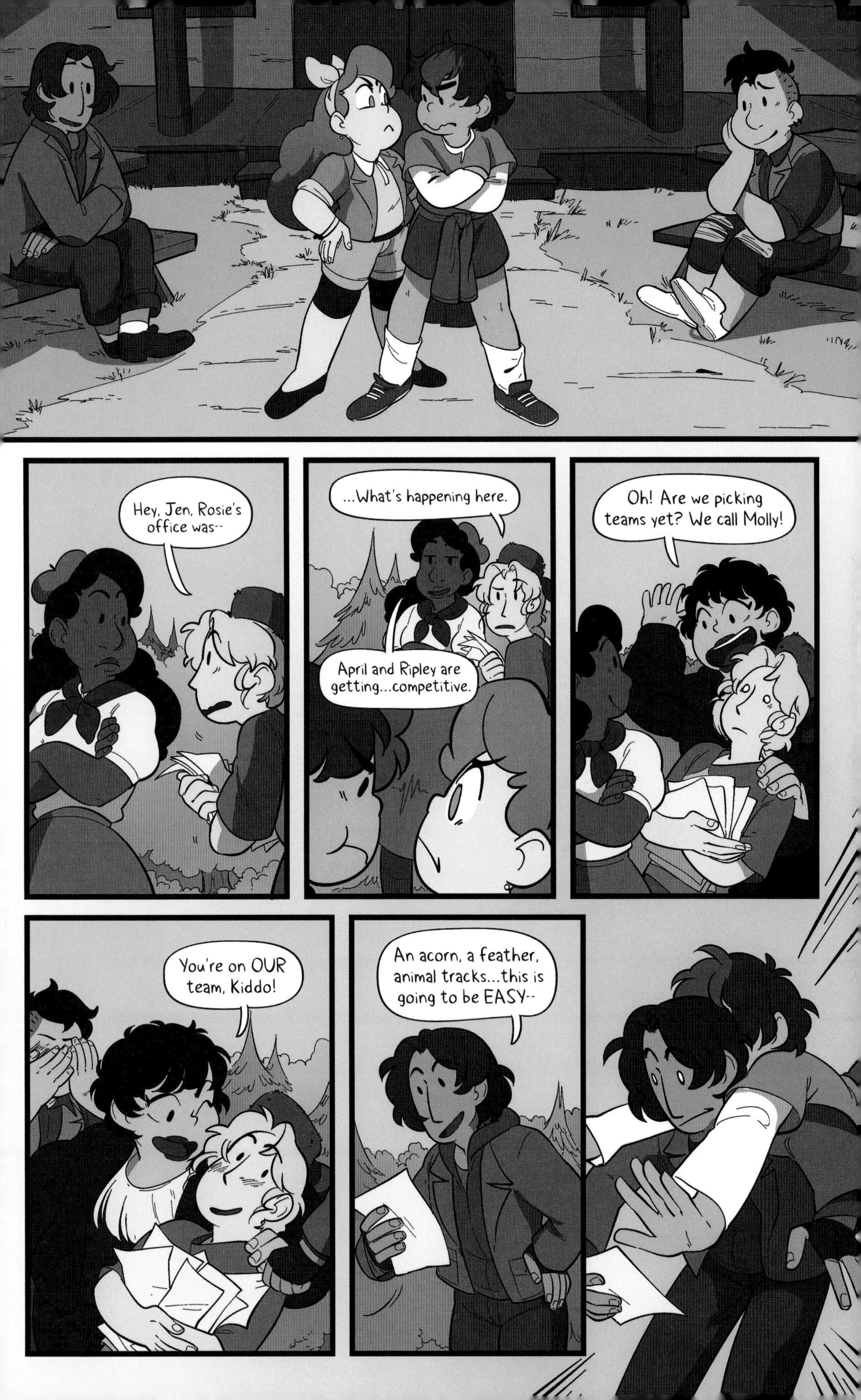
Hey, Jen, Rosie's office was--
...What's happening here.
April and Ripley are getting...competitive.
Oh! Are we picking teams yet? We call Molly!
You're on OUR team, Kiddo!
An acorn, a feather, animal tracks...this is going to be EASY--

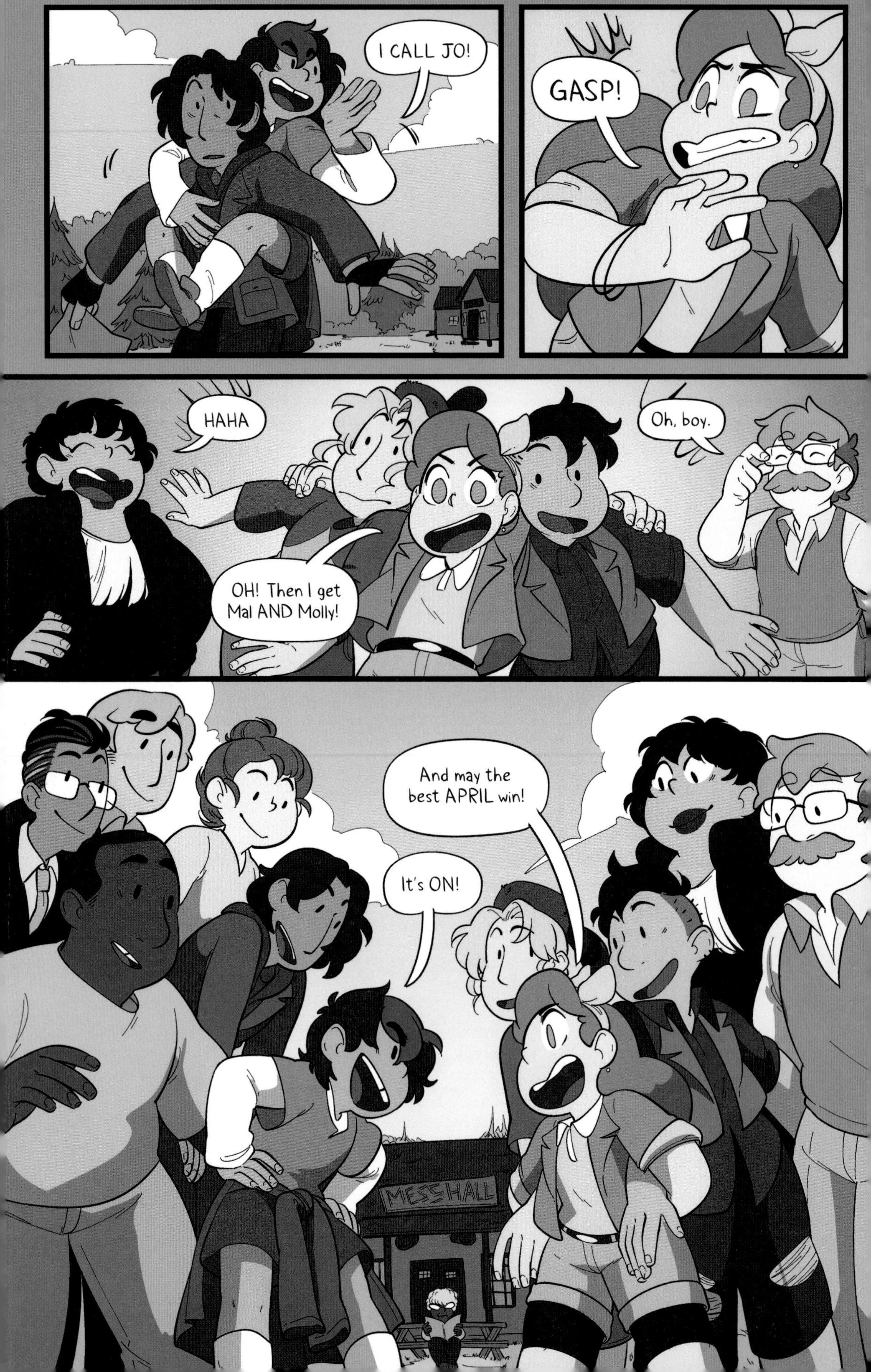
I CALL JO!
GASP!
HAHA
Oh, boy.
OH! Then I get Mal AND Molly!
And may the best APRIL win!
It's ON!
MESSHALL

will comm
The ur
It helps
appearan
dress f
Further
Lumbe
to have
part in
Thiskv
Hardc
have
them

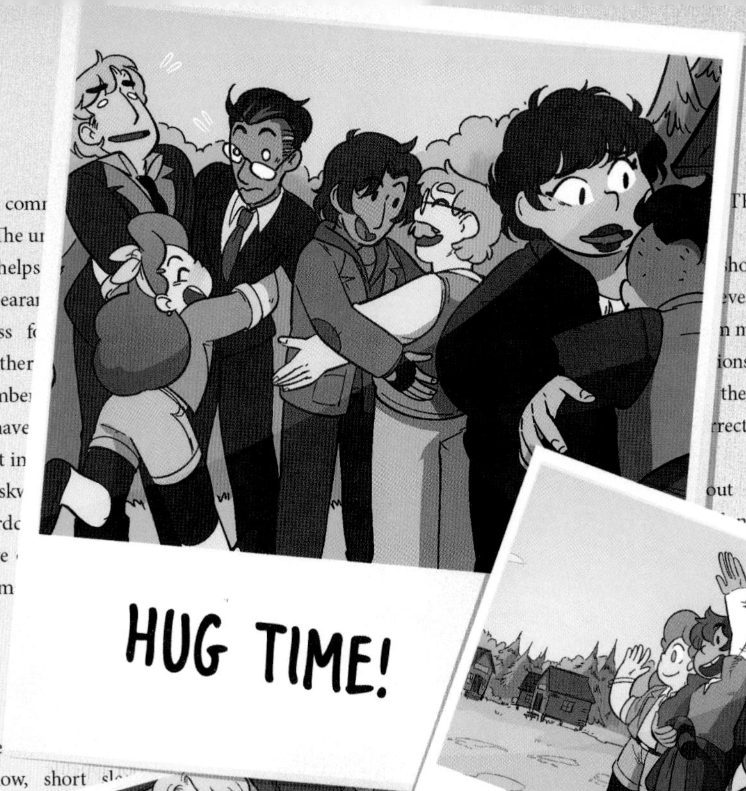
HUG TIME!

THE UNIFORM

should be worn at camp
events when Lumberjanes
n may also be worn at other
ions. It should be worn as a
the uniform dress with
rrect shoes, and stocking or

out grows her uniform or
ng to anoter Lumberjane.
insignia she has
her
her

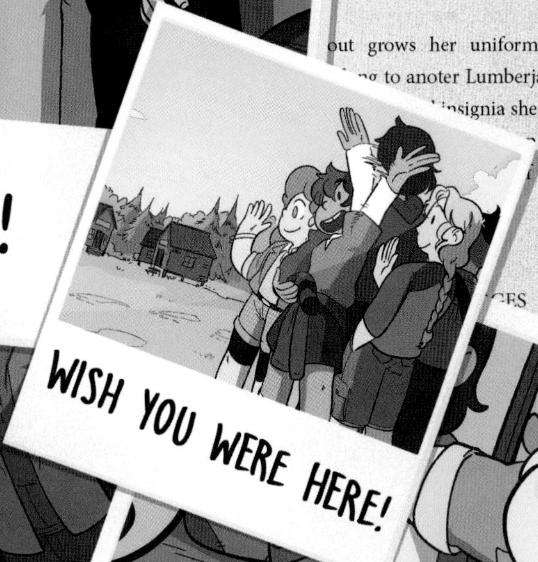
WISH YOU WERE HERE!

The
yellow, short sl
emb
the w
choose
slacks,
made o
out-of-do
green bere
the collar a
Shoes may b
heels, round t … ings or
socks should c … with the shoes or wit
the uniform. Ne… es, bracelets, or other jewelry do
belong with a Lumberjane uniform.

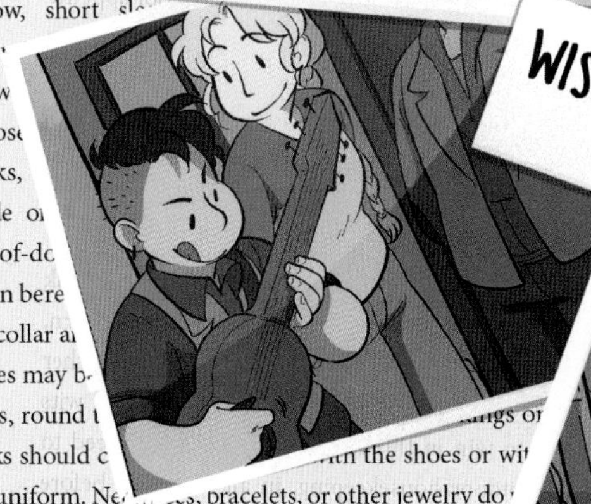

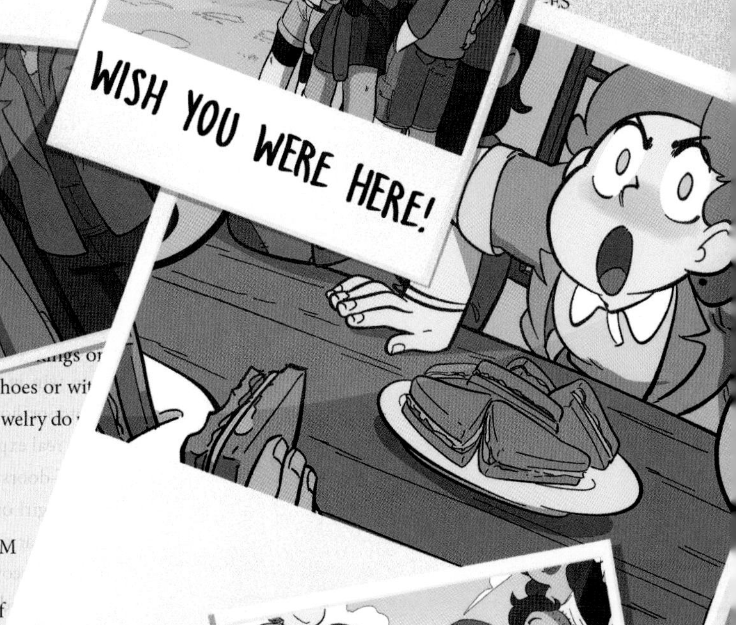

HOW TO WEAR THE UNIFORM

To look well in a uniform demands first of … uniform be kept in good condition—clean … pressed. See that the skirt is the right length for your own height and build, that the belt is adjusted to your waist, that your shoes and stockings are in keeping with the uniform, that you watch your posture and carry yourself with dignity and grace. If the beret is removed indoors, be sure that your hair is neat and kept in place with an insonspicuous clip or ribbon. When you wear a Lumberjane uniform you are identified as a member of this organization and you should be doubly careful to conduct yourself in a way that will show everyone that courtesy and thoughtfullness are part of being a Lumberjane. People are likely to judge a whole nation by the selfishness of a few individuals, to criticize a whole family because of the misconduct of one member, and to feel unkindly toward and organization because of the

The unifor
helps to cre
in a group.
active life th
another bond
future, and pr
in order to b
Lumberjane pr
Penniquiqul Thi … re Lady
Types, but most L… will wish to have one. They
can either buy the uniform, or make it themselves from
materials available at the trading post.

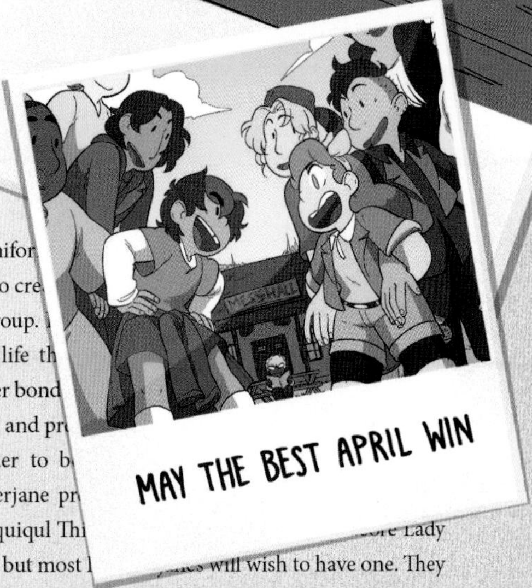
MESS HALL
MAY THE BEST APRIL WIN

LUMBERJANES FIELD MANUAL

CHAPTER
THIRTY-EIGHT

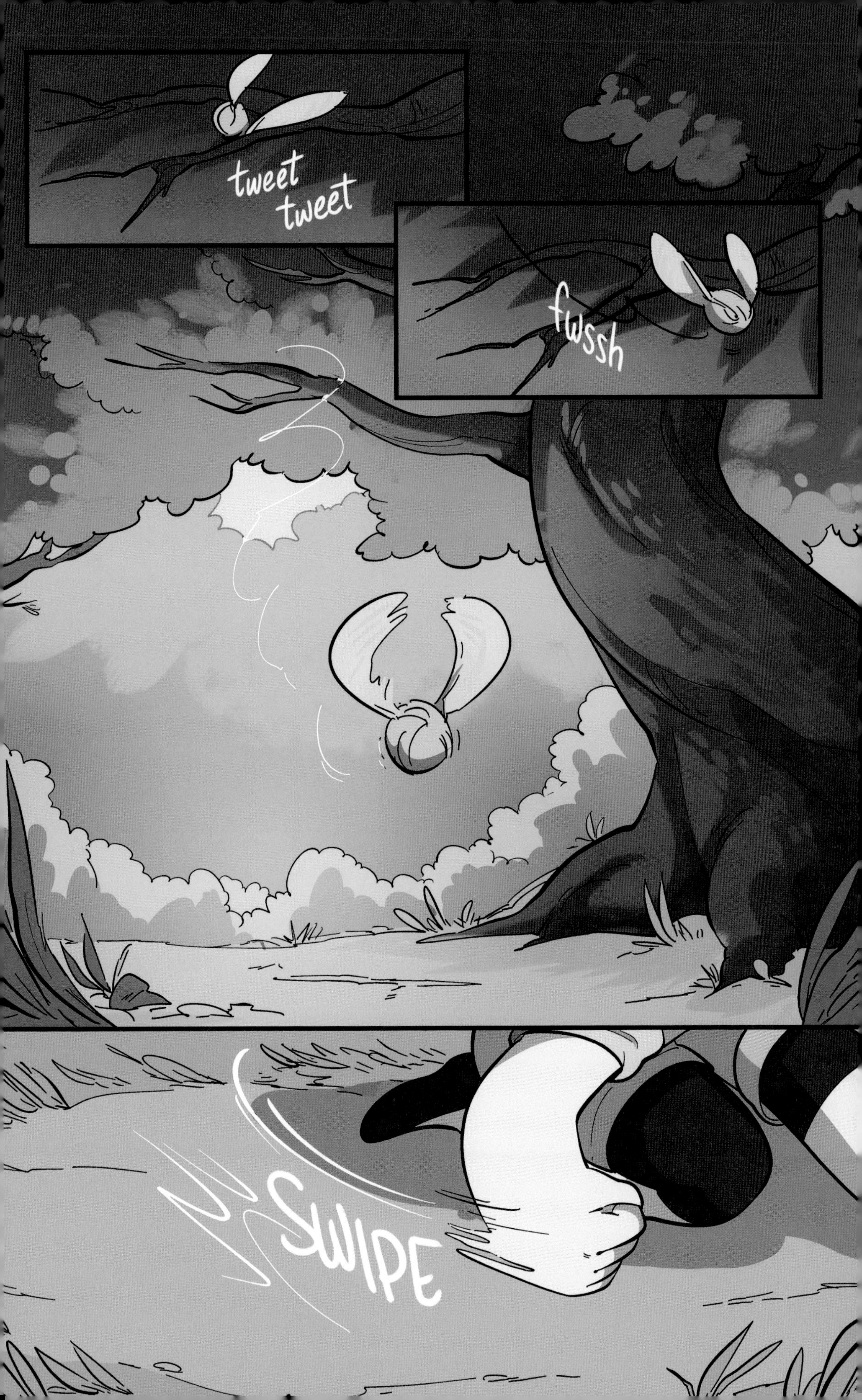
tweet
tweet
fwssh
SWIPE

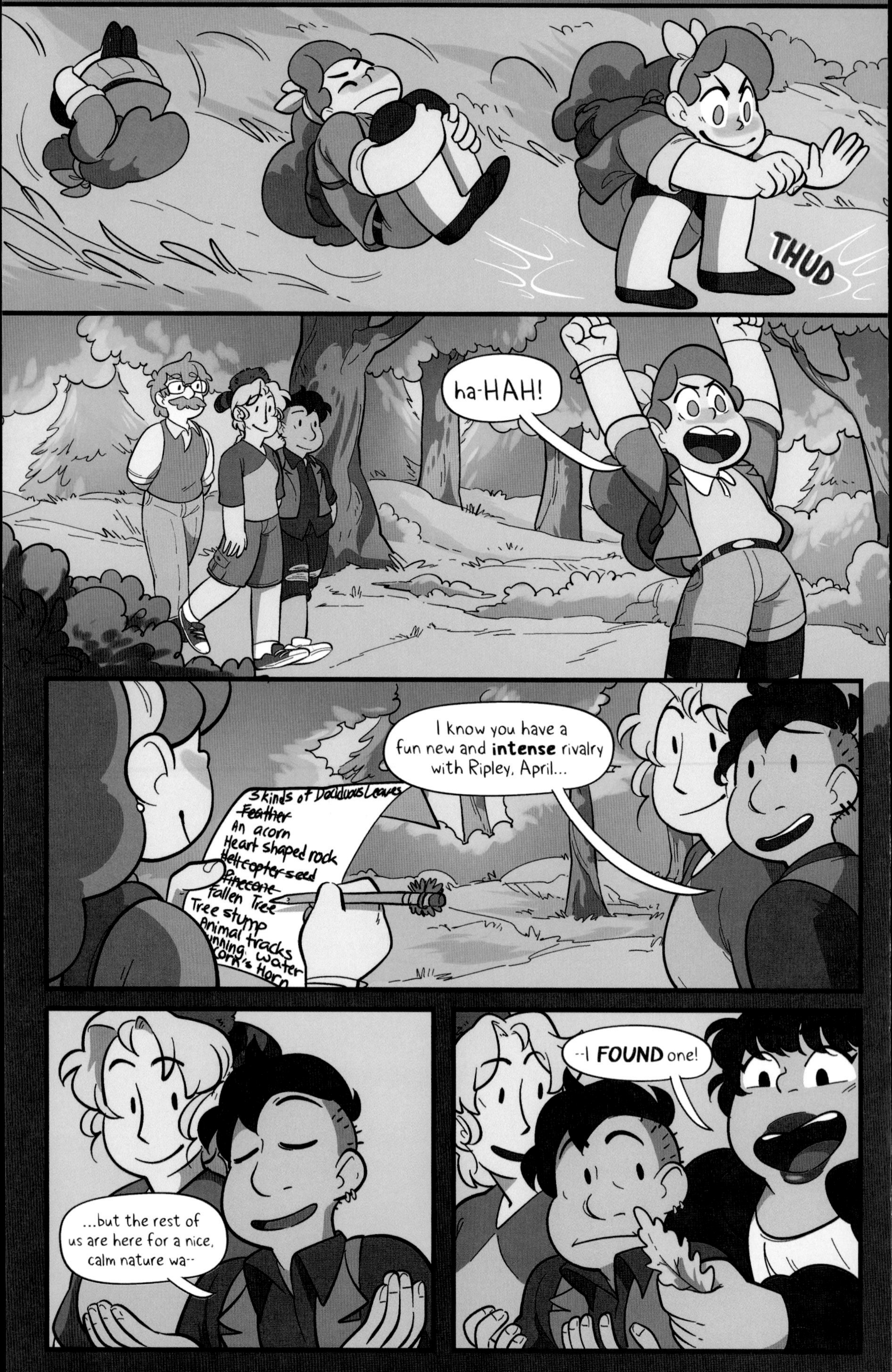
THUD
ha-HAH!
I know you have a fun new and **intense** rivalry with Ripley, April...
5 kinds of Deciduous Leaves
~~Feather~~
An acorn
Heart shaped rock
~~Helicopter seed~~
~~Pinecone~~
Fallen Tree
Tree stump
Animal tracks
...but the rest of us are here for a nice, calm nature wa--
--I **FOUND** one!

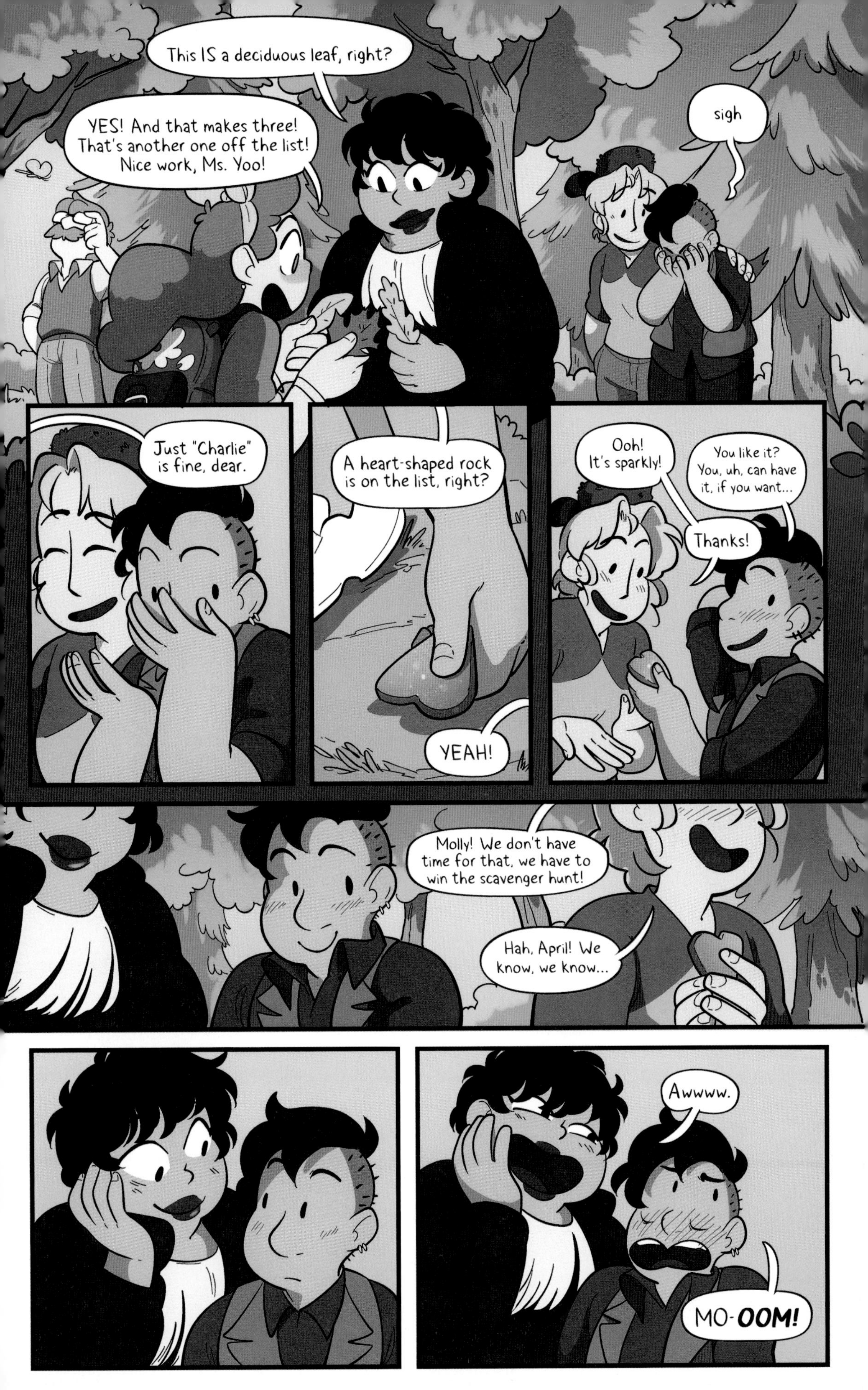
This IS a deciduous leaf, right?
YES! And that makes three! That's another one off the list! Nice work, Ms. Yoo!
sigh
Just "Charlie" is fine, dear.
A heart-shaped rock is on the list, right?
YEAH!
Ooh! It's sparkly!
You like it? You, uh, can have it, if you want...
Thanks!
Molly! We don't have time for that, we have to win the scavenger hunt!
Hah, April! We know, we know...
Awwww.
MO-**OOM!**

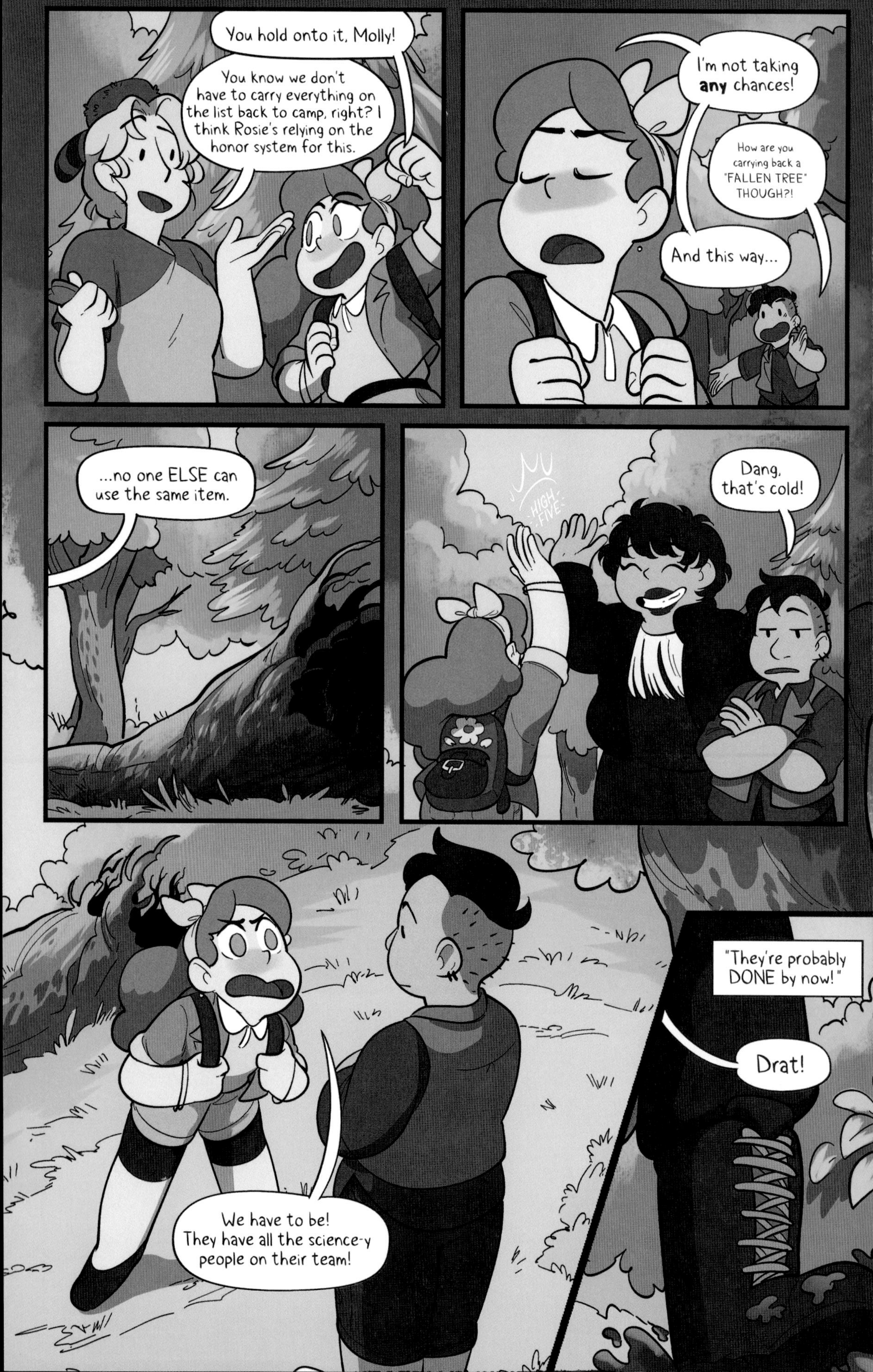
You hold onto it, Molly!
You know we don't have to carry everything on the list back to camp, right? I think Rosie's relying on the honor system for this.
I'm not taking **any** chances!
How are you carrying back a "FALLEN TREE" THOUGH?!
And this way...
...no one ELSE can use the same item.
HIGH FIVE
Dang, that's cold!
"They're probably DONE by now!"
Drat!
We have to be! They have all the science-y people on their team!

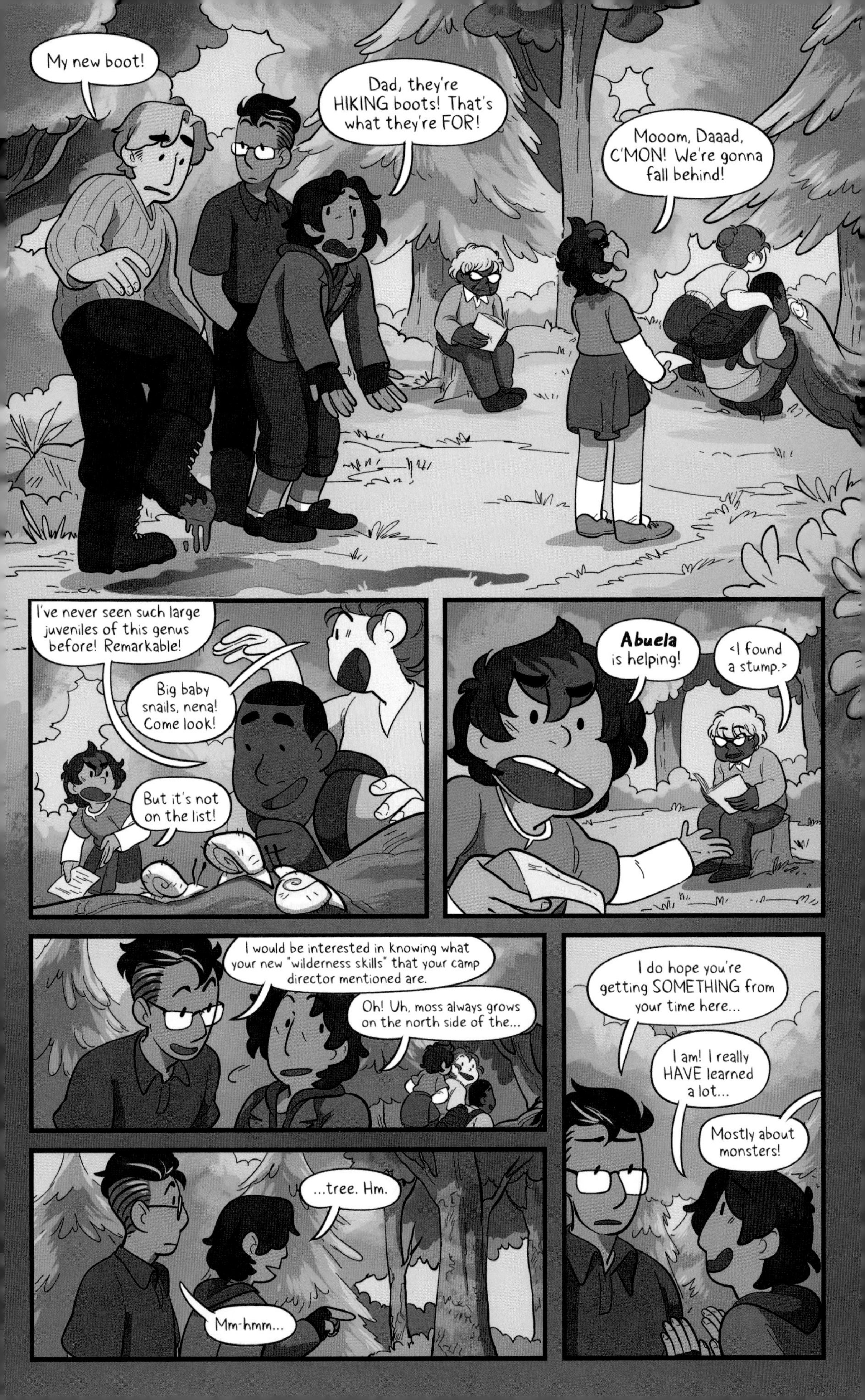
My new boot!
Dad, they're HIKING boots! That's what they're FOR!
Mooom, Daaad, C'MON! We're gonna fall behind!
I've never seen such large juveniles of this genus before! Remarkable!
Big baby snails, nena! Come look!
But it's not on the list!
Abuela is helping!
<I found a stump.>
I would be interested in knowing what your new "wilderness skills" that your camp director mentioned are.
Oh! Uh, moss always grows on the north side of the...
...tree. Hm.
Mm-hmm...
I do hope you're getting SOMETHING from your time here...
I am! I really HAVE learned a lot...
Mostly about monsters!

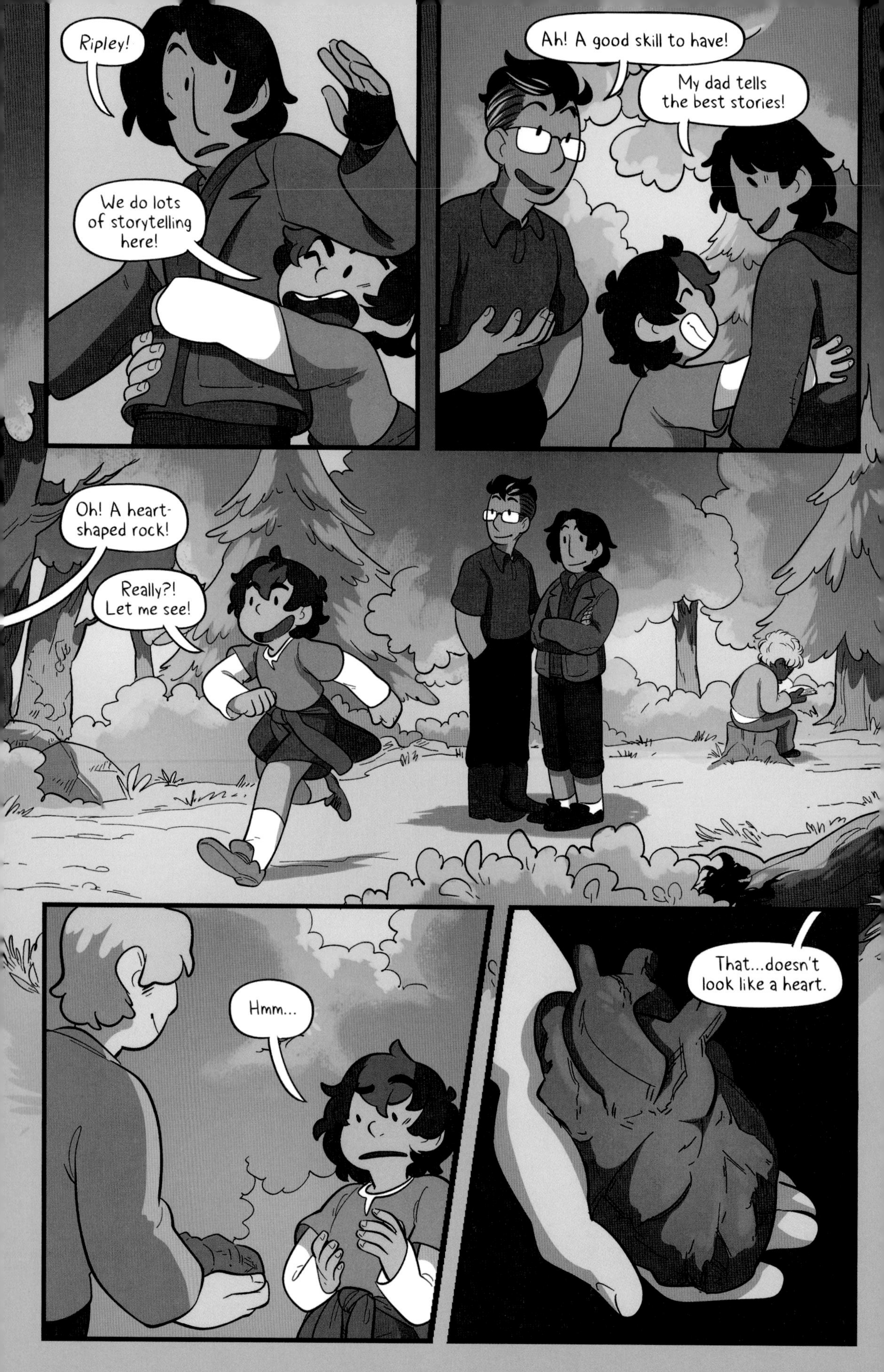
Ripley!
We do lots of storytelling here!
Ah! A good skill to have!
My dad tells the best stories!
Oh! A heart-shaped rock!
Really?! Let me see!
Hmm...
That...doesn't look like a heart.

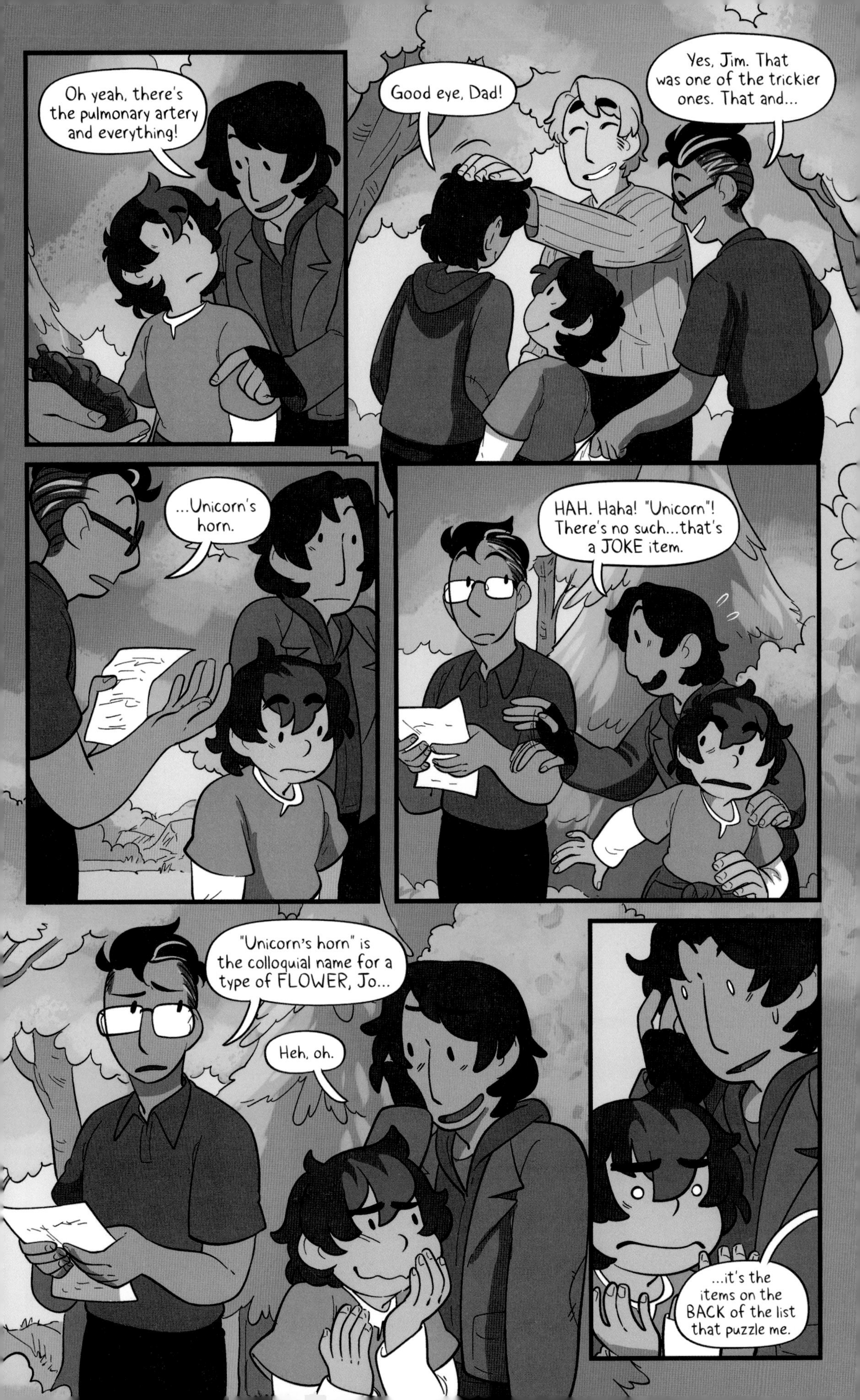
Oh yeah, there's the pulmonary artery and everything!
Good eye, Dad!
Yes, Jim. That was one of the trickier ones. That and...
...Unicorn's horn.
HAH. Haha! "Unicorn"! There's no such...that's a JOKE item.
"Unicorn's horn" is the colloquial name for a type of FLOWER, Jo...
Heh, oh.
...it's the items on the BACK of the list that puzzle me.

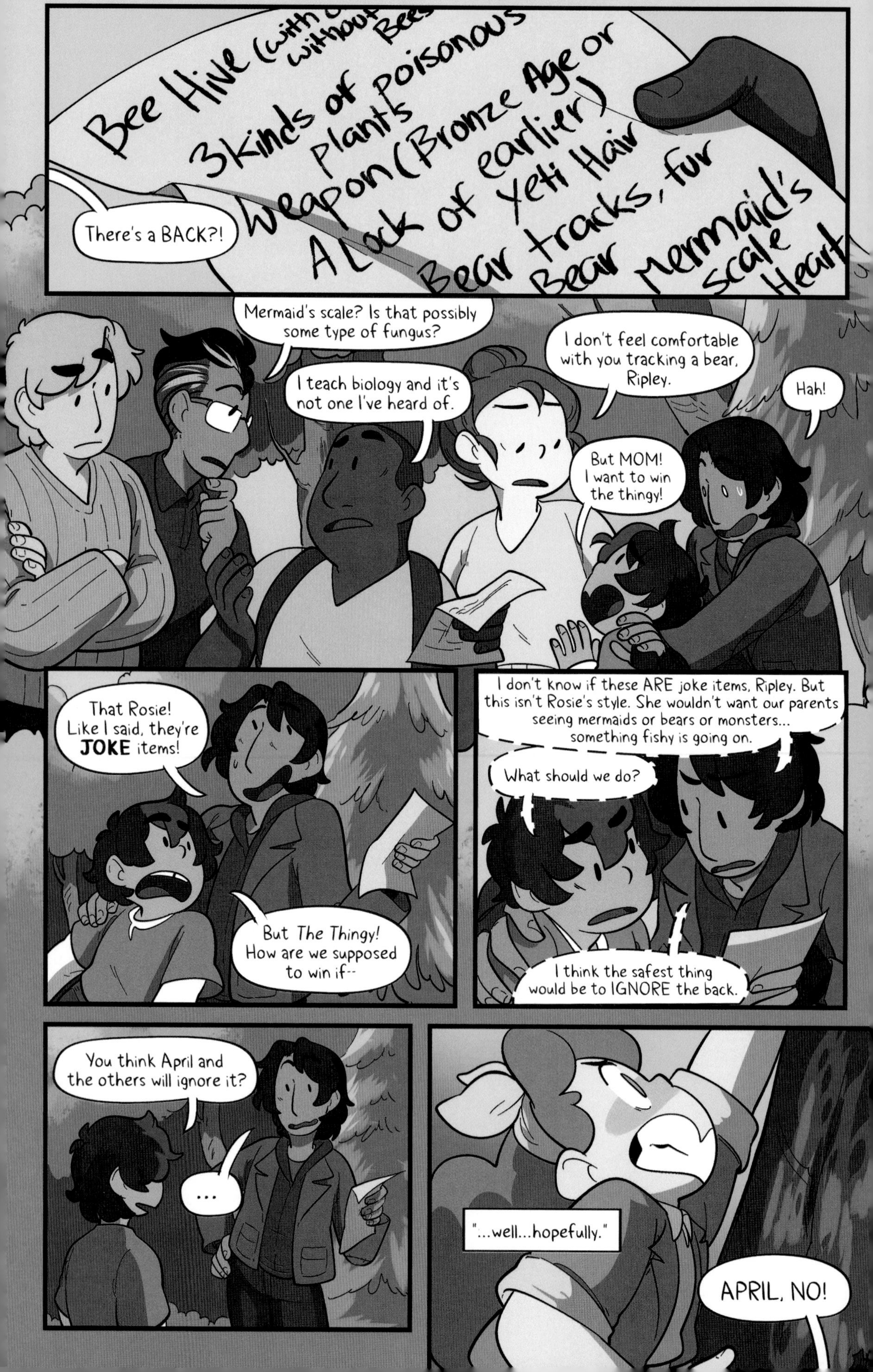
Bee Hive (with or without Bees
3 kinds of poisonous plants
Weapon (Bronze Age or earlier)
A Lock of Yeti Hair
Bear tracks, fur
Bear
Mermaid's scale
Heart
There's a BACK?!
Mermaid's scale? Is that possibly some type of fungus?
I teach biology and it's not one I've heard of.
I don't feel comfortable with you tracking a bear, Ripley.
Hah!
But MOM! I want to win the thingy!
That Rosie! Like I said, they're **JOKE** items!
But *The Thingy*! How are we supposed to win if--
I don't know if these ARE joke items, Ripley. But this isn't Rosie's style. She wouldn't want our parents seeing mermaids or bears or monsters... something fishy is going on.
What should we do?
I think the safest thing would be to IGNORE the back.
You think April and the others will ignore it?
...
"...well...hopefully."
APRIL, NO!

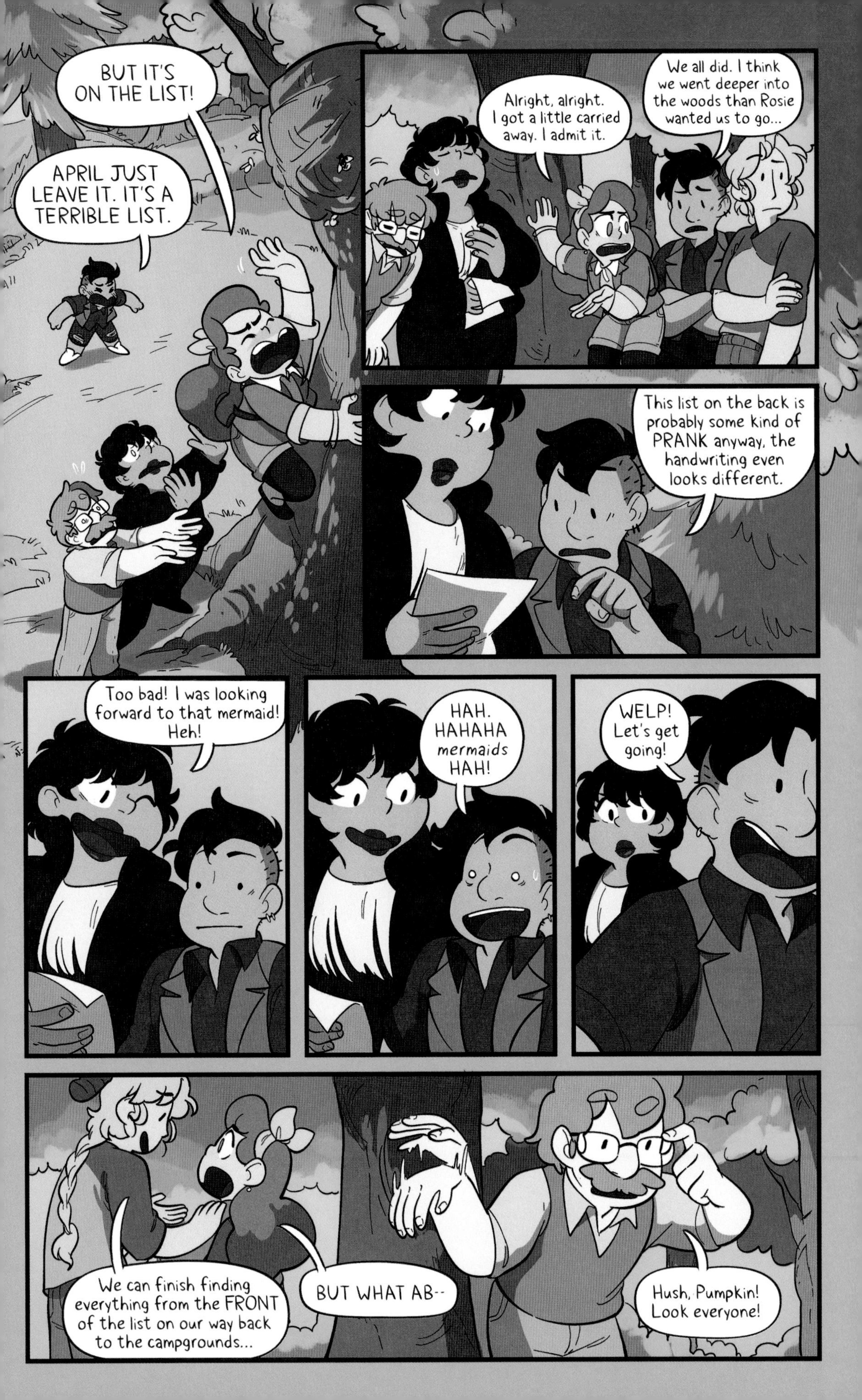
BUT IT'S ON THE LIST!
APRIL JUST LEAVE IT. IT'S A TERRIBLE LIST.
Alright, alright. I got a little carried away. I admit it.
We all did. I think we went deeper into the woods than Rosie wanted us to go...
This list on the back is probably some kind of PRANK anyway, the handwriting even looks different.
Too bad! I was looking forward to that mermaid! Heh!
HAH. HAHAHA mermaids HAH!
WELP! Let's get going!
We can finish finding everything from the FRONT of the list on our way back to the campgrounds...
BUT WHAT AB--
Hush, Pumpkin! Look everyone!

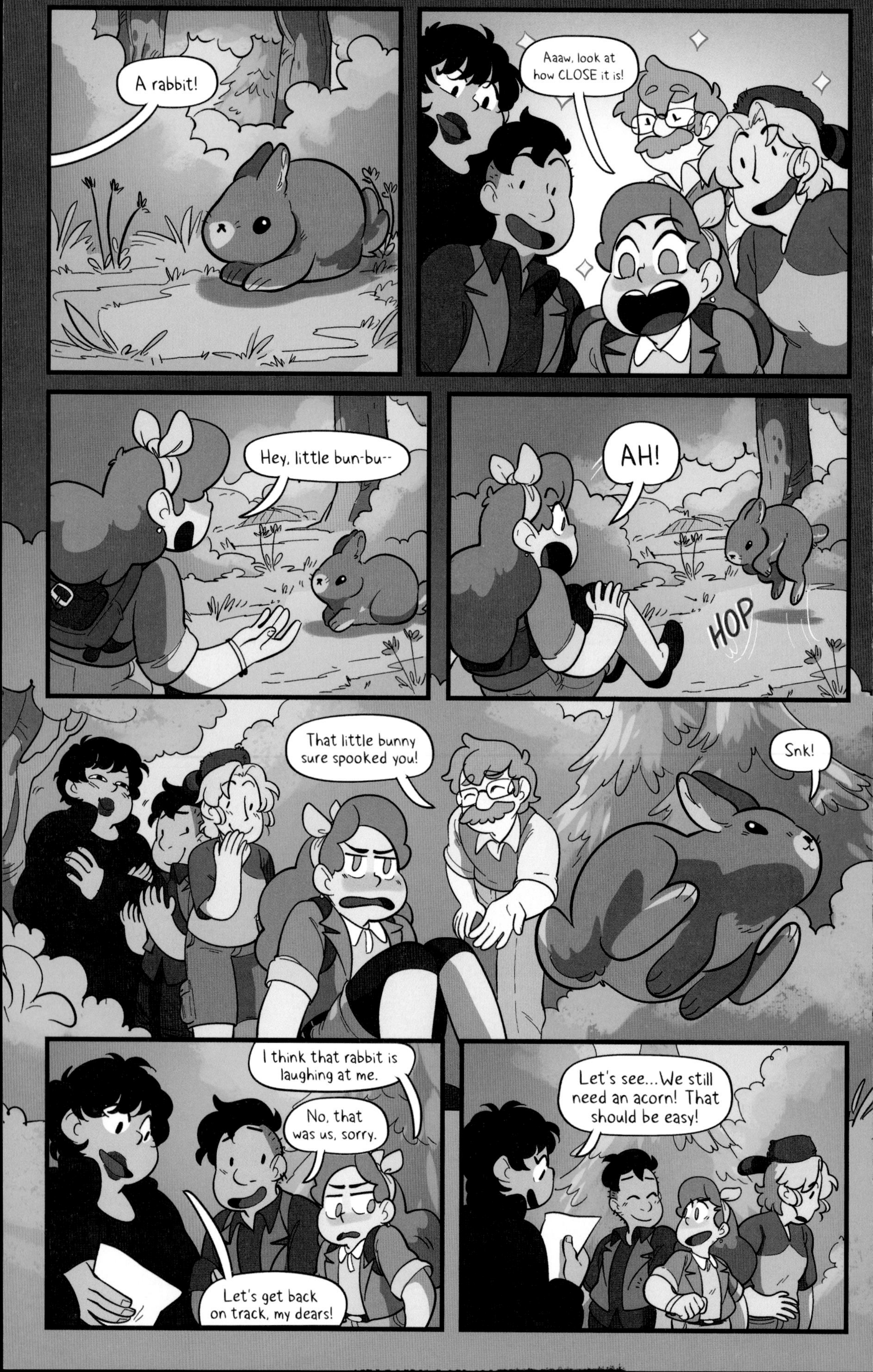
A rabbit!
Aaaw, look at how CLOSE it is!
Hey, little bun-bu--
AH!
HOP
That little bunny sure spooked you!
Snk!
I think that rabbit is laughing at me.
No, that was us, sorry.
Let's get back on track, my dears!
Let's see...We still need an acorn! That should be easy!

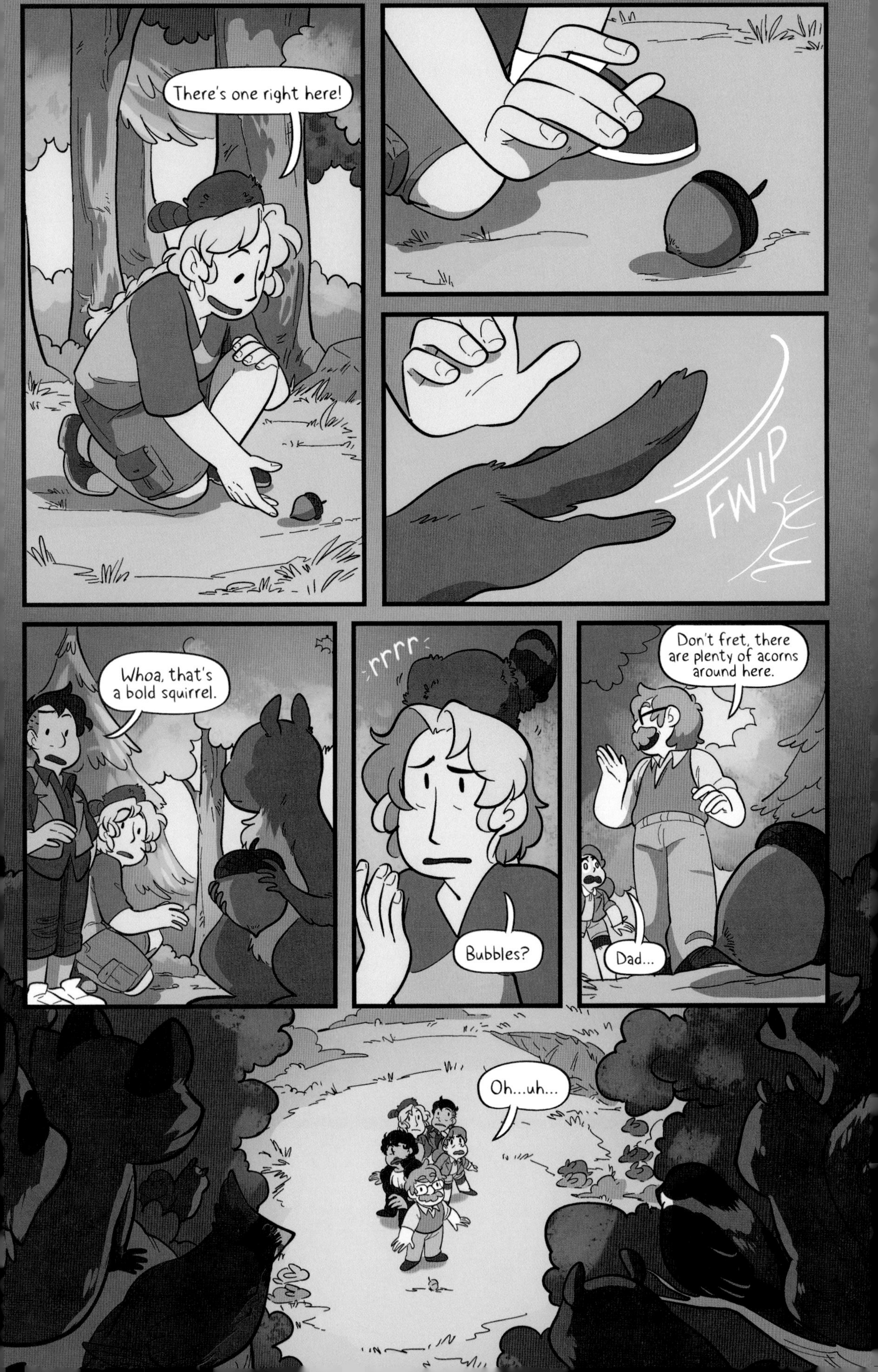
There's one right here!
FWIP
Whoa, that's a bold squirrel.
rrrr
Bubbles?
Don't fret, there are plenty of acorns around here.
Dad...
Oh...uh...

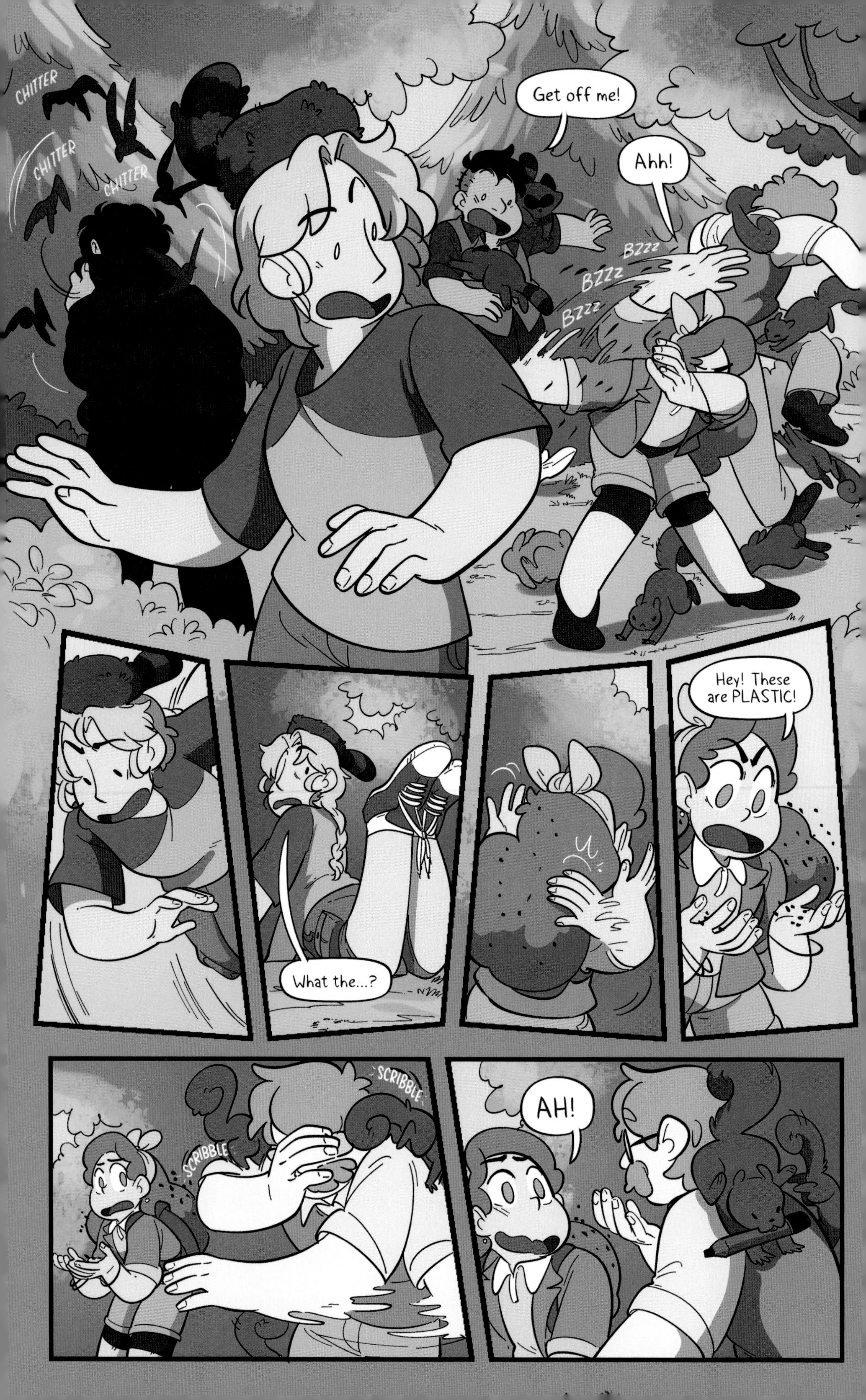
CHITTER
CHITTER
CHITTER
Get off me!
Ahh!
BZZZ
BZZZ
BZZZ
What the...?
Hey! These are PLASTIC!
SCRIBBLE
SCRIBBLE
AH!

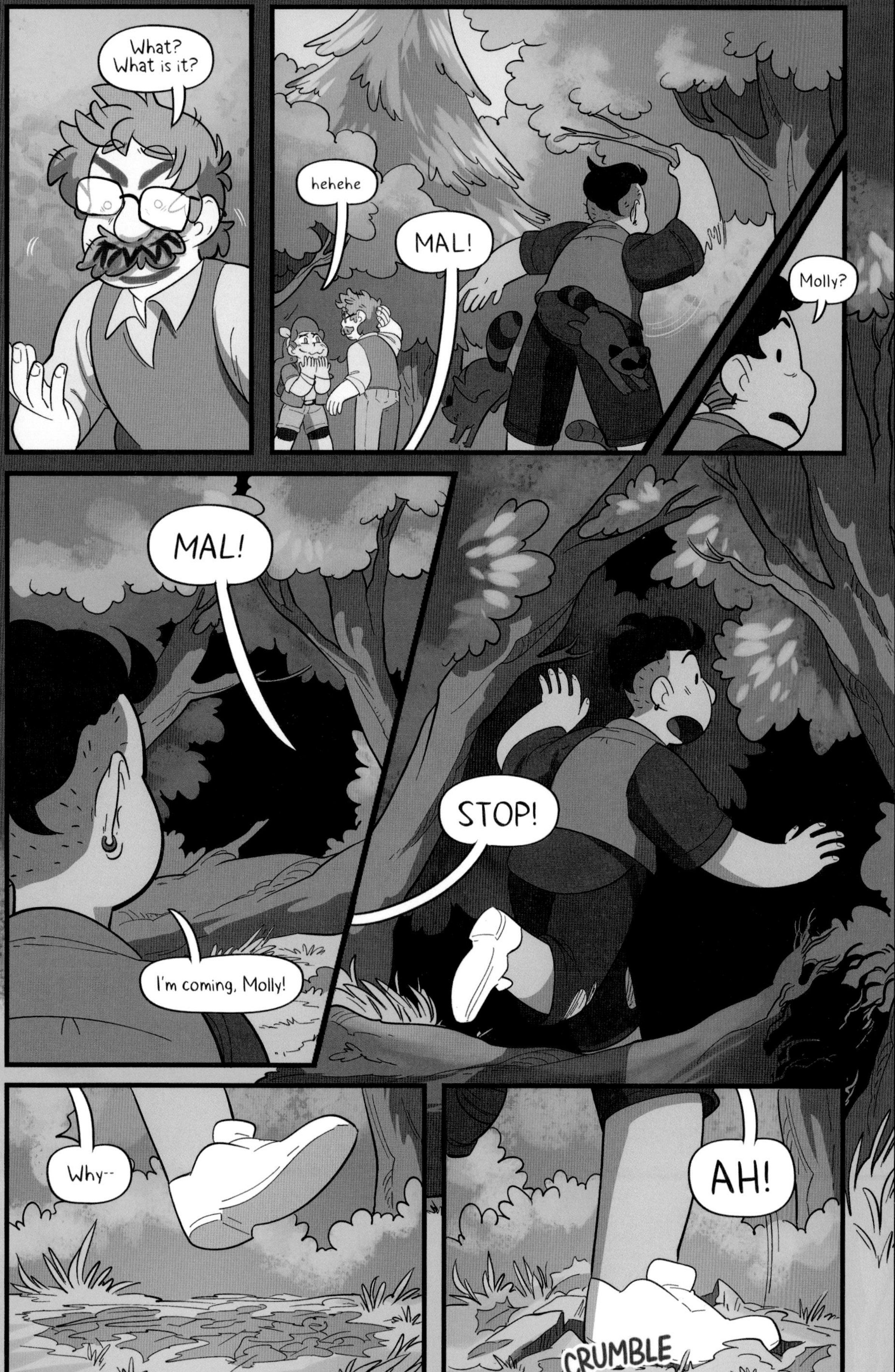
What? What is it?
hehehe
MAL!
Molly?
MAL!
STOP!
I'm coming, Molly!
Why--
AH!
CRUMBLE

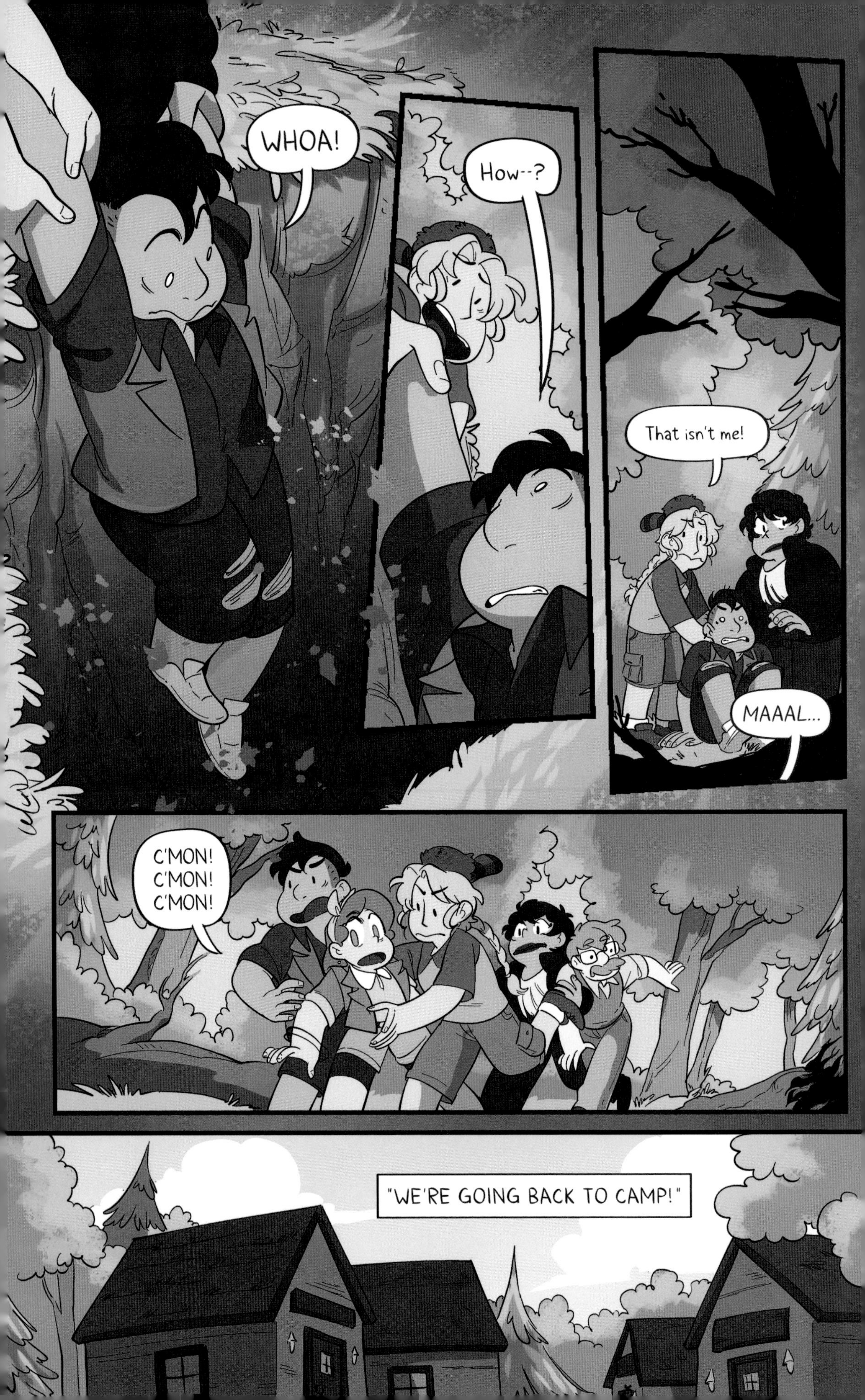
WHOA!
How--?
That isn't me!
MAAAL...
C'MON! C'MON! C'MON!
"WE'RE GOING BACK TO CAMP!"

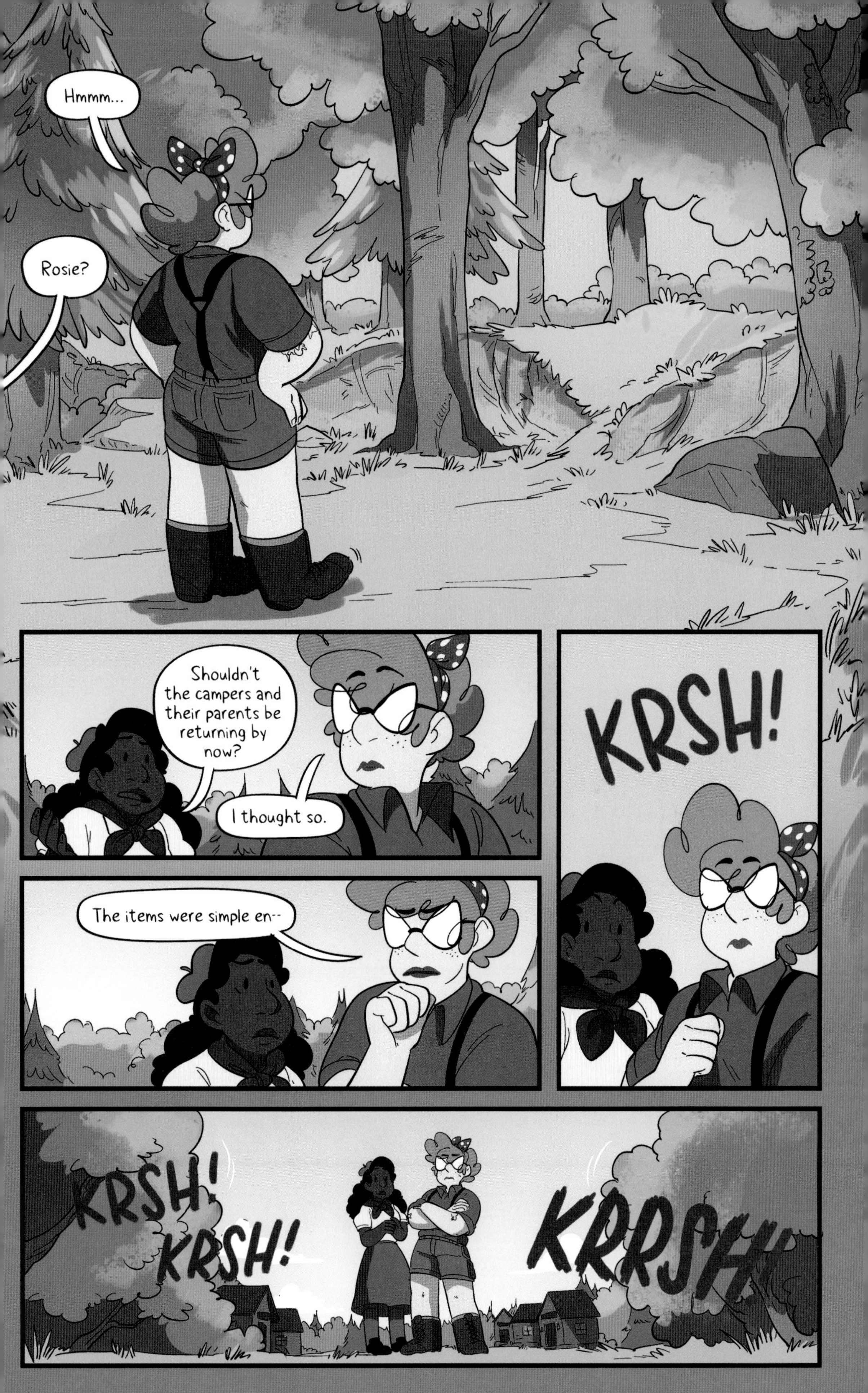
Hmmm...
Rosie?
Shouldn't the campers and their parents be returning by now?
I thought so.
The items were simple en--
KRSH!
KRSH!
KRSH!
KRRSH!

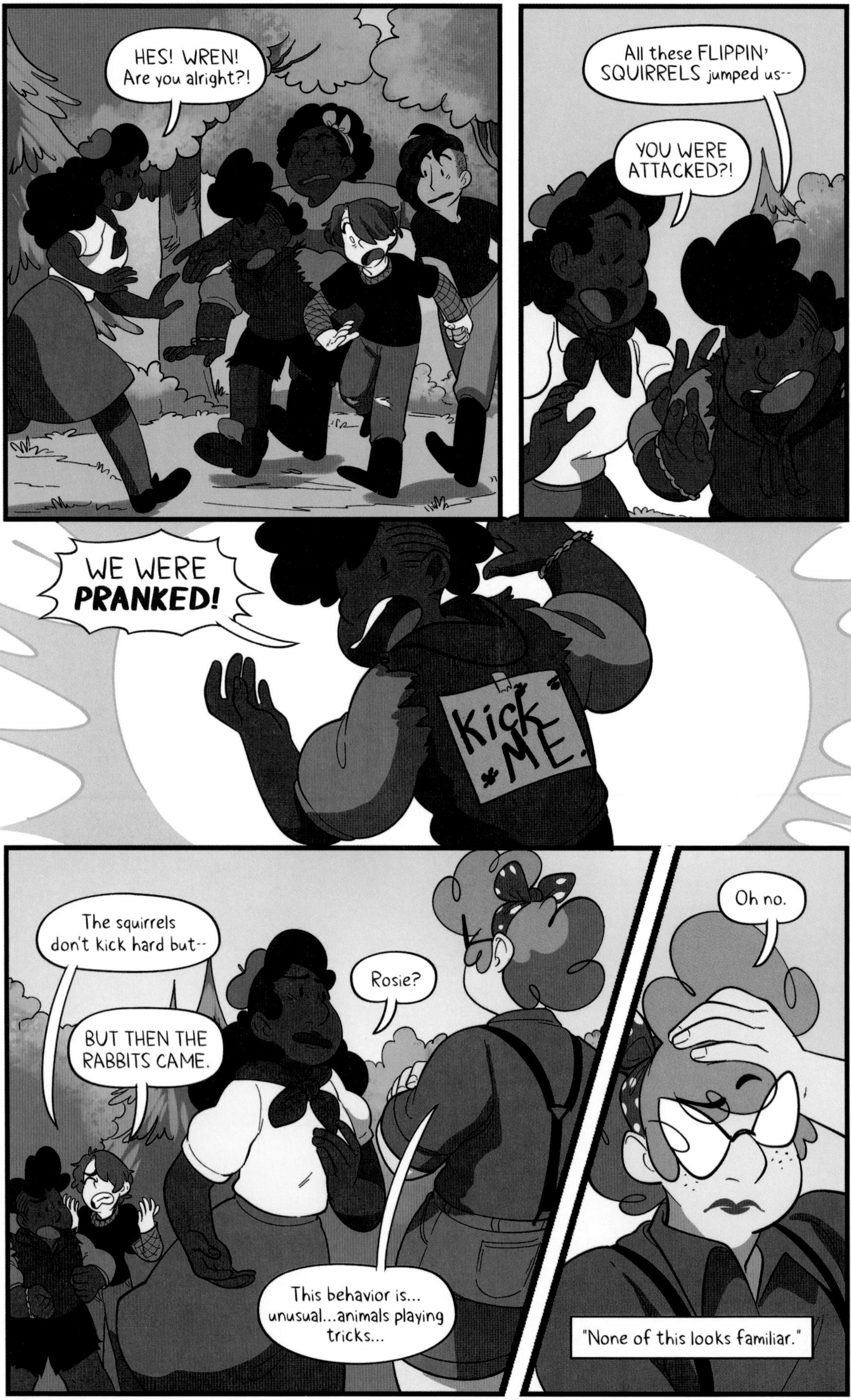
HES! WREN!
Are you alright?!
All these FLIPPIN' SQUIRRELS jumped us--
YOU WERE ATTACKED?!
WE WERE PRANKED!
KICK ME
The squirrels don't kick hard but--
BUT THEN THE RABBITS CAME.
Rosie?
This behavior is... unusual...animals playing tricks...
Oh no.
"None of this looks familiar."

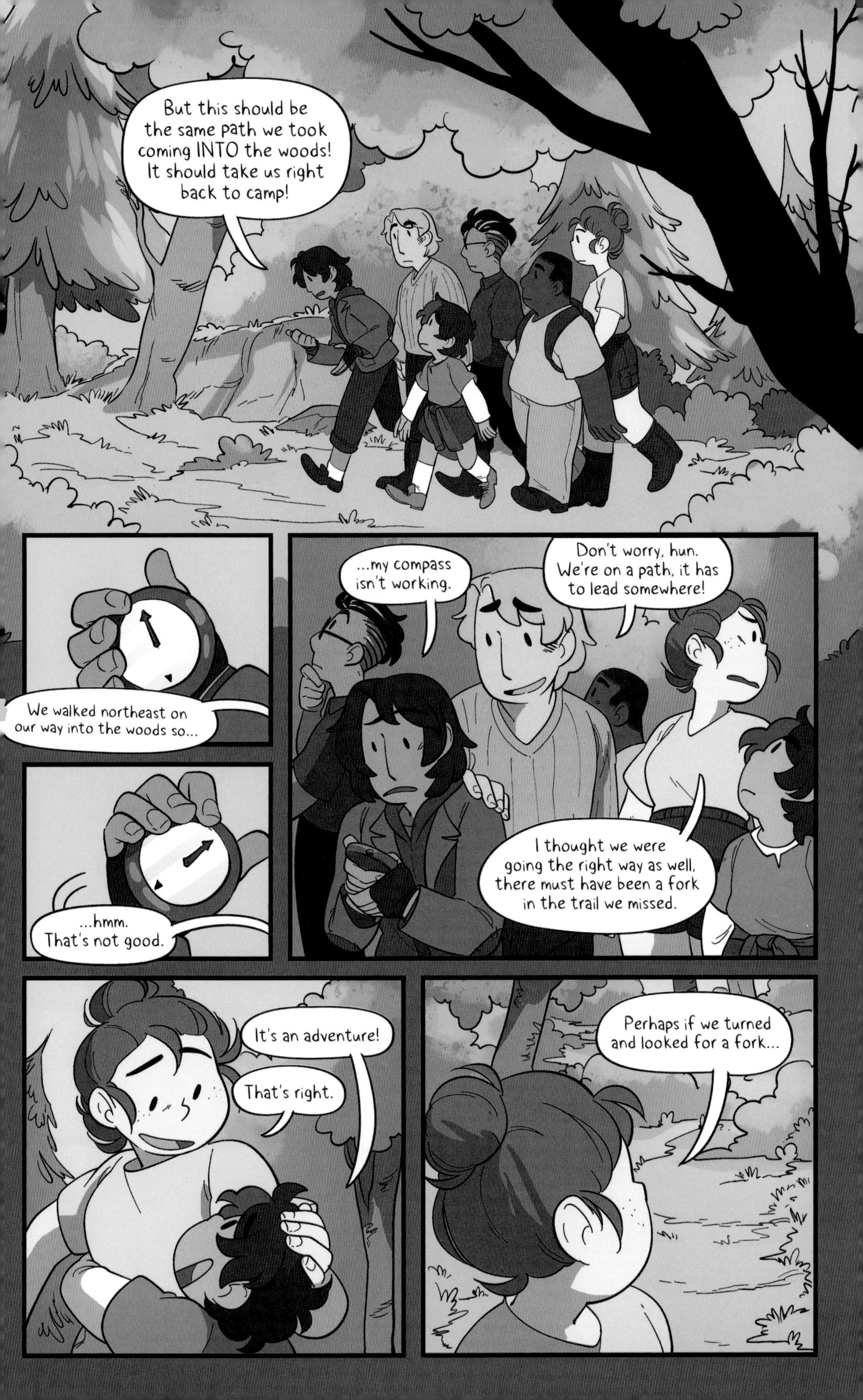
But this should be the same path we took coming INTO the woods! It should take us right back to camp!
We walked northeast on our way into the woods so...
...hmm. That's not good.
...my compass isn't working.
Don't worry, hun. We're on a path, it has to lead somewhere!
I thought we were going the right way as well, there must have been a fork in the trail we missed.
It's an adventure!
That's right.
Perhaps if we turned and looked for a fork...

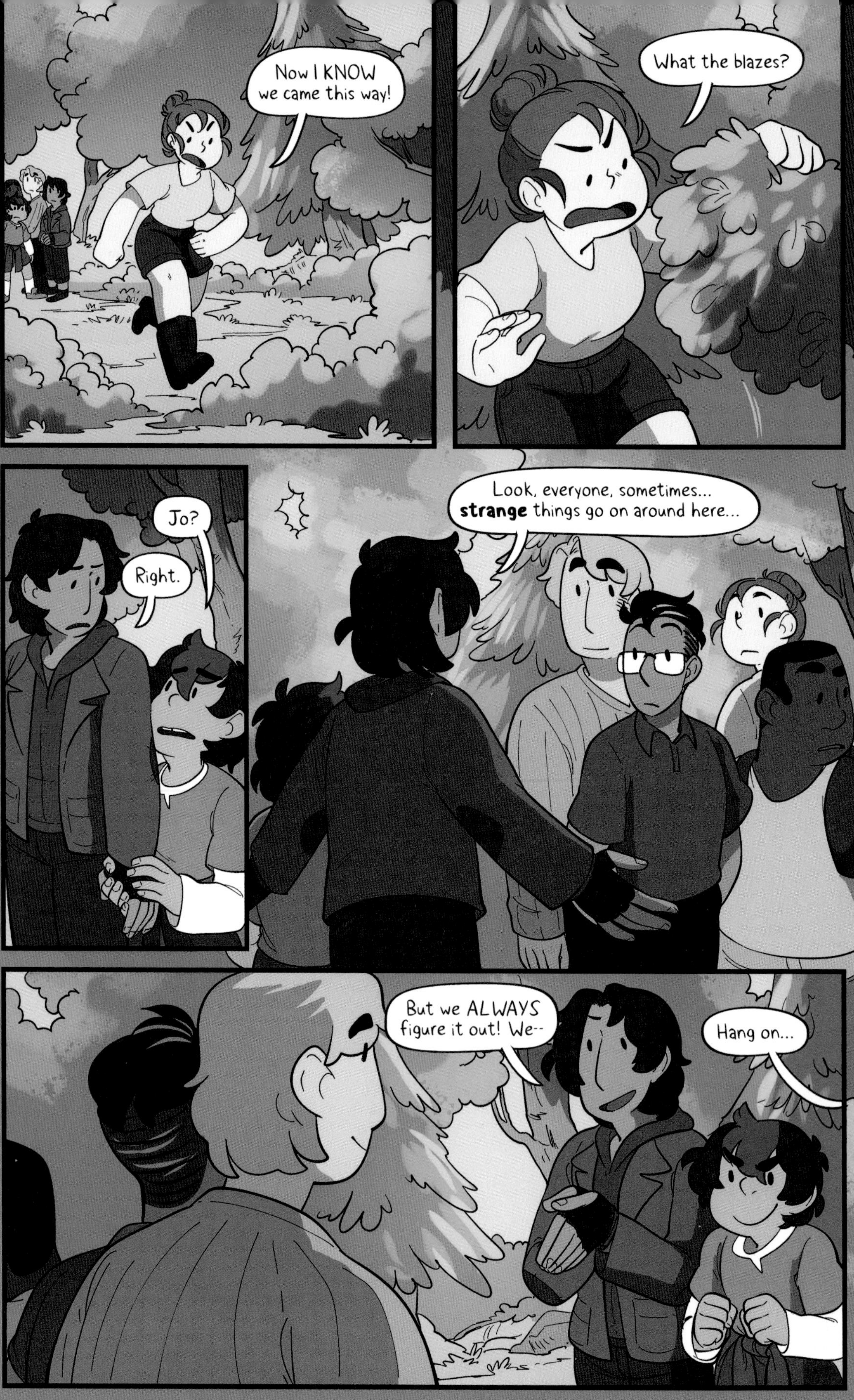
Now I KNOW we came this way!
What the blazes?
Jo?
Right.
Look, everyone, sometimes... **strange** things go on around here...
But we ALWAYS figure it out! We--
Hang on...

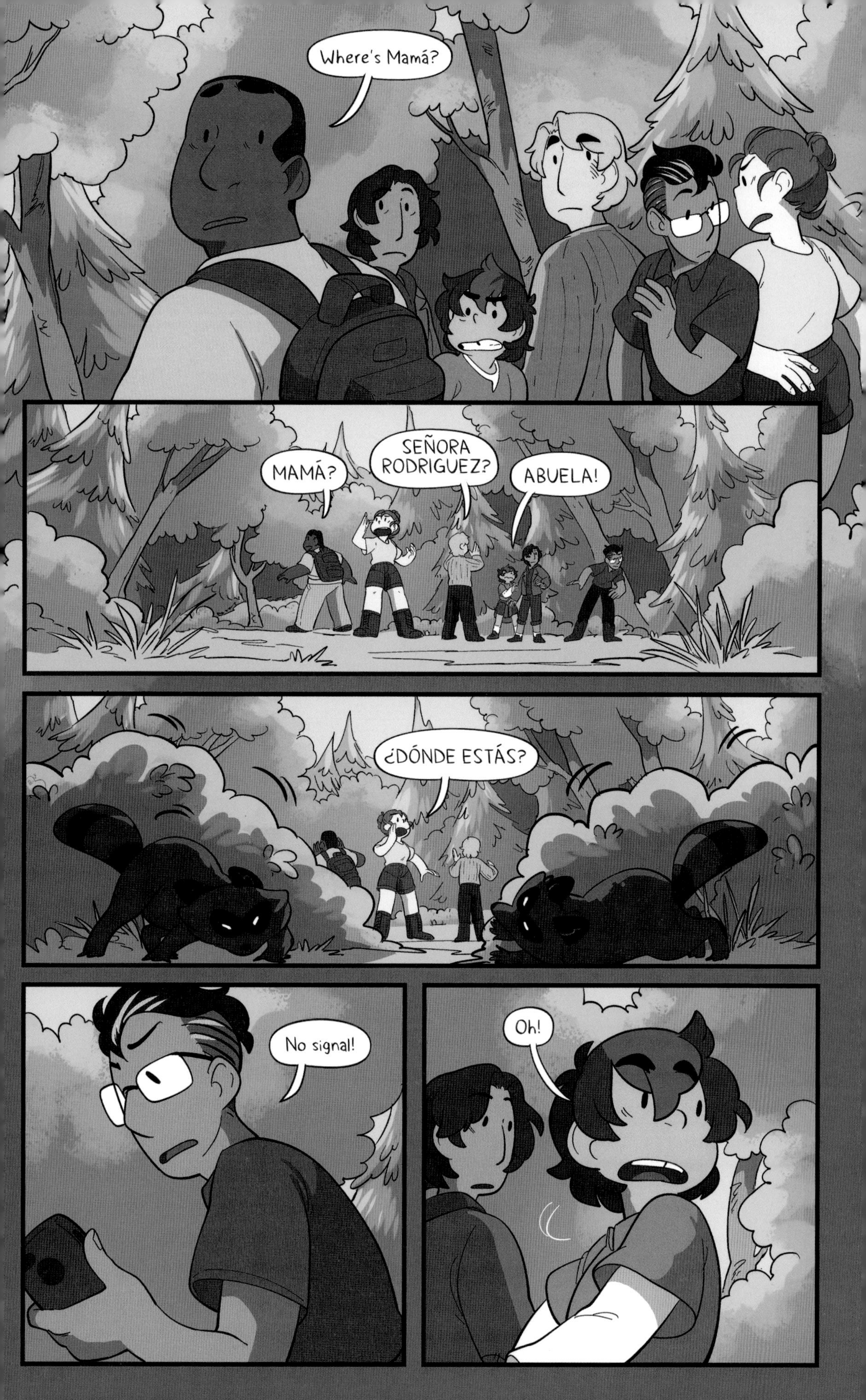
Where's Mamá?
MAMÁ?
SEÑORA RODRIGUEZ?
ABUELA!
¿DÓNDE ESTÁS?
No signal!
Oh!

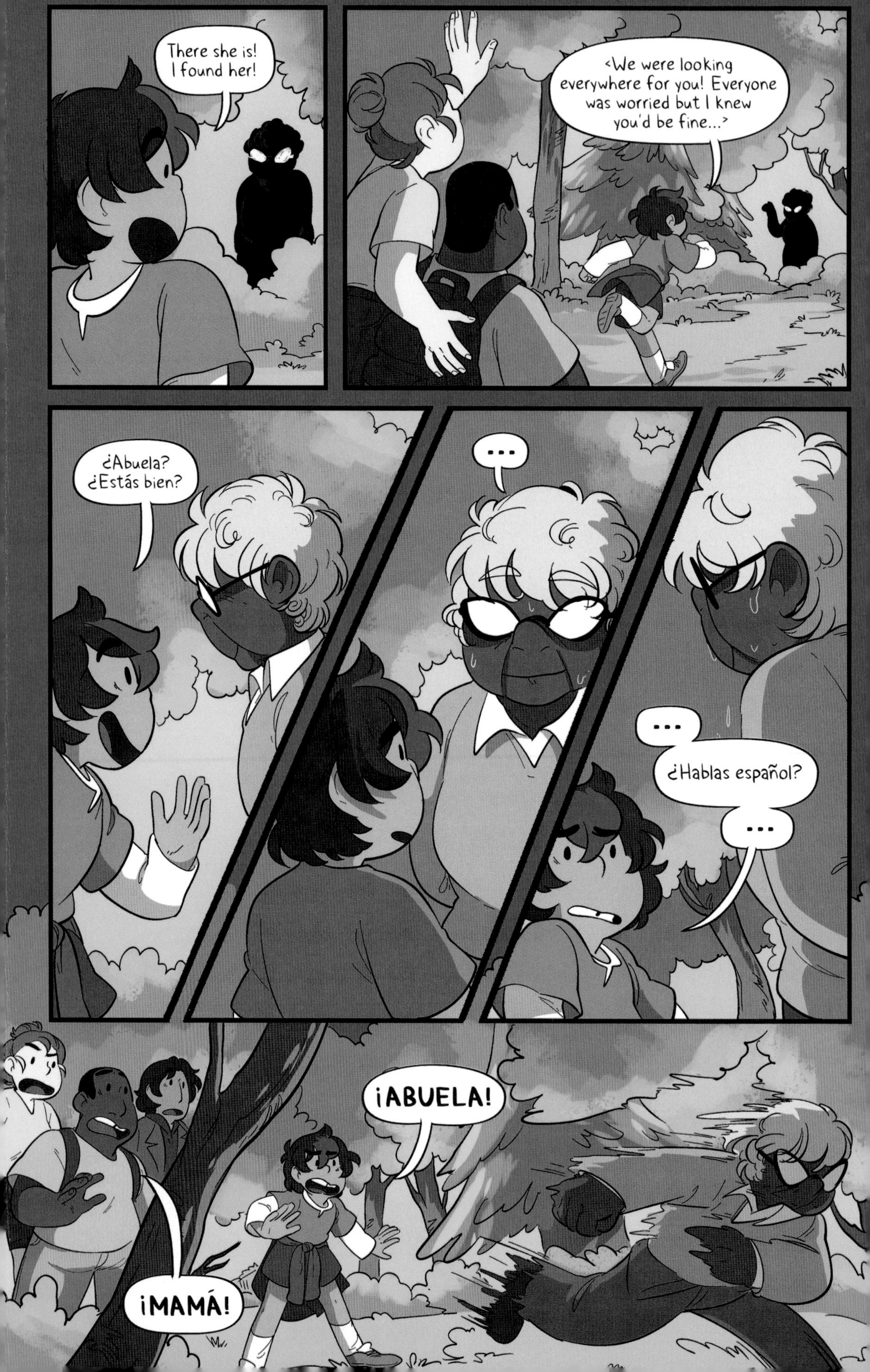
There she is! I found her!
<We were looking everywhere for you! Everyone was worried but I knew you'd be fine...>
¿Abuela? ¿Estás bien?
...
...
¿Hablas español?
...
¡ABUELA!
¡MAMÁ!

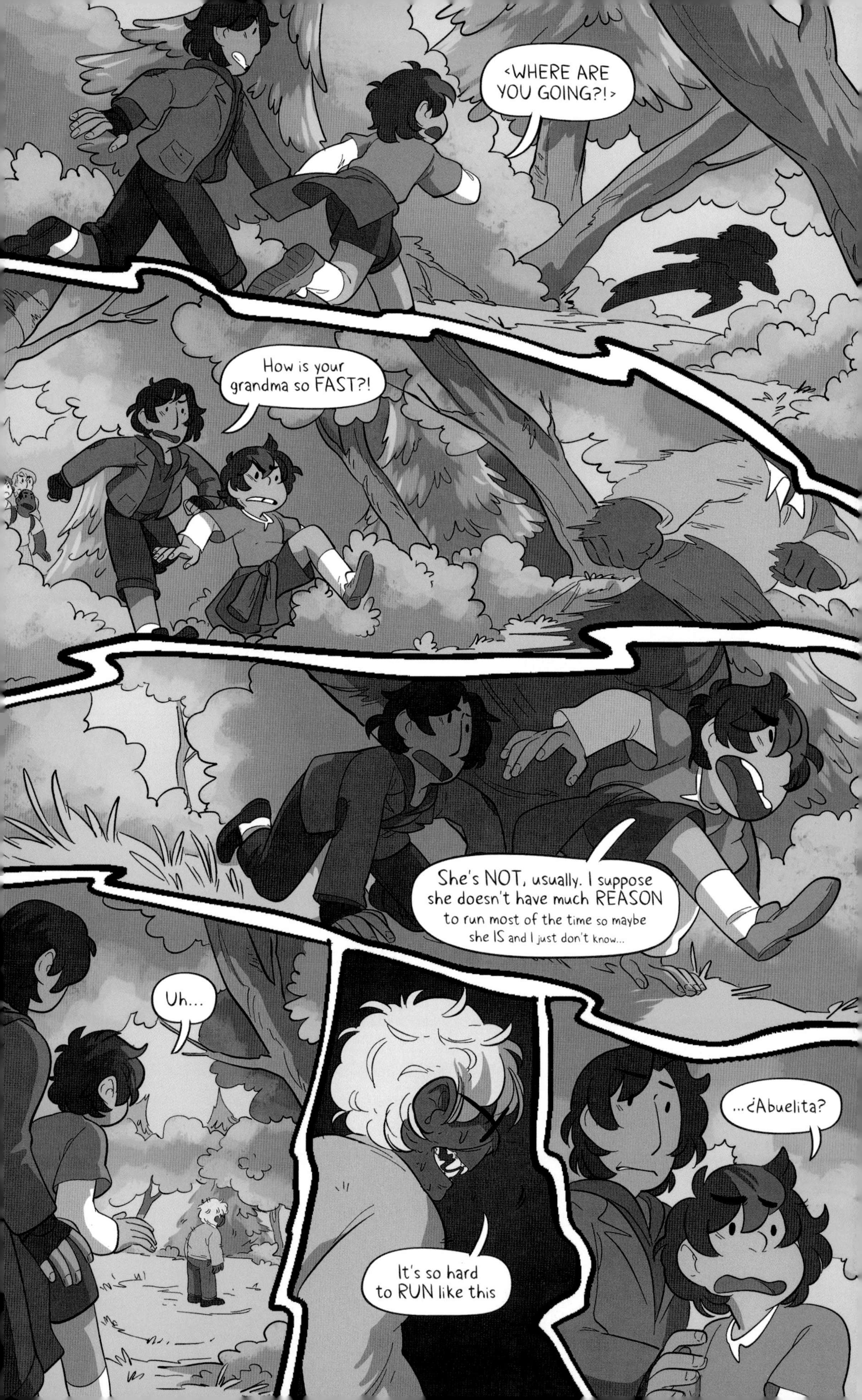

<WHERE ARE YOU GOING?!>
How is your grandma so FAST?!
She's NOT, usually. I suppose she doesn't have much REASON to run most of the time so maybe she IS and I just don't know...
Uh...
It's so hard to RUN like this
...¿Abuelita?

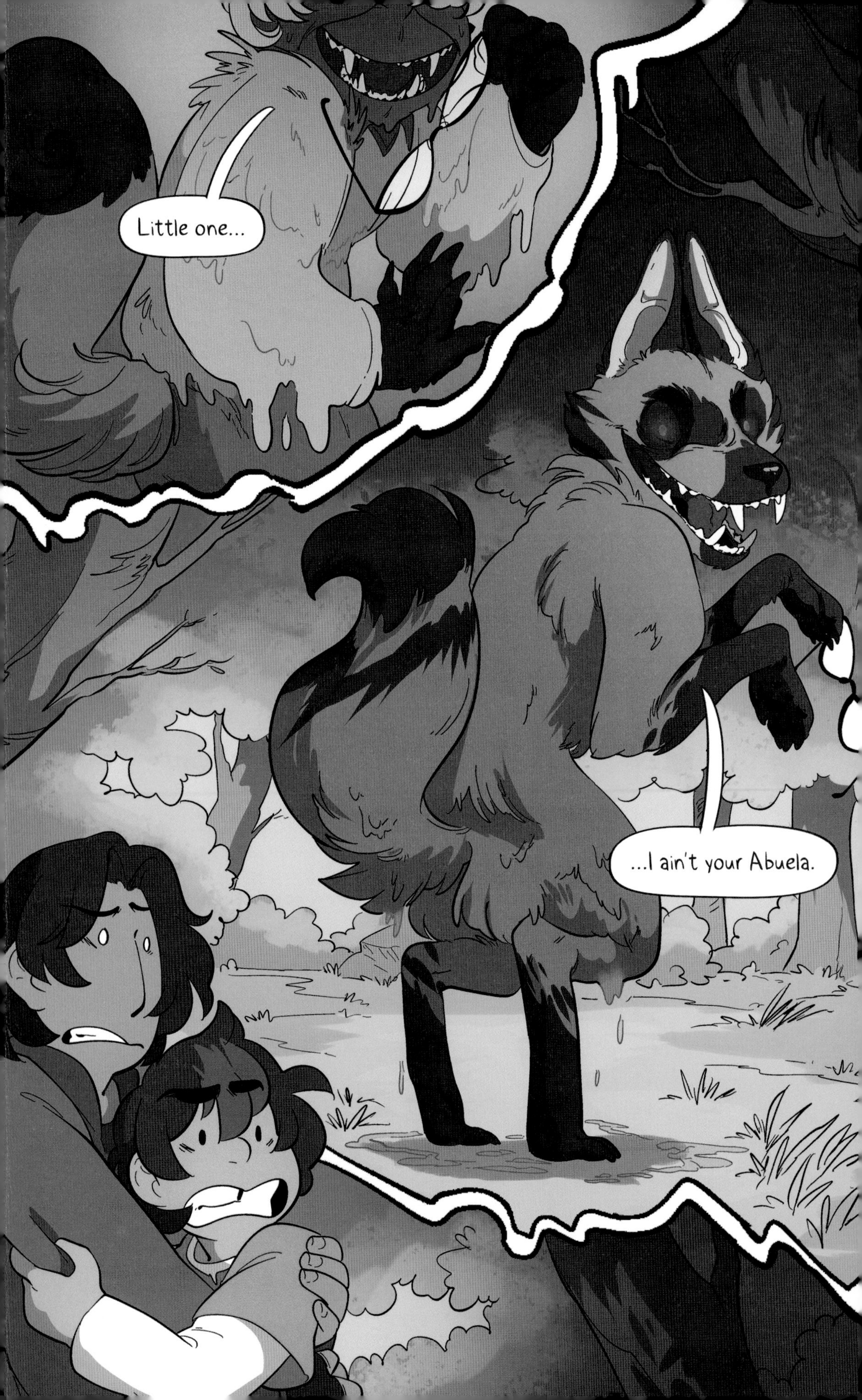
Little one...
...I ain't your Abuela.

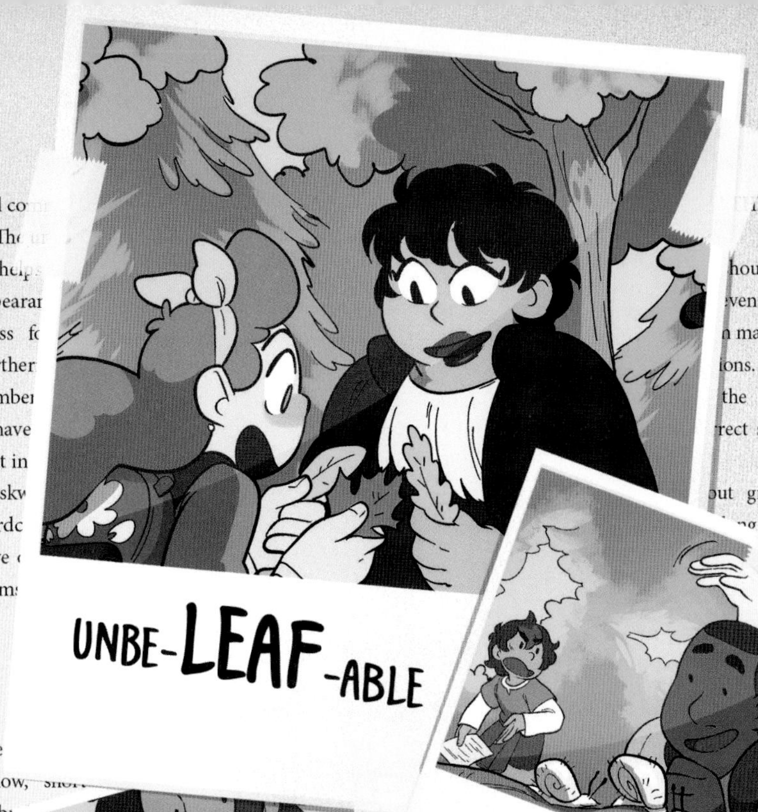
UNBE-LEAF-ABLE

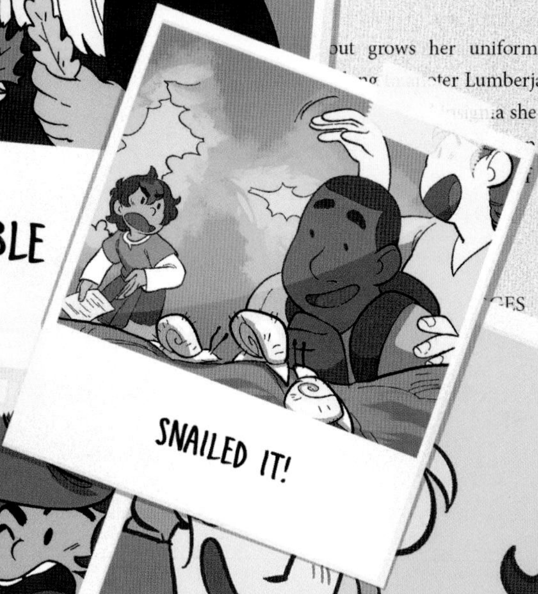
SNAILED IT!

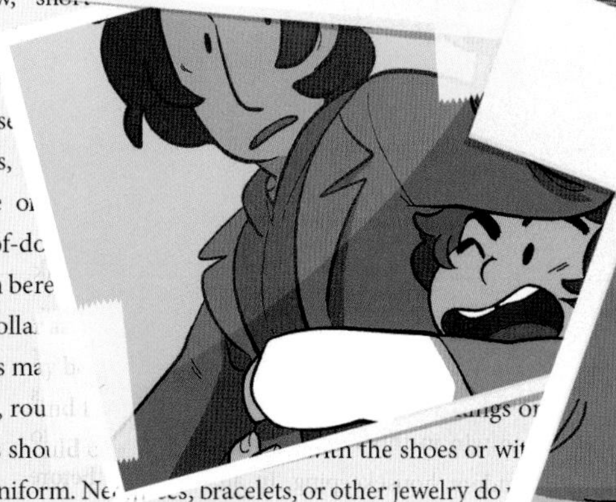

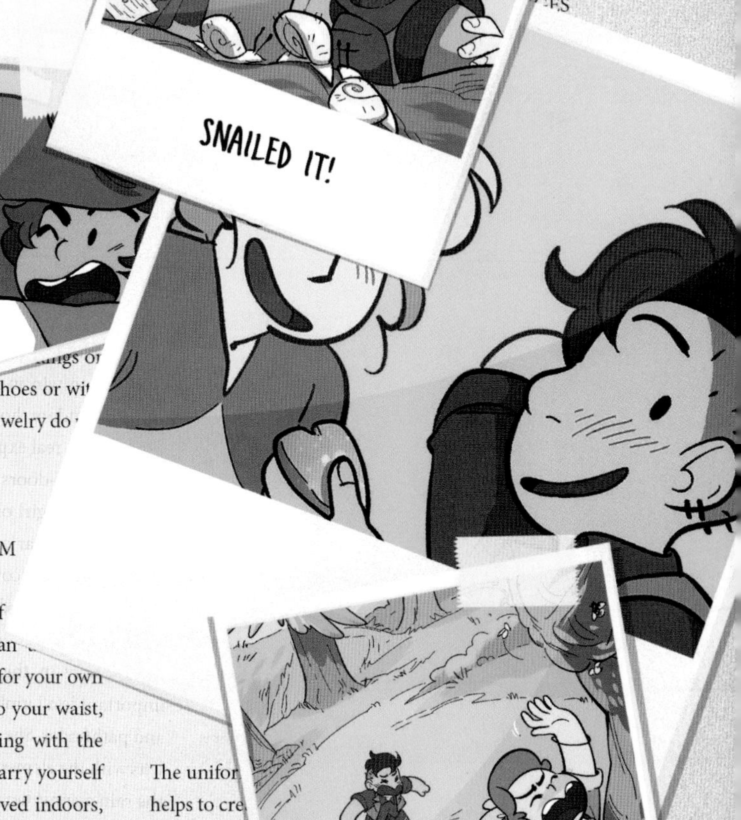

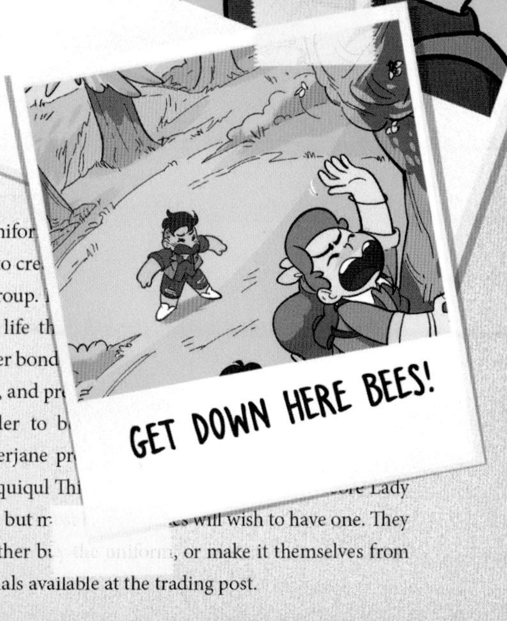
GET DOWN HERE BEES!

will co
The u
It helps
appearan
dress fo
Further
Lumber
to have
part in
Thiskw
Hardc
have
thems

HE UNIFORM

hould be worn at camp
vents when Lumberjanes
n may also be worn at other
ions. It should be worn as a
the uniform dress with
rrect shoes, and stocking or
out grows her uniform or
ter Lumberjane.
a she has
her
her

The
yellow,
emb
the w
choose
slacks,
made o
out-of-dc
green bere
the colla
Shoes ma
heels, rou kings or
socks shou with the shoes or wit
the uniform. Ne bracelets, or other jewelry do
belong with a Lumberjane uniform.

HOW TO WEAR THE UNIFORM

To look well in a uniform demands first of uniform be kept in good condition—clean pressed. See that the skirt is the right length for your own height and build, that the belt is adjusted to your waist, that your shoes and stockings are in keeping with the uniform, that you watch your posture and carry yourself with dignity and grace. If the beret is removed indoors, be sure that your hair is neat and kept in place with an insonspicuous clip or ribbon. When you wear a Lumberjane uniform you are identified as a member of this organization and you should be doubly careful to conduct yourself in a way that will show everyone that courtesy and thoughtfullness are part of being a Lumberjane. People are likely to judge a whole nation by the selfishness of a few individuals, to criticize a whole family because of the misconduct of one member, and to feel unkindly toward and organization because of the

The unifor
helps to cre
in a group.
active life th
another bond
future, and pr
in order to b
Lumberjane pr
Penniquiqul Thi ore Lady
Types, but m es will wish to have one. They
can either bu the uniform, or make it themselves from
materials available at the trading post.

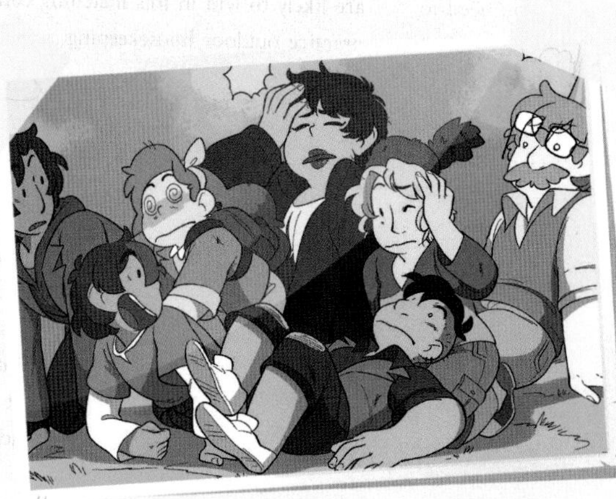

LUMBERJANES FIELD MANUAL

CHAPTER THIRTY-NINE

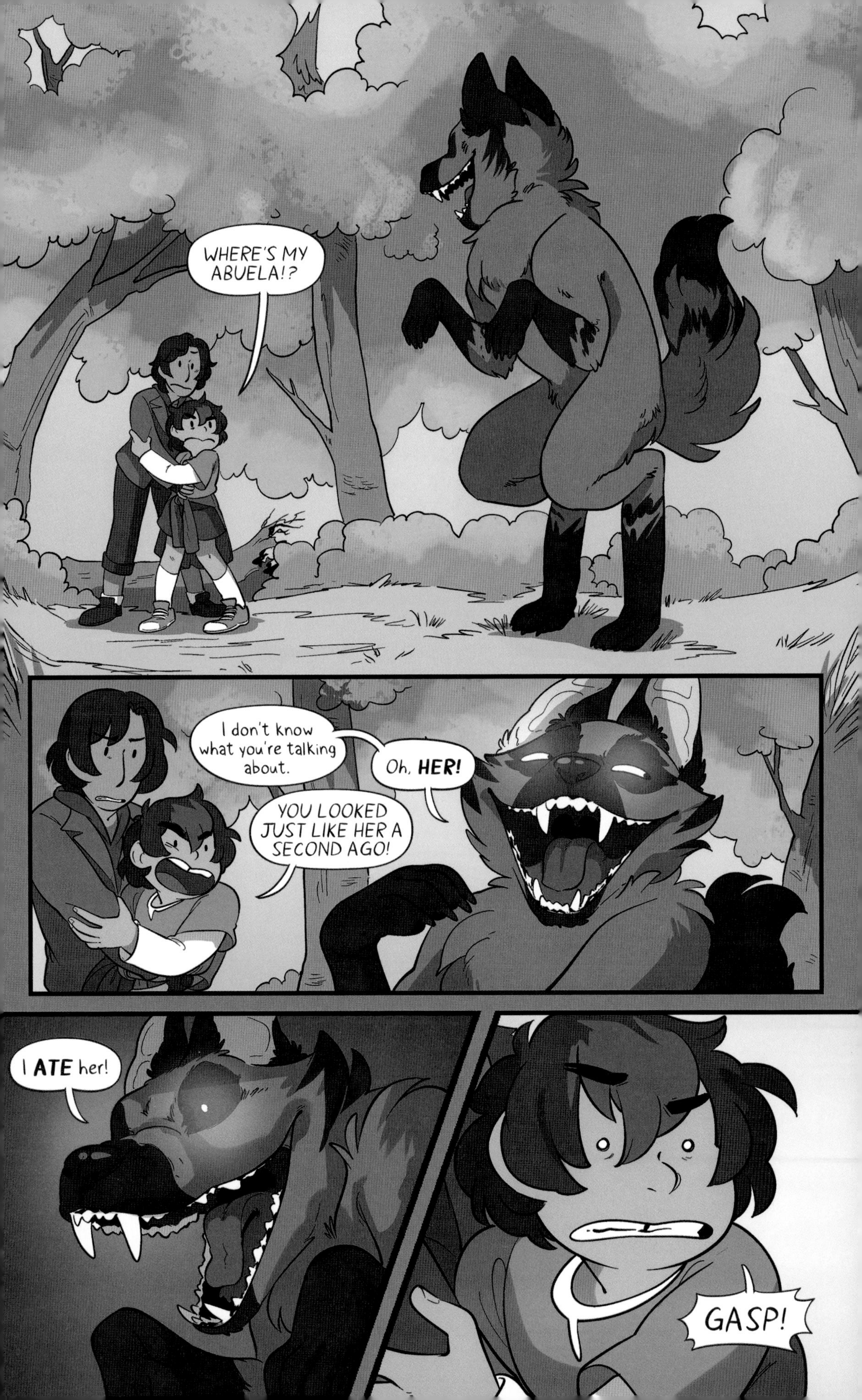
WHERE'S MY ABUELA!?
I don't know what you're talking about.
Oh, **HER!**
YOU LOOKED JUST LIKE HER A SECOND AGO!
I **ATE** her!
GASP!

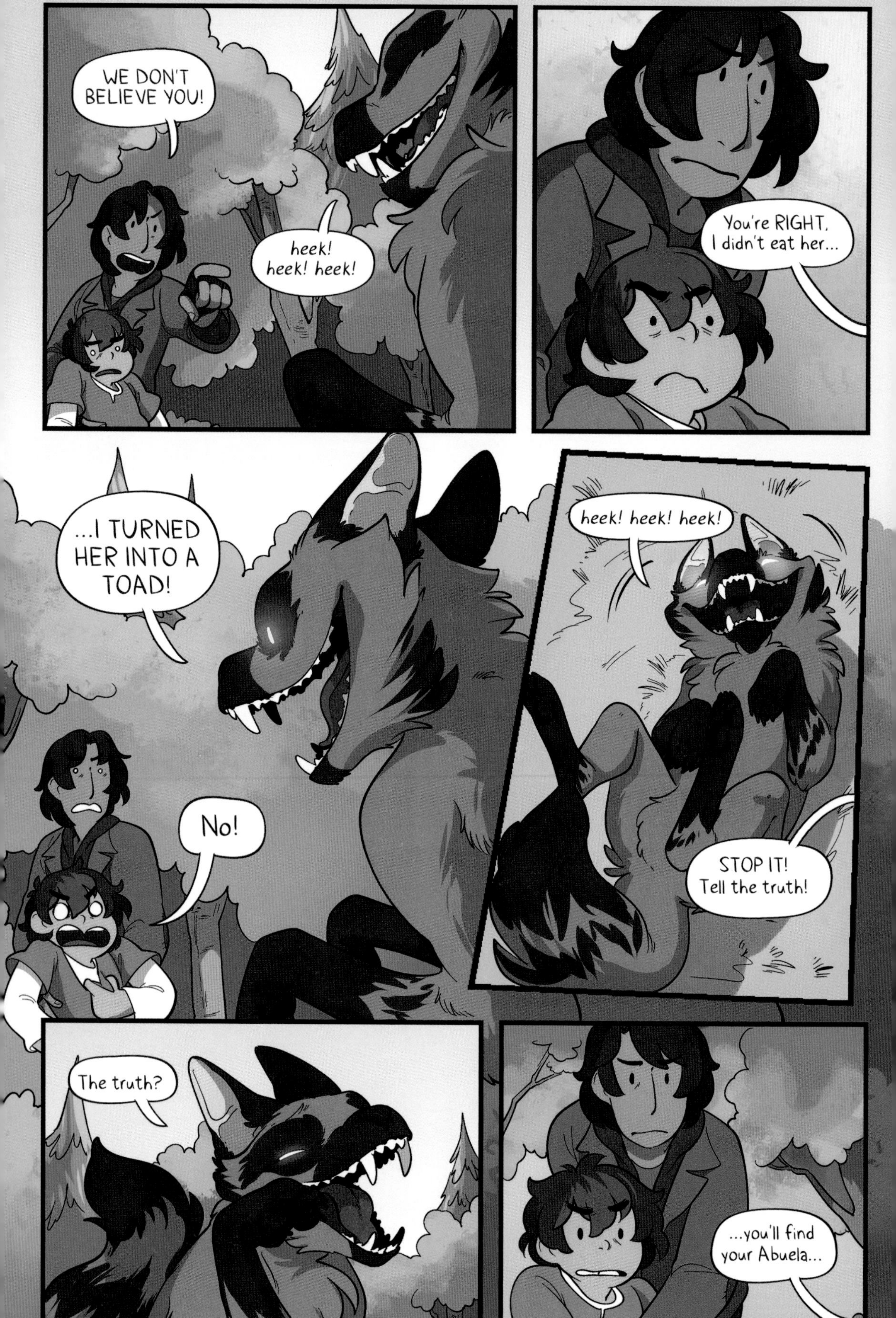
WE DON'T BELIEVE YOU!
heek! heek! heek!
You're RIGHT, I didn't eat her...
...I TURNED HER INTO A TOAD!
No!
heek! heek! heek!
STOP IT! Tell the truth!
The truth?
...you'll find your Abuela...

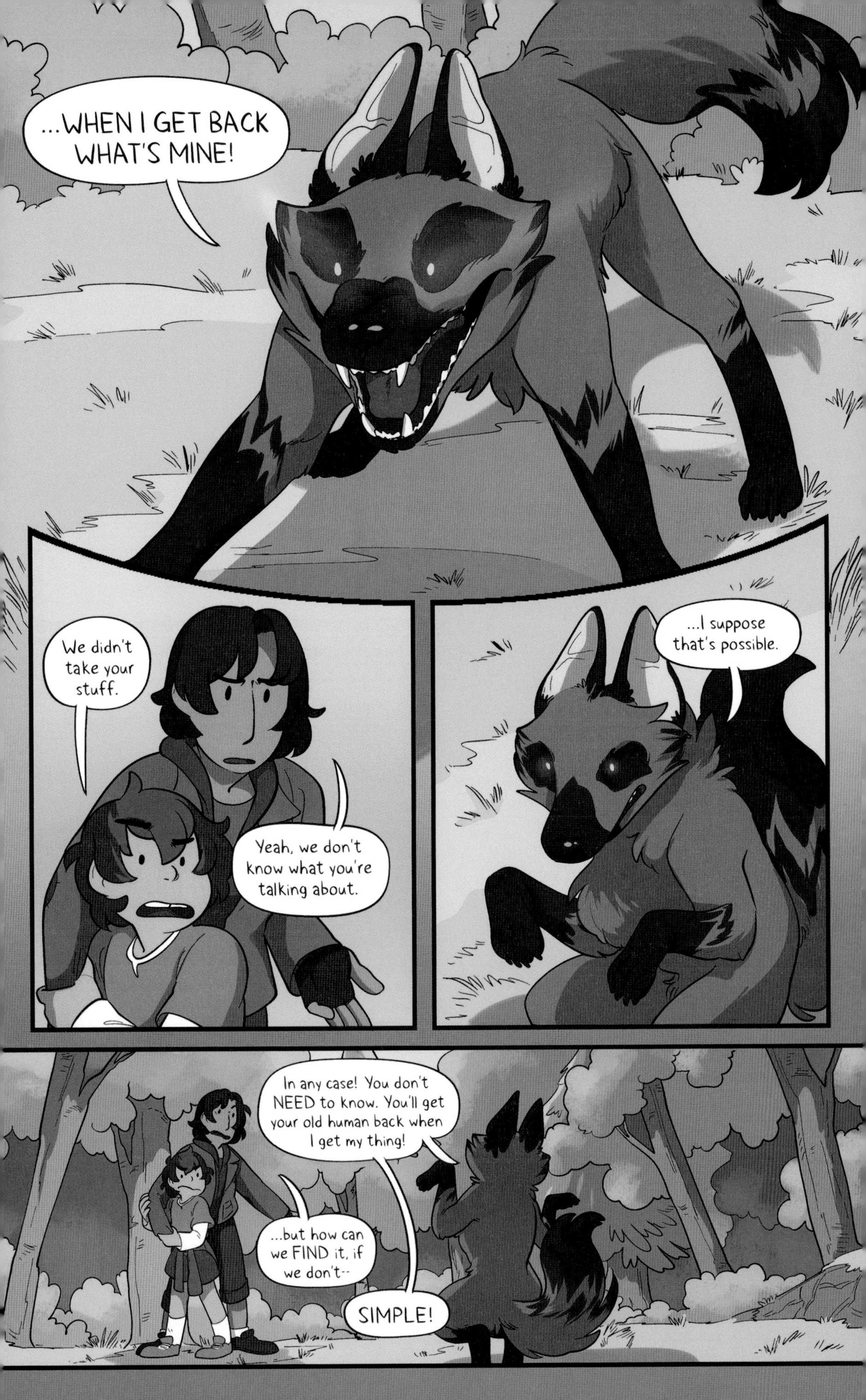
...WHEN I GET BACK WHAT'S MINE!
We didn't take your stuff.
Yeah, we don't know what you're talking about.
...I suppose that's possible.
In any case! You don't NEED to know. You'll get your old human back when I get my thing!
...but how can we FIND it, if we don't--
SIMPLE!

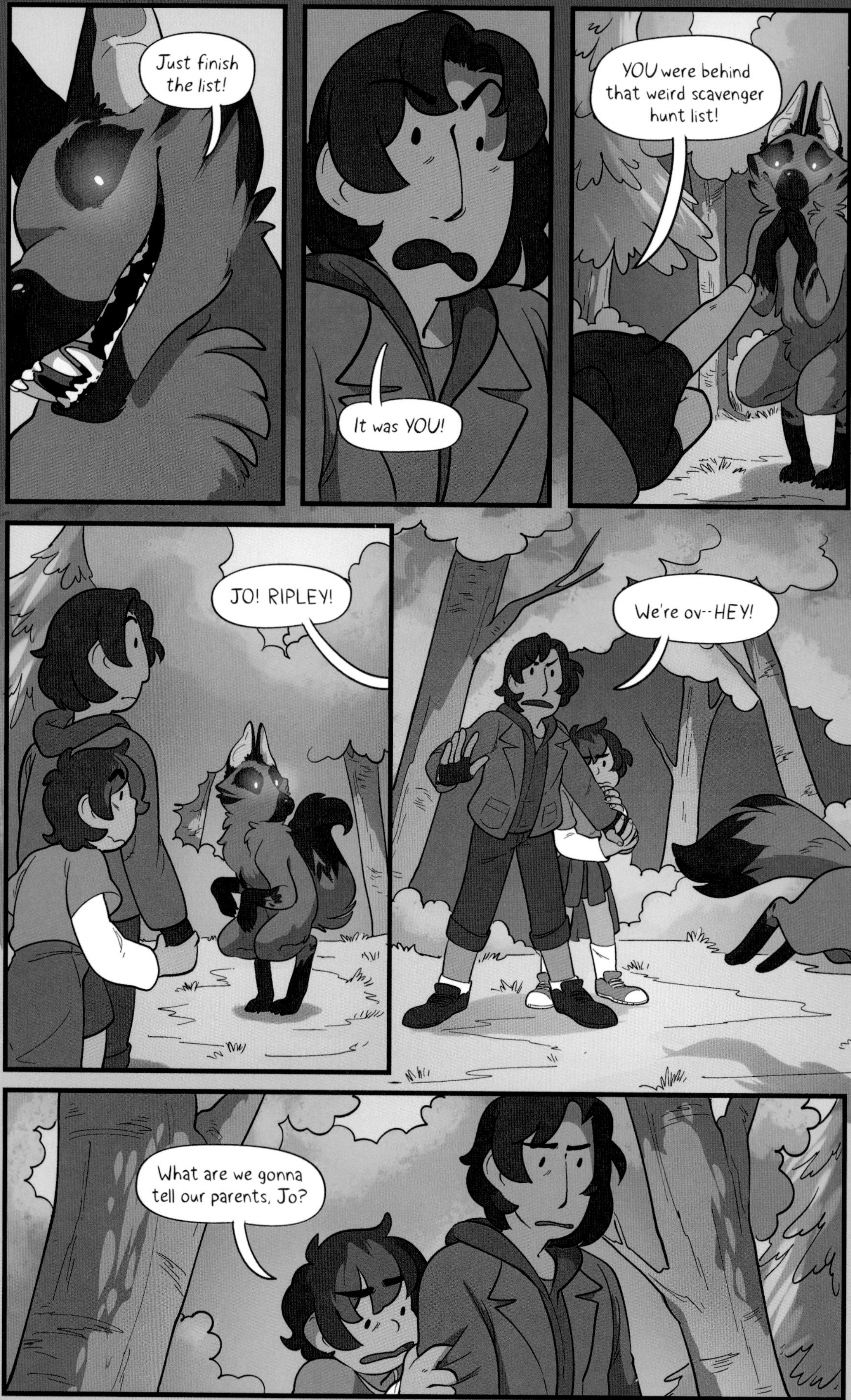
Just finish the list!
It was YOU!
YOU were behind that weird scavenger hunt list!
JO! RIPLEY!
We're ov--HEY!
What are we gonna tell our parents, Jo?

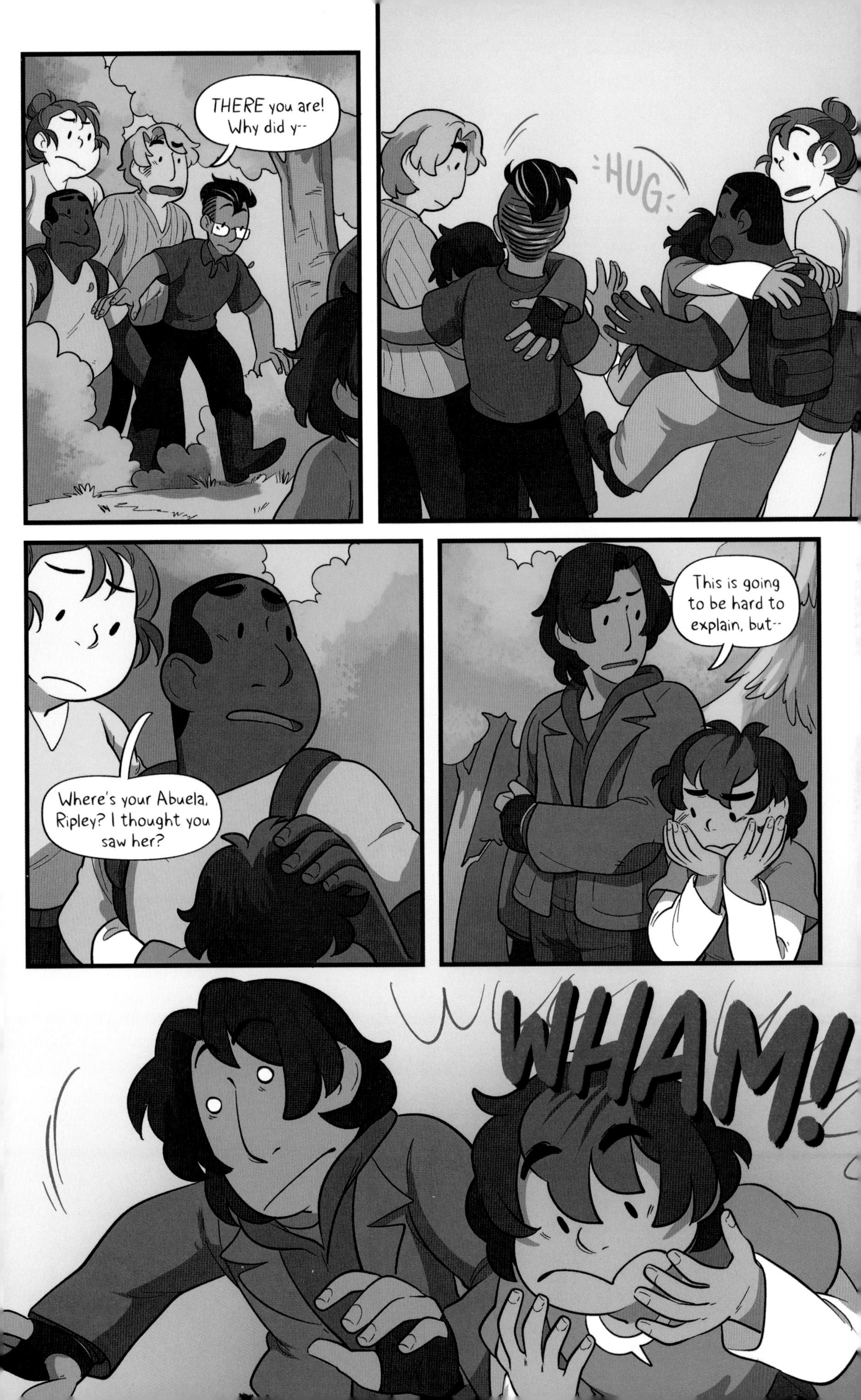
THERE you are! Why did y--
HUG
Where's your Abuela, Ripley? I thought you saw her?
This is going to be hard to explain, but--
WHAM!

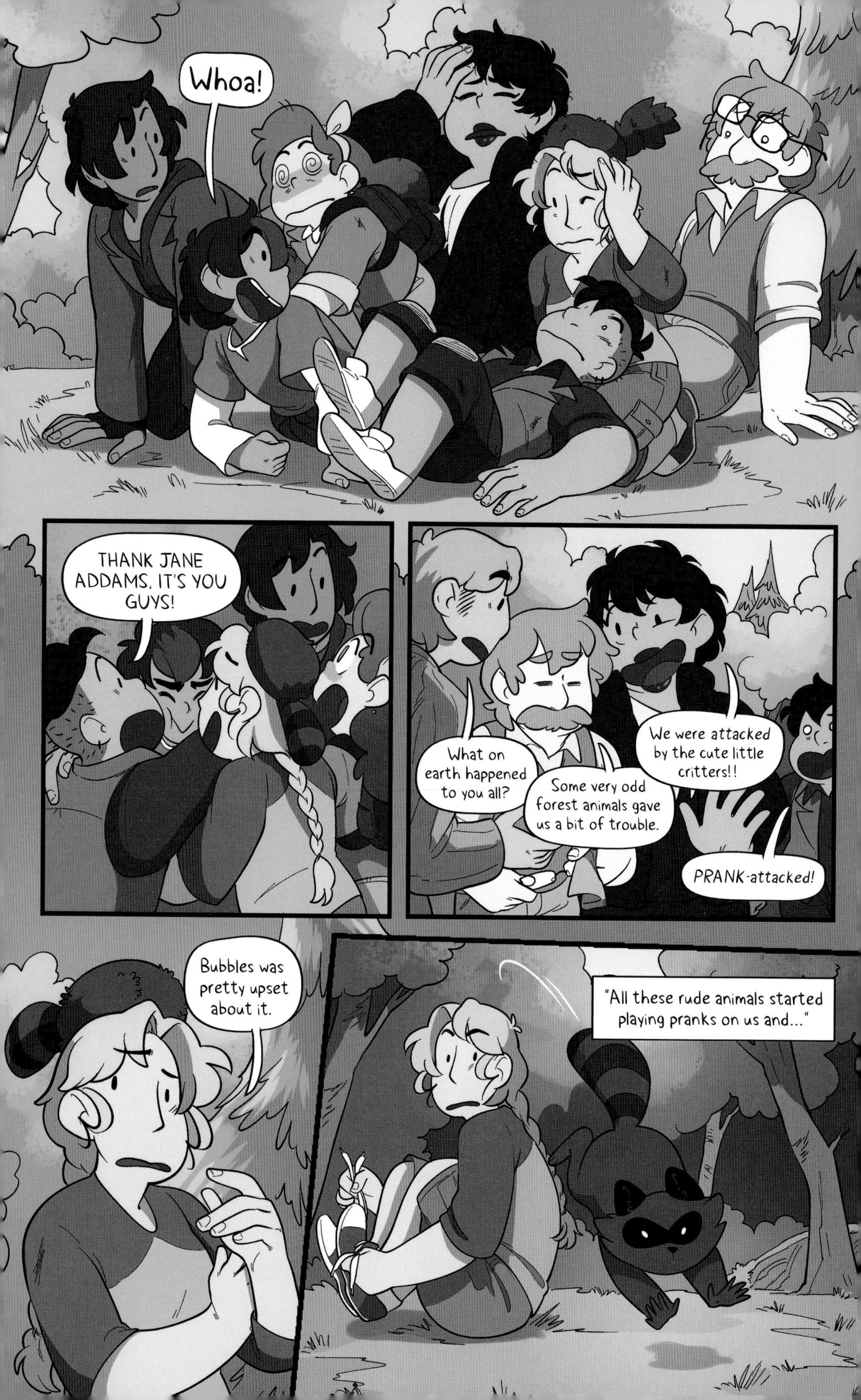
Whoa!
THANK JANE ADDAMS, IT'S YOU GUYS!
What on earth happened to you all?
Some very odd forest animals gave us a bit of trouble.
We were attacked by the cute little critters!!
PRANK-attacked!
Bubbles was pretty upset about it.
"All these rude animals started playing pranks on us and..."

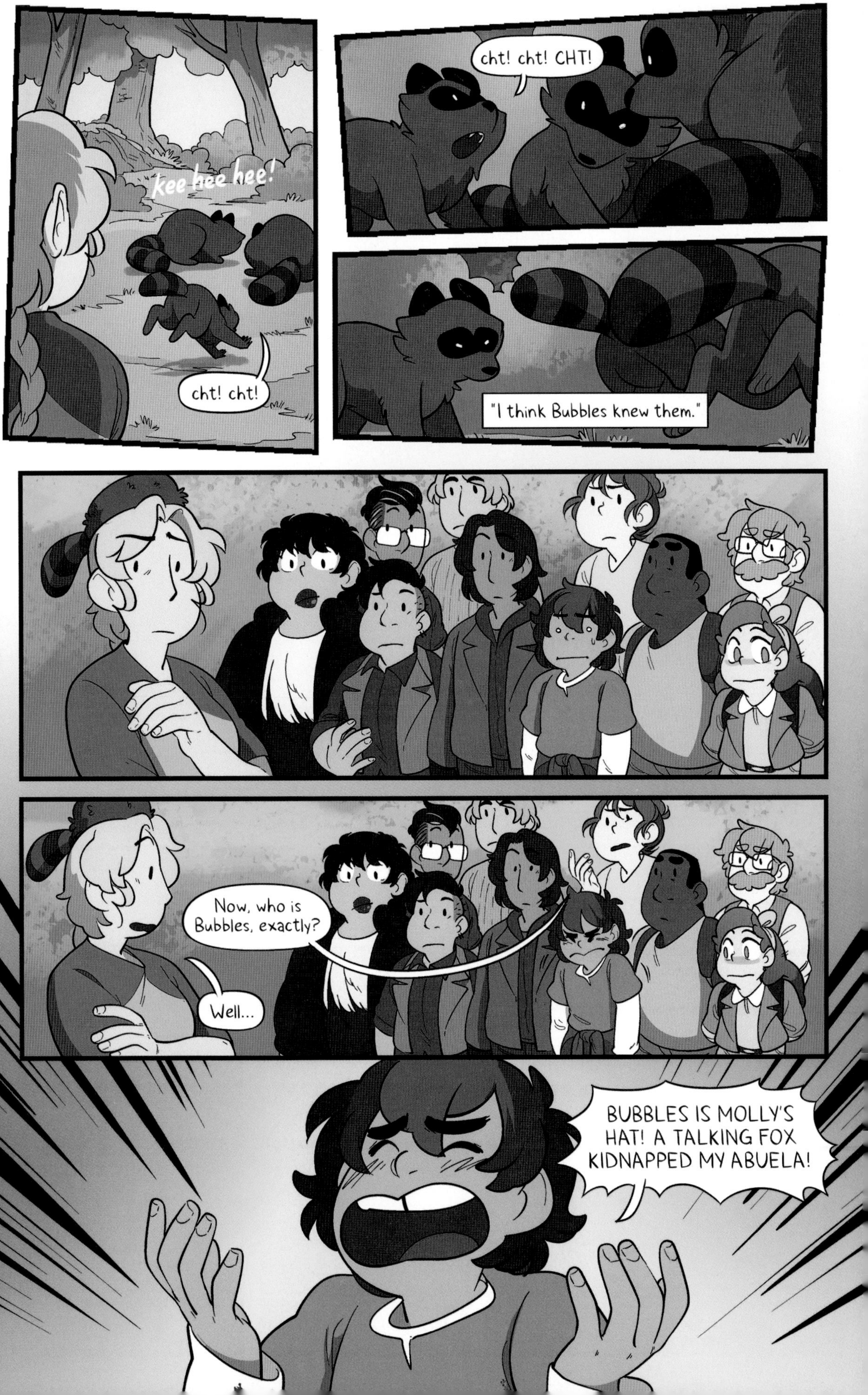
kee hee hee!
cht! cht!
cht! cht! CHT!
"I think Bubbles knew them."
Now, who is Bubbles, exactly?
Well...
BUBBLES IS MOLLY'S HAT! A TALKING FOX KIDNAPPED MY ABUELA!

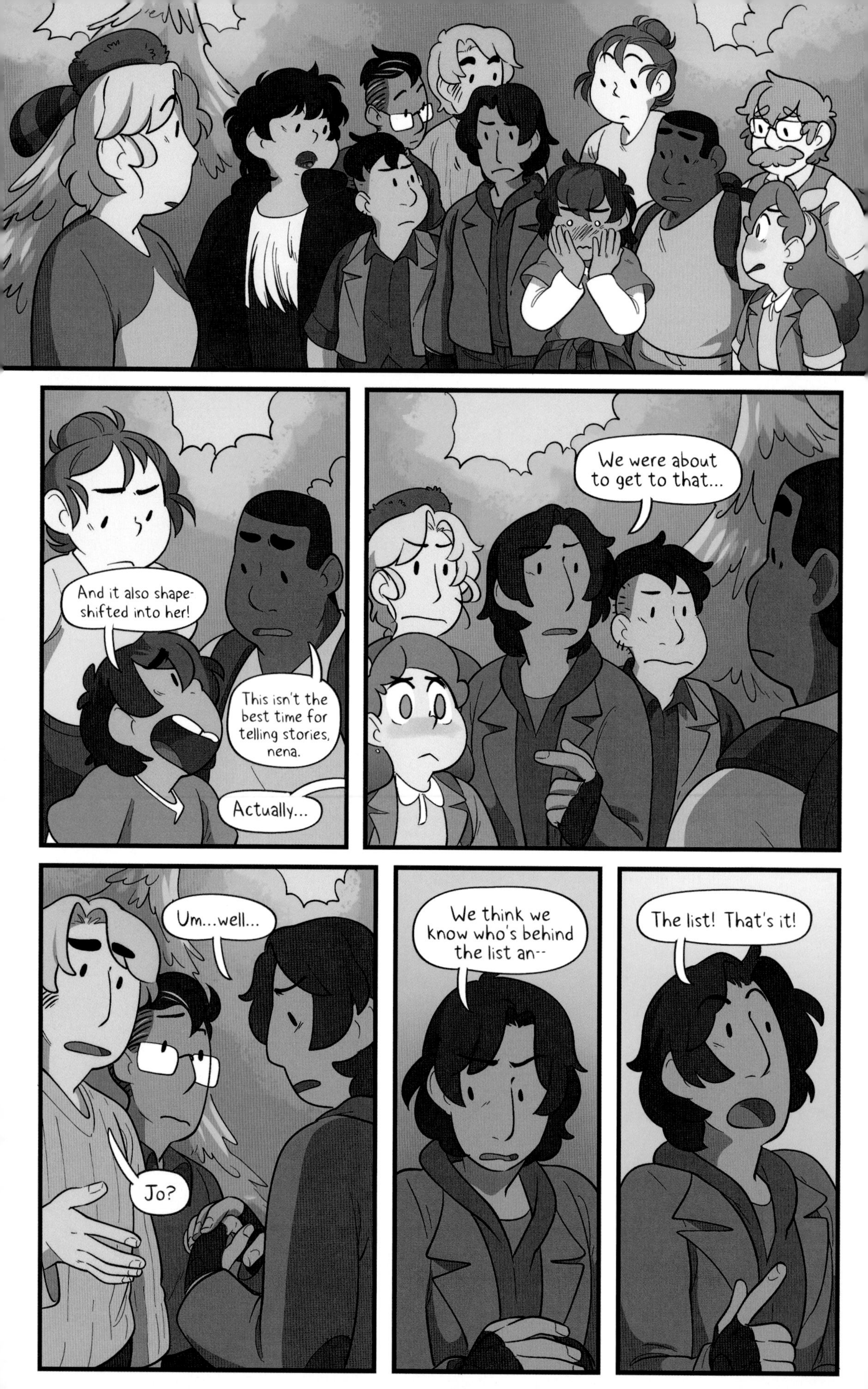
And it also shape-shifted into her!
This isn't the best time for telling stories, nena.
Actually...
We were about to get to that...
Um...well...
Jo?
We think we know who's behind the list an--
The list! That's it!

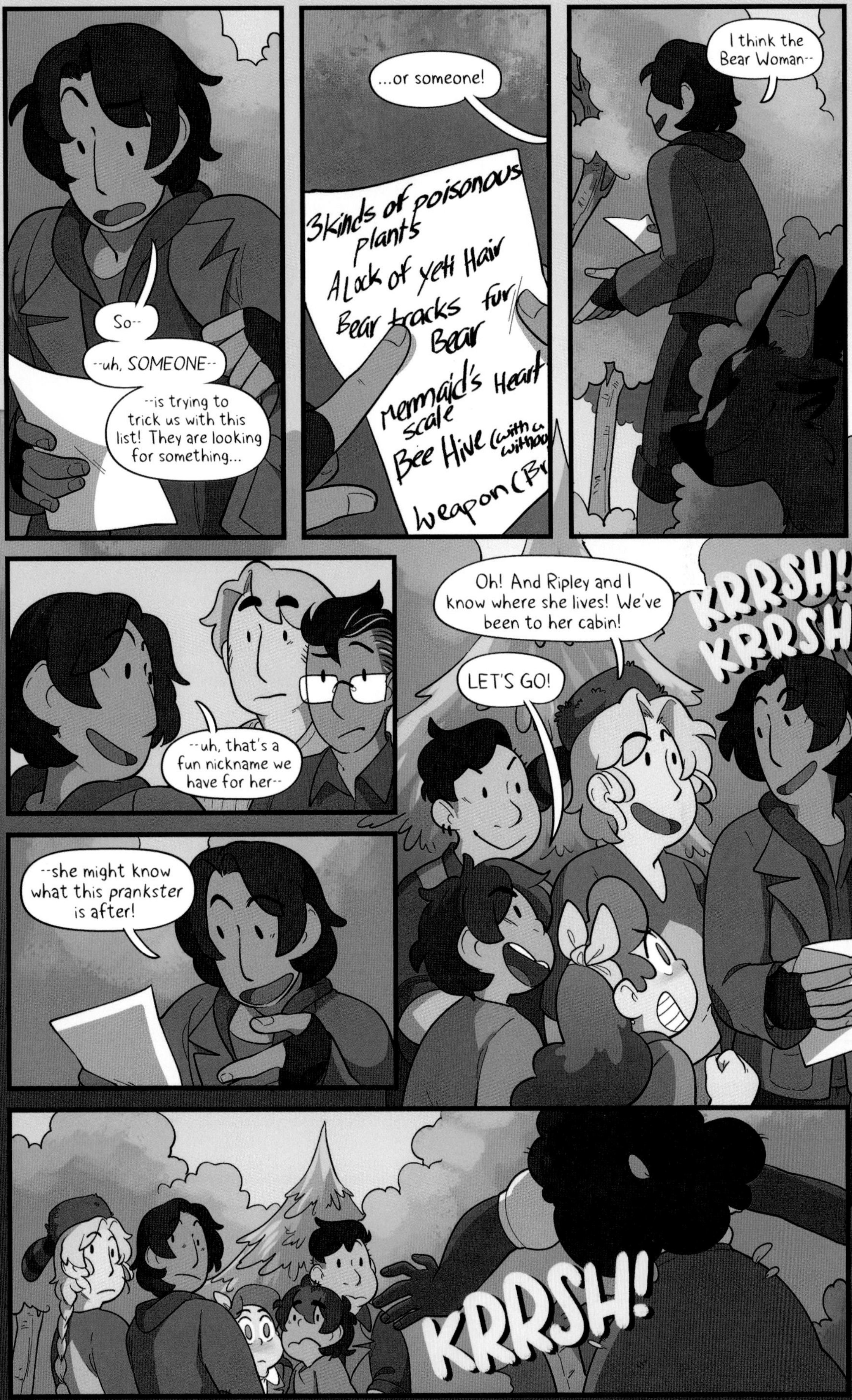
So--
--uh, SOMEONE--
--is trying to trick us with this list! They are looking for something...
...or someone!
3 kinds of poisonous plants
A Lock of yeti Hair
Bear tracks fur Bear
Mermaid's Heart scale
Bee Hive
Weapon
I think the Bear Woman--
--uh, that's a fun nickname we have for her--
--she might know what this prankster is after!
Oh! And Ripley and I know where she lives! We've been to her cabin!
LET'S GO!
KRRSH! KRRSH!
KRRSH!

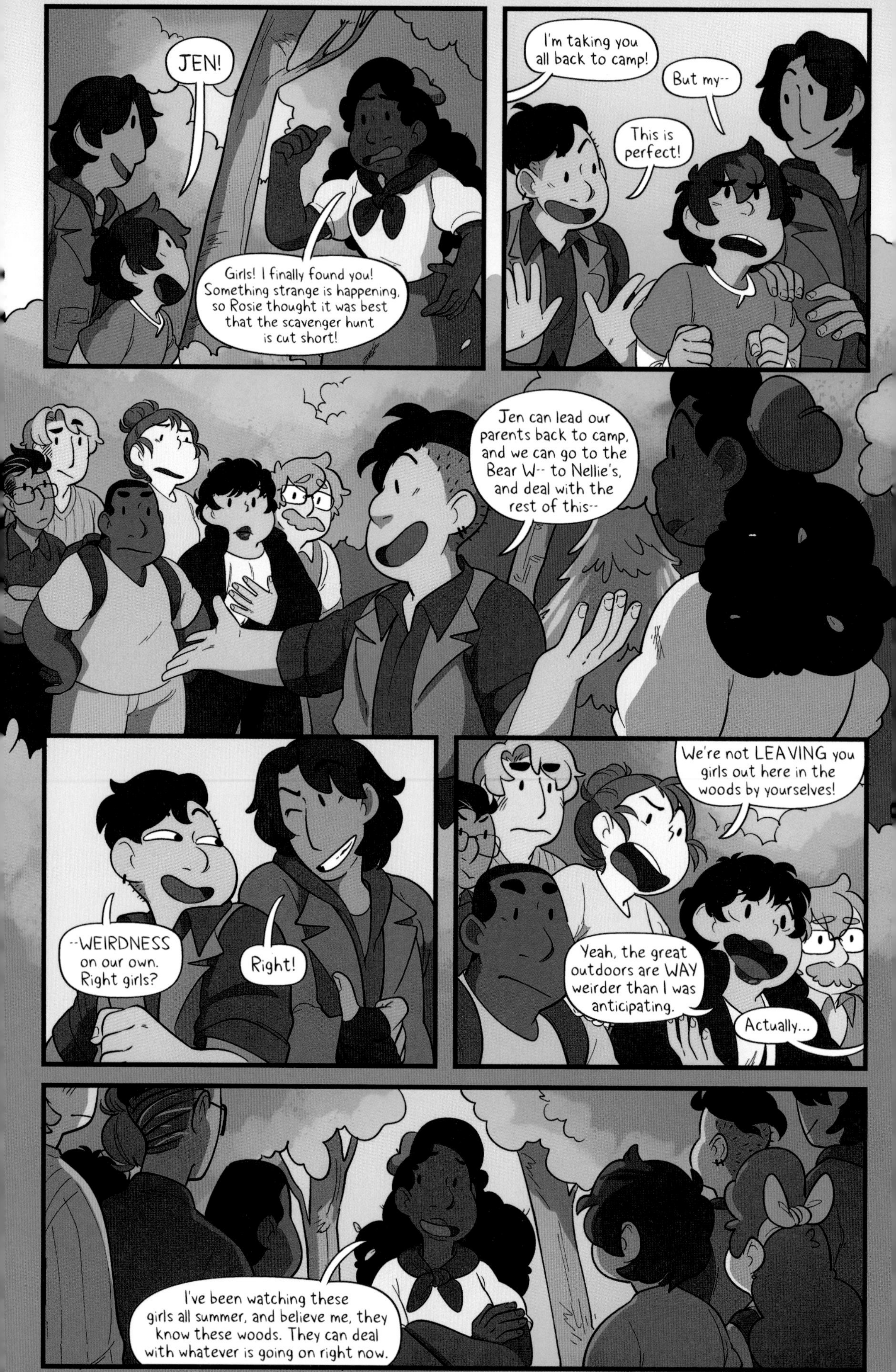
JEN!
Girls! I finally found you! Something strange is happening, so Rosie thought it was best that the scavenger hunt is cut short!
I'm taking you all back to camp!
But my--
This is perfect!
Jen can lead our parents back to camp, and we can go to the Bear W-- to Nellie's, and deal with the rest of this--
--WEIRDNESS on our own. Right girls?
Right!
We're not LEAVING you girls out here in the woods by yourselves!
Yeah, the great outdoors are WAY weirder than I was anticipating.
Actually...
I've been watching these girls all summer, and believe me, they know these woods. They can deal with whatever is going on right now.

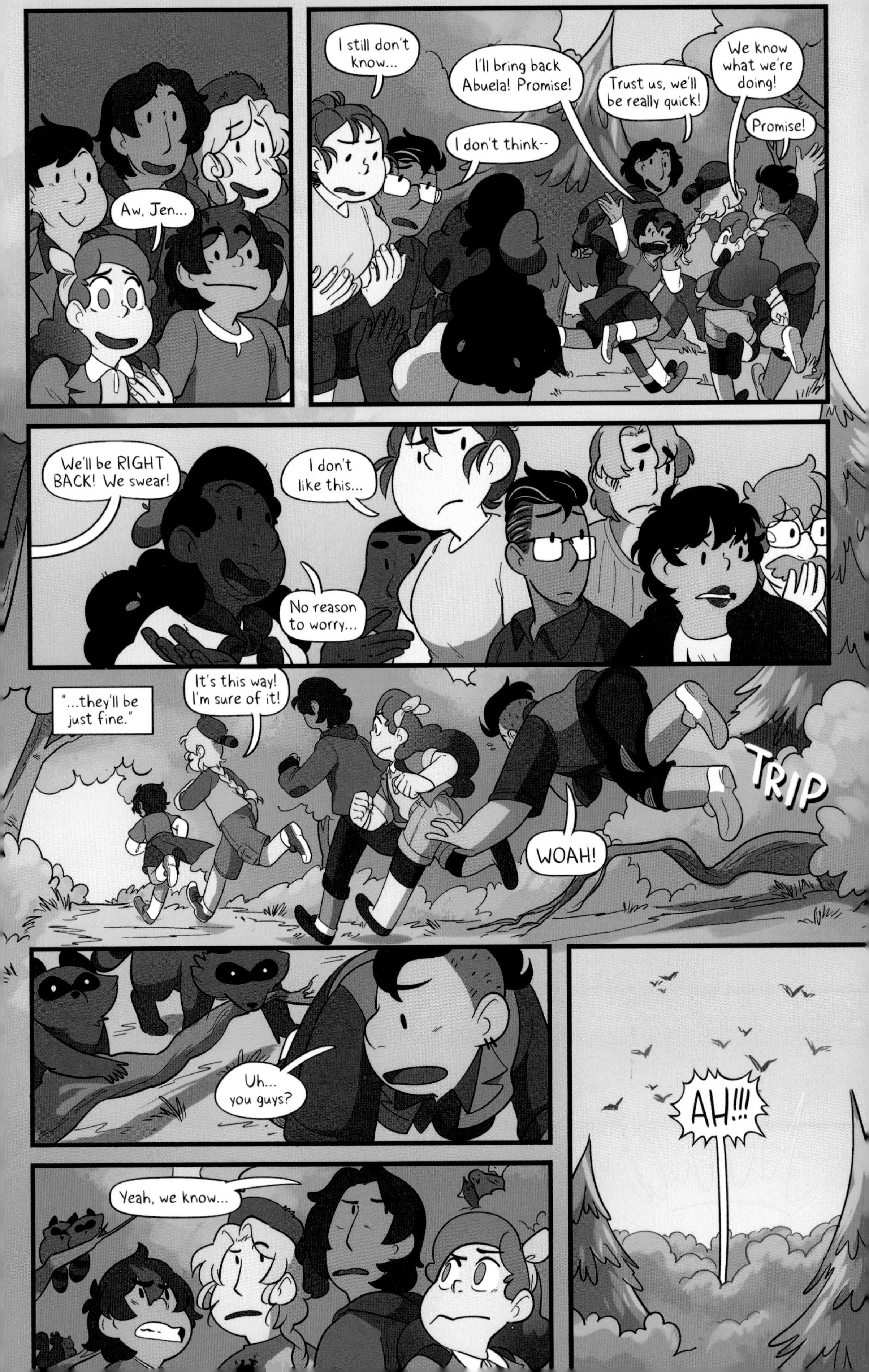
Aw, Jen...
I still don't know...
I'll bring back Abuela! Promise!
I don't think--
Trust us, we'll be really quick!
We know what we're doing!
Promise!
We'll be RIGHT BACK! We swear!
I don't like this...
No reason to worry...
"...they'll be just fine."
It's this way! I'm sure of it!
TRIP
WOAH!
Uh... you guys?
Yeah, we know...
AH!!!

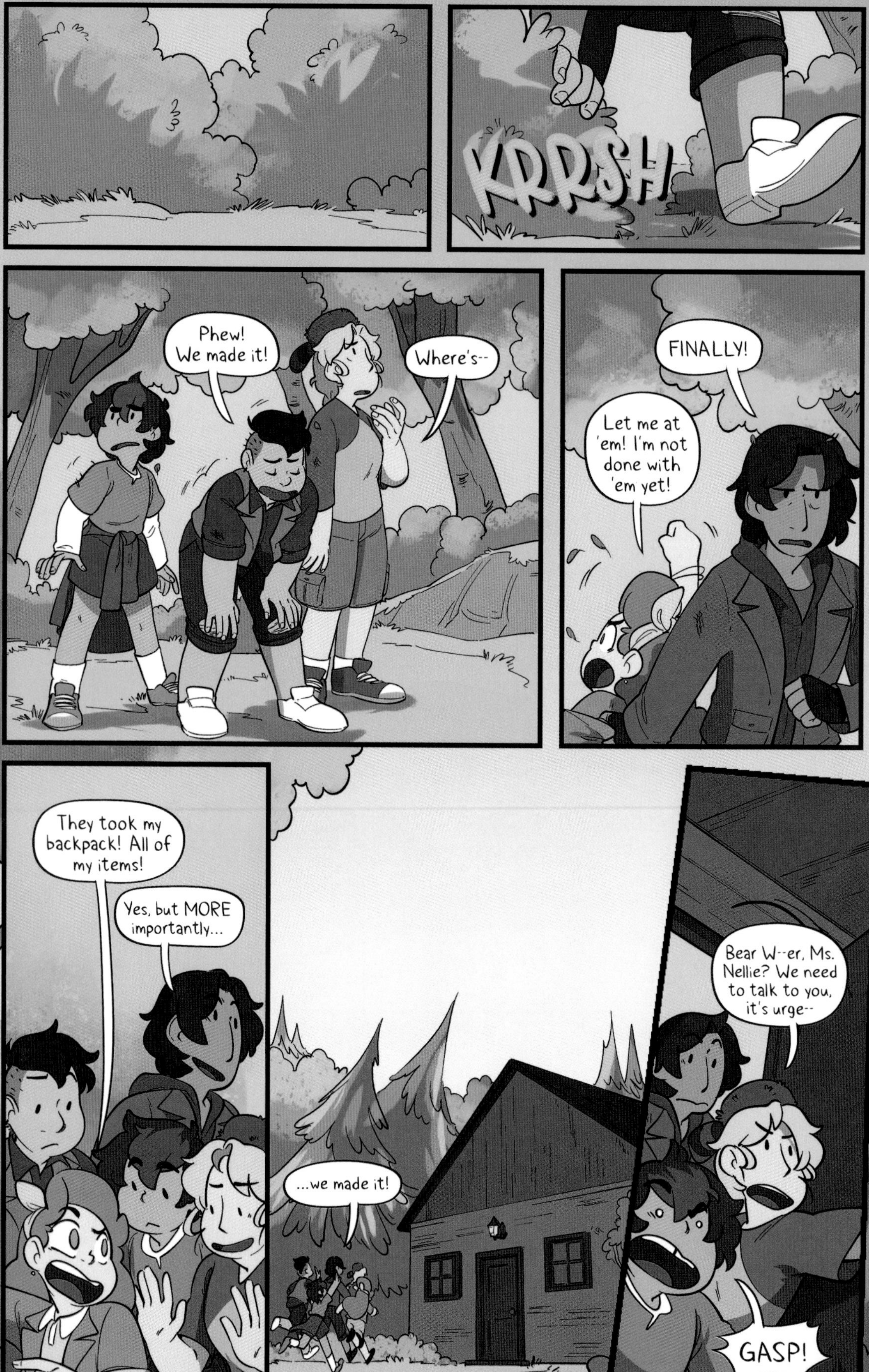
KRRSH
Phew! We made it!
Where's--
FINALLY!
Let me at 'em! I'm not done with 'em yet!
They took my backpack! All of my items!
Yes, but MORE importantly...
...we made it!
Bear W--er, Ms. Nellie? We need to talk to you, it's urge--
GASP!

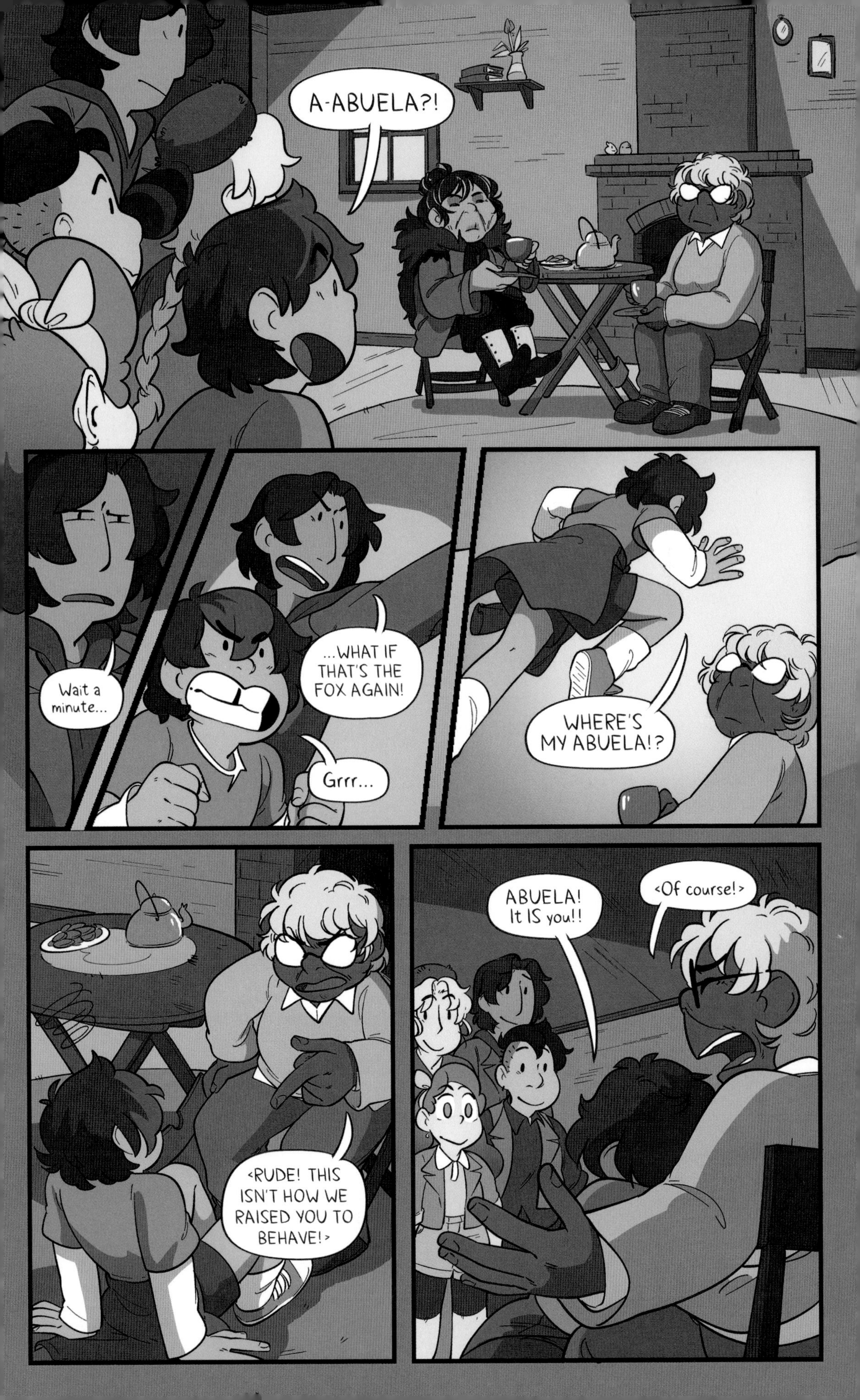
A-ABUELA?!
Wait a minute...
...WHAT IF THAT'S THE FOX AGAIN!
Grrr...
WHERE'S MY ABUELA!?
<RUDE! THIS ISN'T HOW WE RAISED YOU TO BEHAVE!>
ABUELA! It IS you!!
<Of course!>

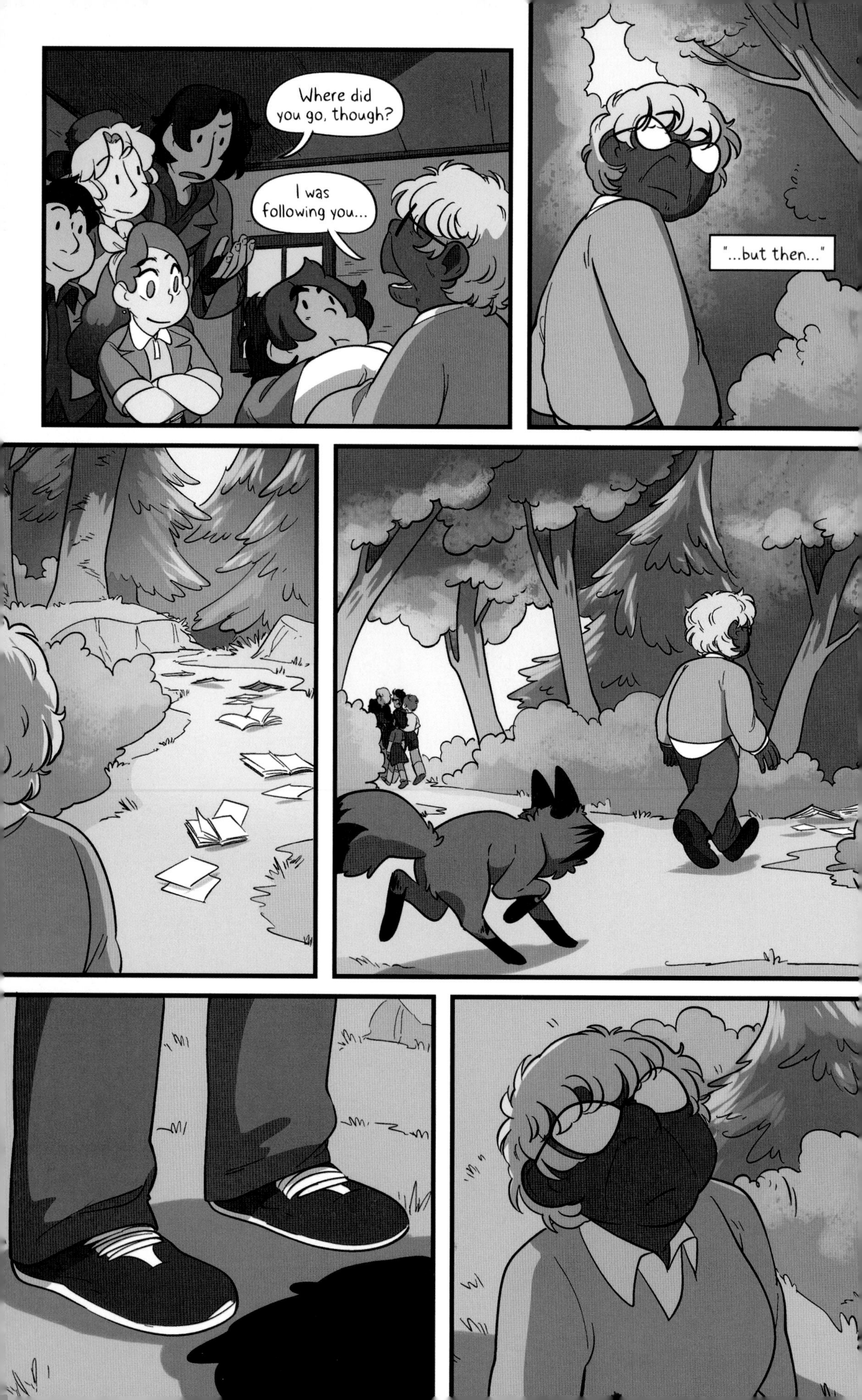
Where did you go, though?
I was following you...
"...but then..."

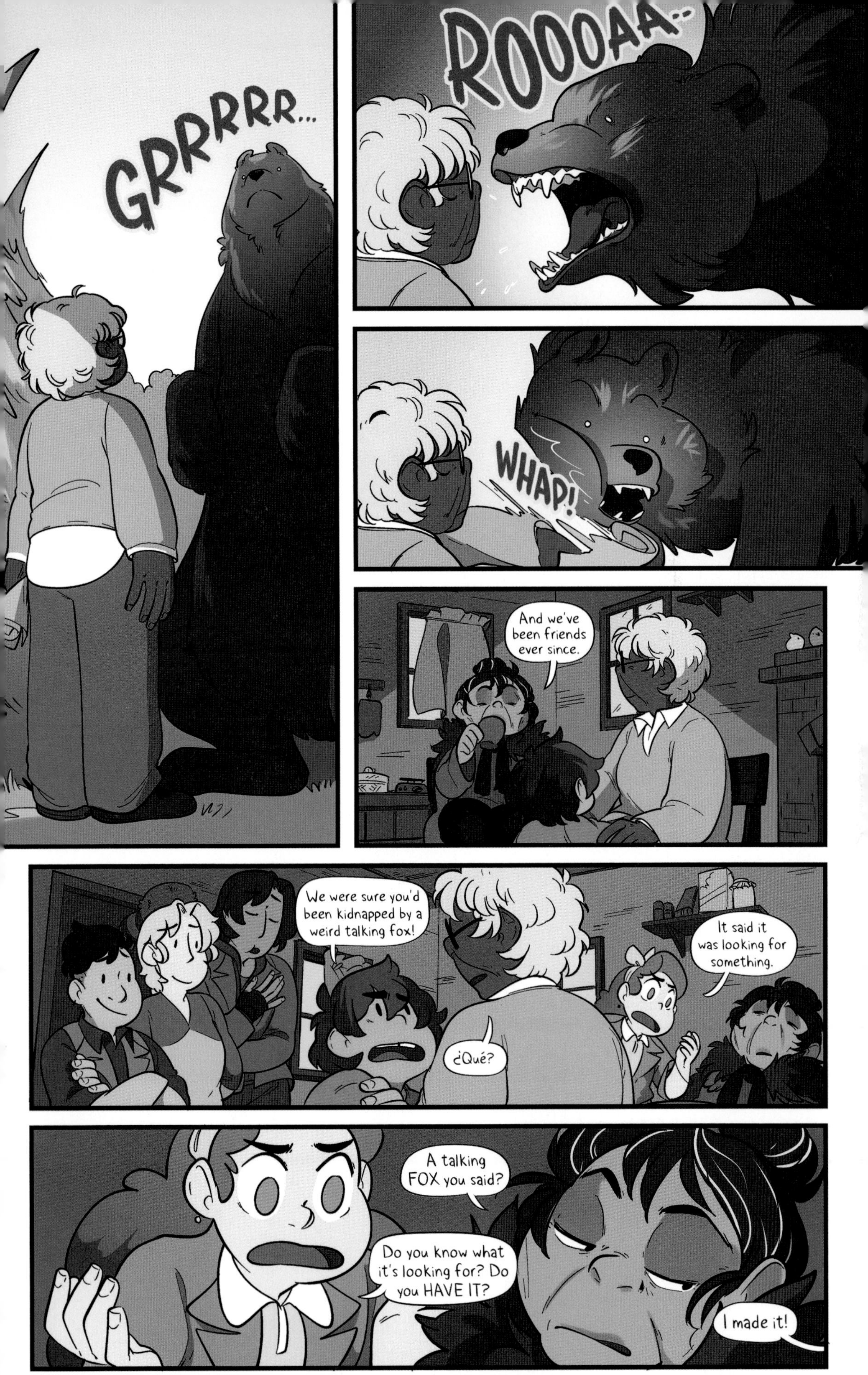
GRRRRR...
ROOOAA..
WHAP!
And we've been friends ever since.
We were sure you'd been kidnapped by a weird talking fox!
¿Qué?
It said it was looking for something.
A talking FOX you said?
Do you know what it's looking for? Do you HAVE IT?
I made it!

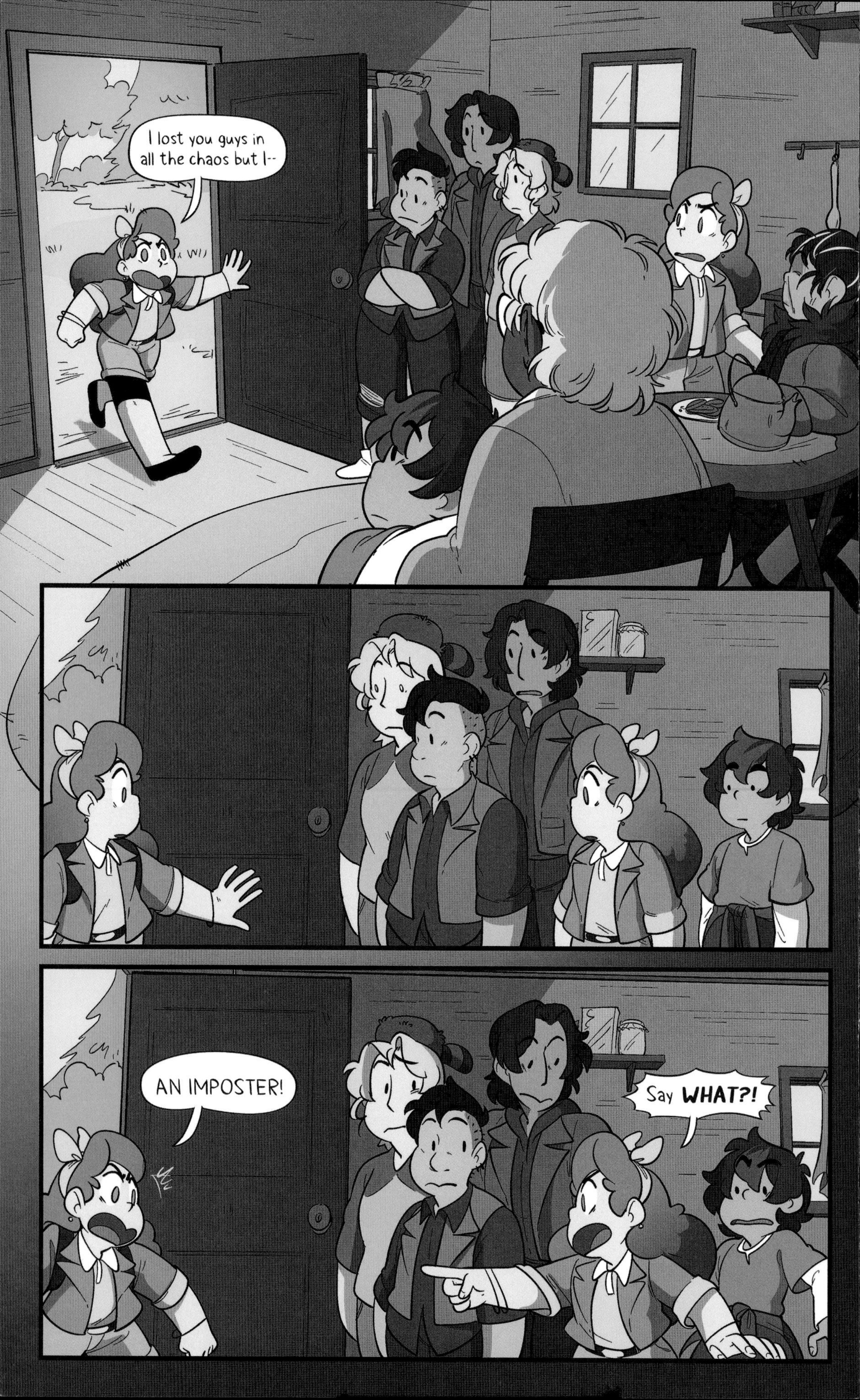

I lost you guys in all the chaos but I--
AN IMPOSTER!
Say **WHAT?!**

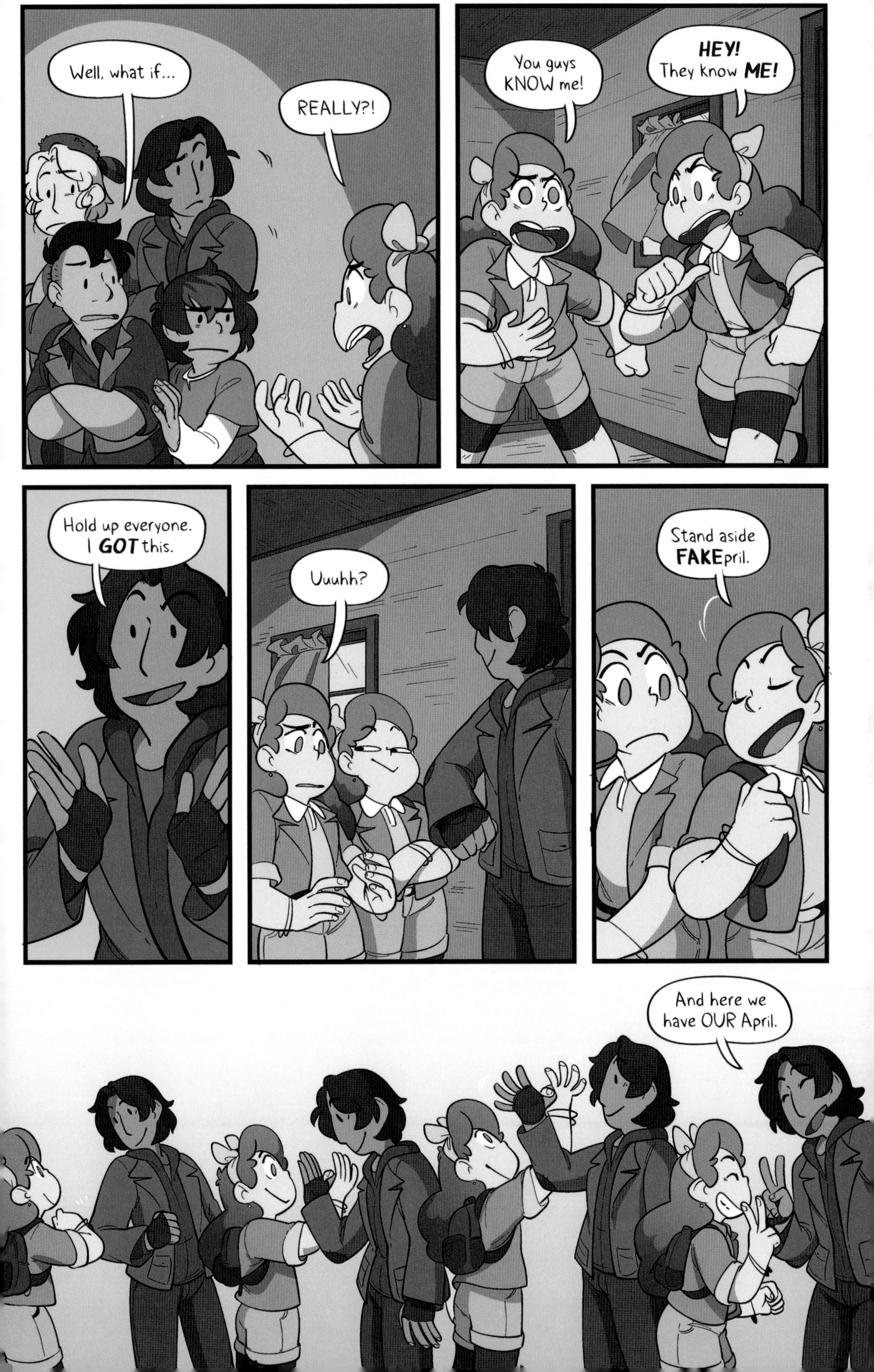
Well, what if...
REALLY?!
You guys KNOW me!
HEY! They know ME!
Hold up everyone. I GOT this.
Uuuhh?
Stand aside FAKEpril.
And here we have OUR April.

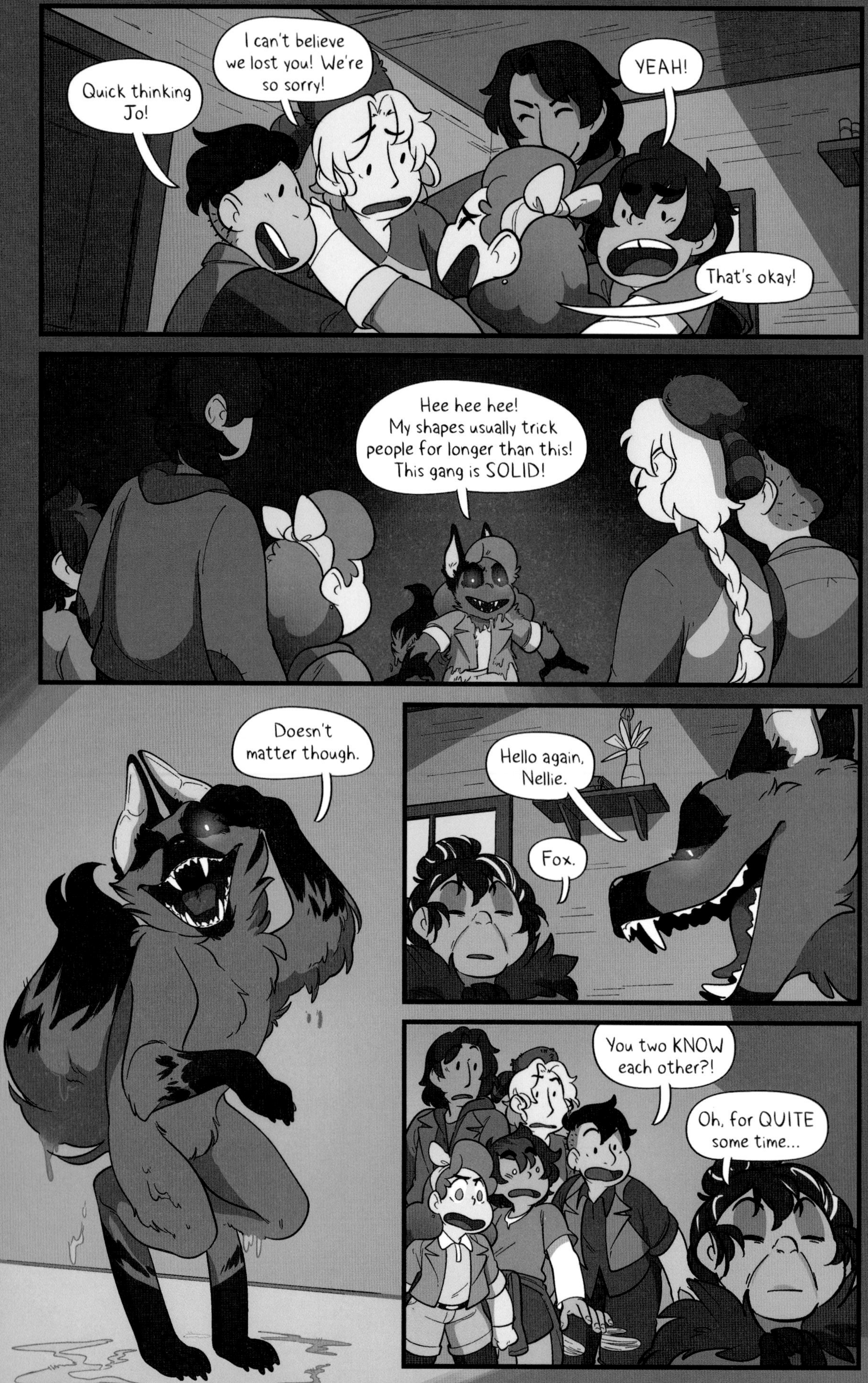
Quick thinking Jo!
I can't believe we lost you! We're so sorry!
YEAH!
That's okay!
Hee hee hee! My shapes usually trick people for longer than this! This gang is SOLID!
Doesn't matter though.
Hello again, Nellie.
Fox.
You two KNOW each other?!
Oh, for QUITE some time...

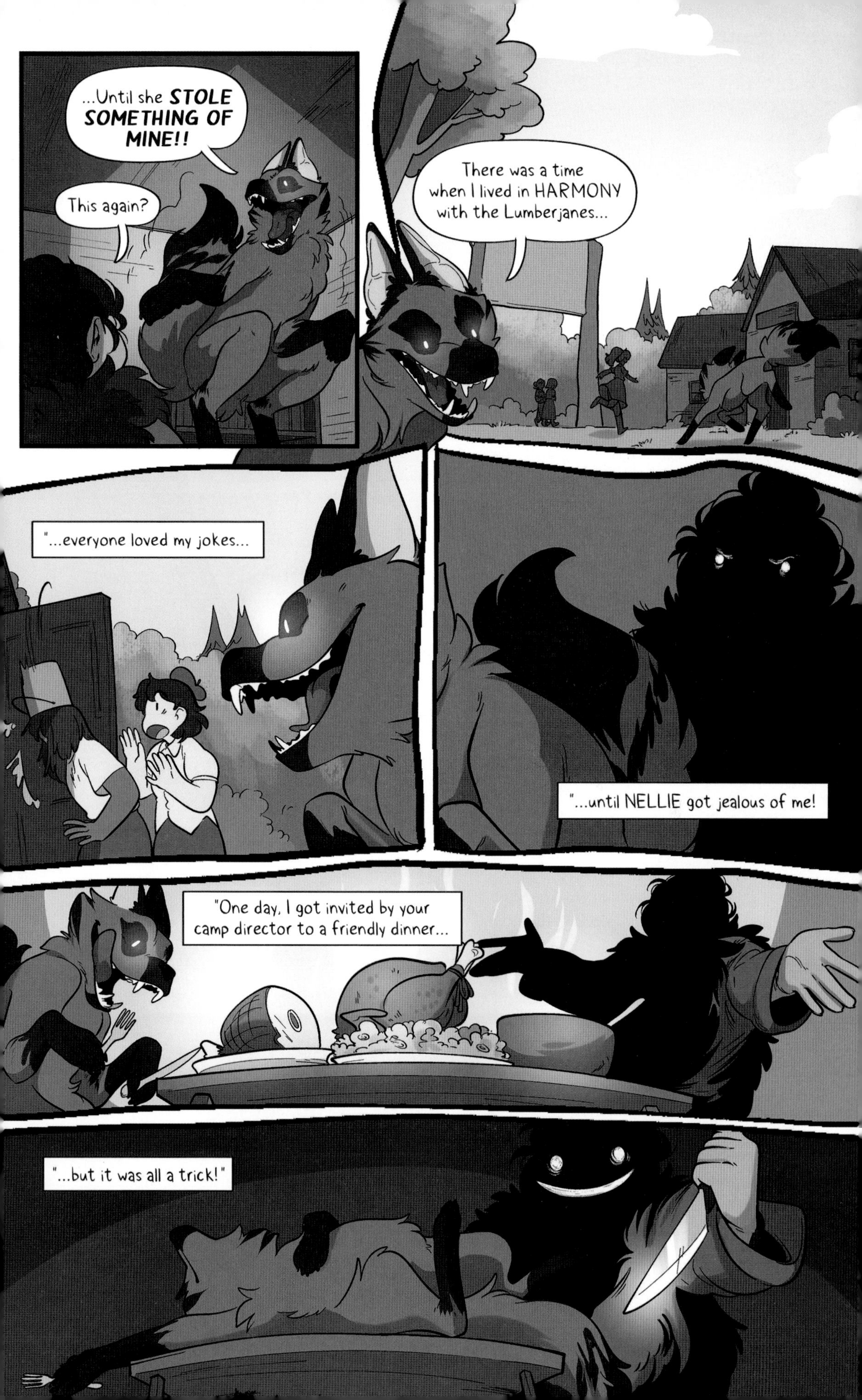
...Until she STOLE SOMETHING OF MINE!!
This again?
There was a time when I lived in HARMONY with the Lumberjanes...
"...everyone loved my jokes...
"...until NELLIE got jealous of me!
"One day, I got invited by your camp director to a friendly dinner...
"...but it was all a trick!"

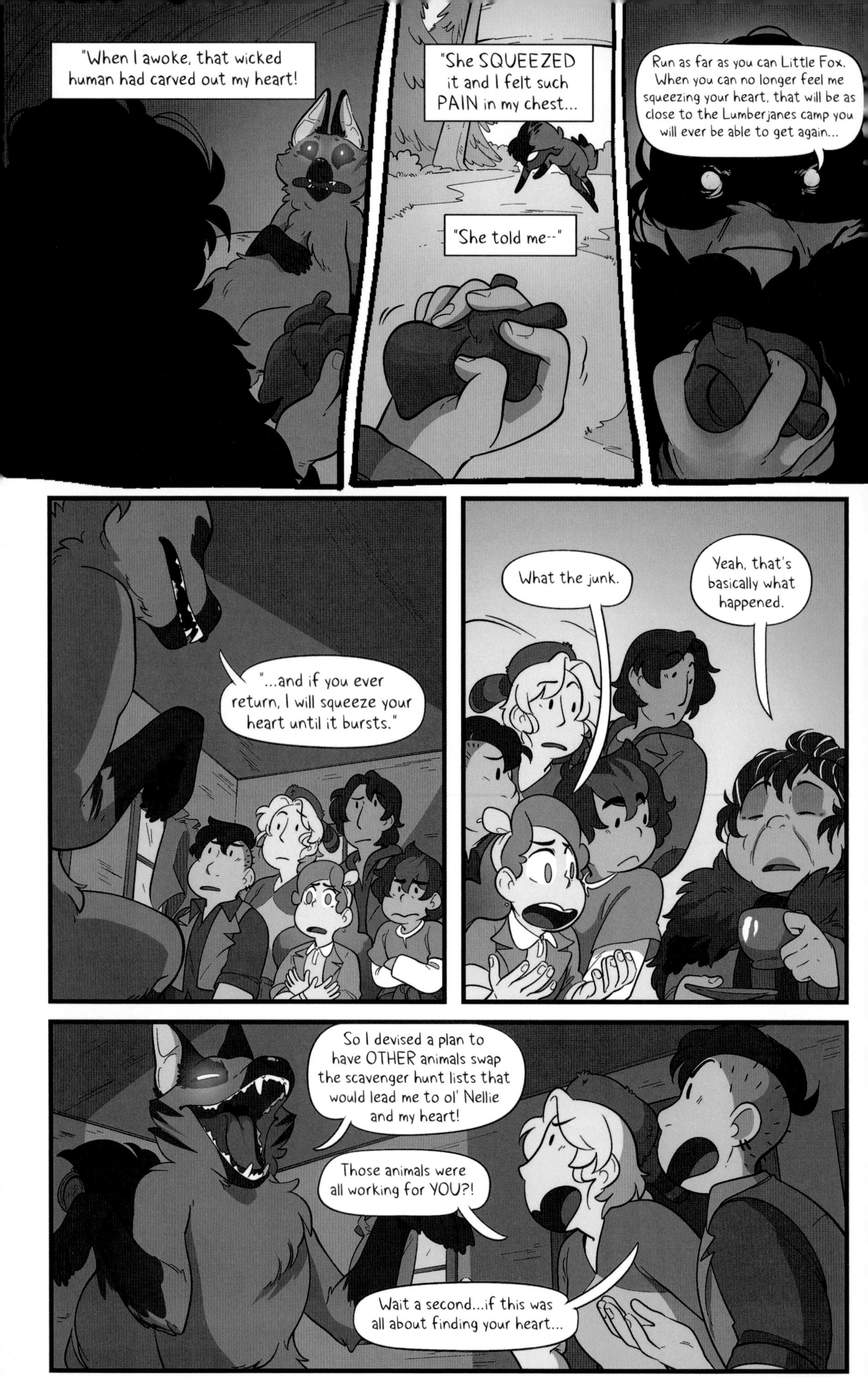
"When I awoke, that wicked human had carved out my heart!
"She SQUEEZED it and I felt such PAIN in my chest...
"She told me--"
Run as far as you can Little Fox. When you can no longer feel me squeezing your heart, that will be as close to the Lumberjanes camp you will ever be able to get again...
"...and if you ever return, I will squeeze your heart until it bursts."
What the junk.
Yeah, that's basically what happened.
So I devised a plan to have OTHER animals swap the scavenger hunt lists that would lead me to ol' Nellie and my heart!
Those animals were all working for YOU?!
Wait a second...if this was all about finding your heart...

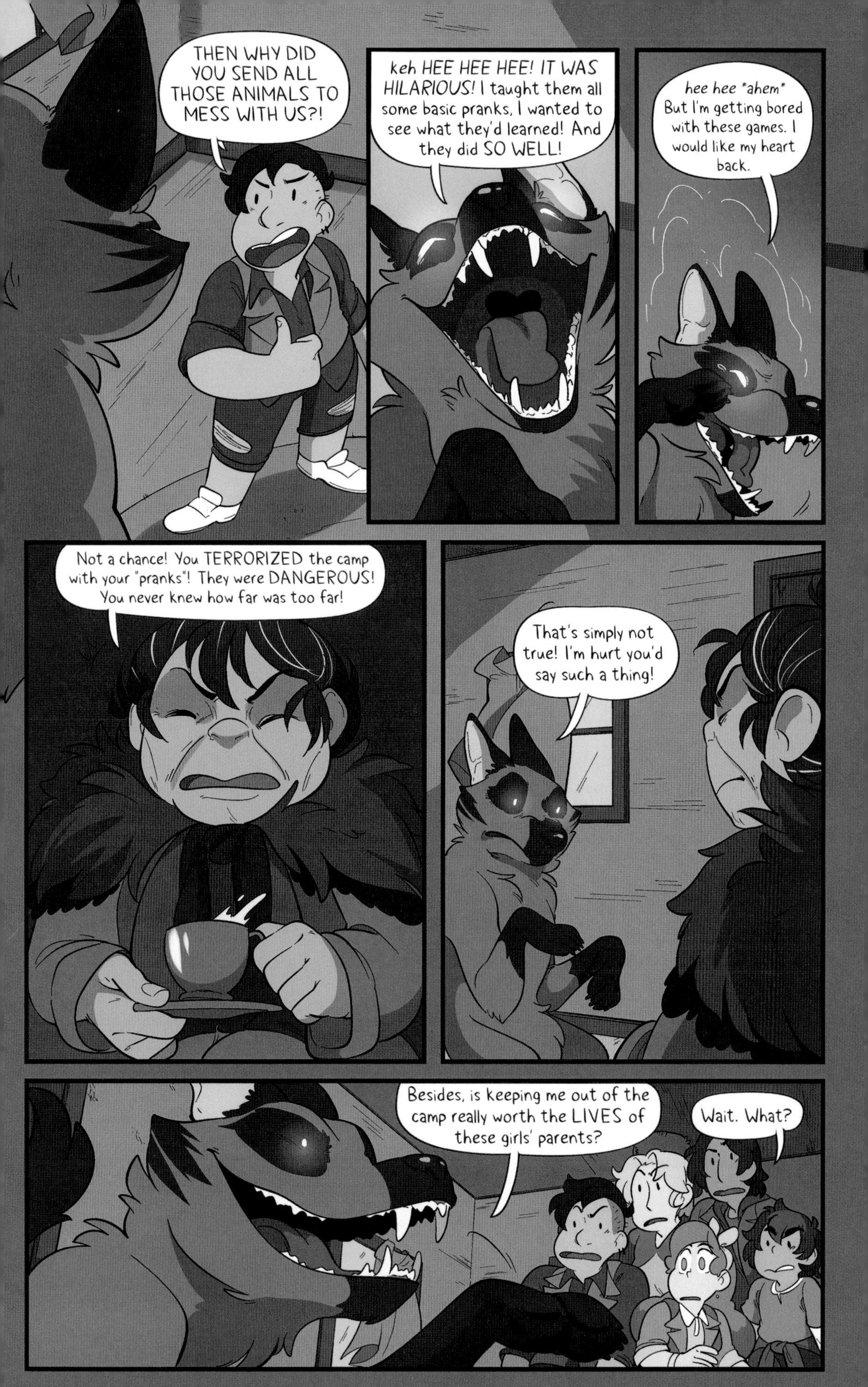
THEN WHY DID YOU SEND ALL THOSE ANIMALS TO MESS WITH US?!
keh HEE HEE HEE! IT WAS HILARIOUS! I taught them all some basic pranks, I wanted to see what they'd learned! And they did SO WELL!
hee hee *ahem* But I'm getting bored with these games. I would like my heart back.
Not a chance! You TERRORIZED the camp with your "pranks"! They were DANGEROUS! You never knew how far was too far!
That's simply not true! I'm hurt you'd say such a thing!
Besides, is keeping me out of the camp really worth the LIVES of these girls' parents?
Wait. What?

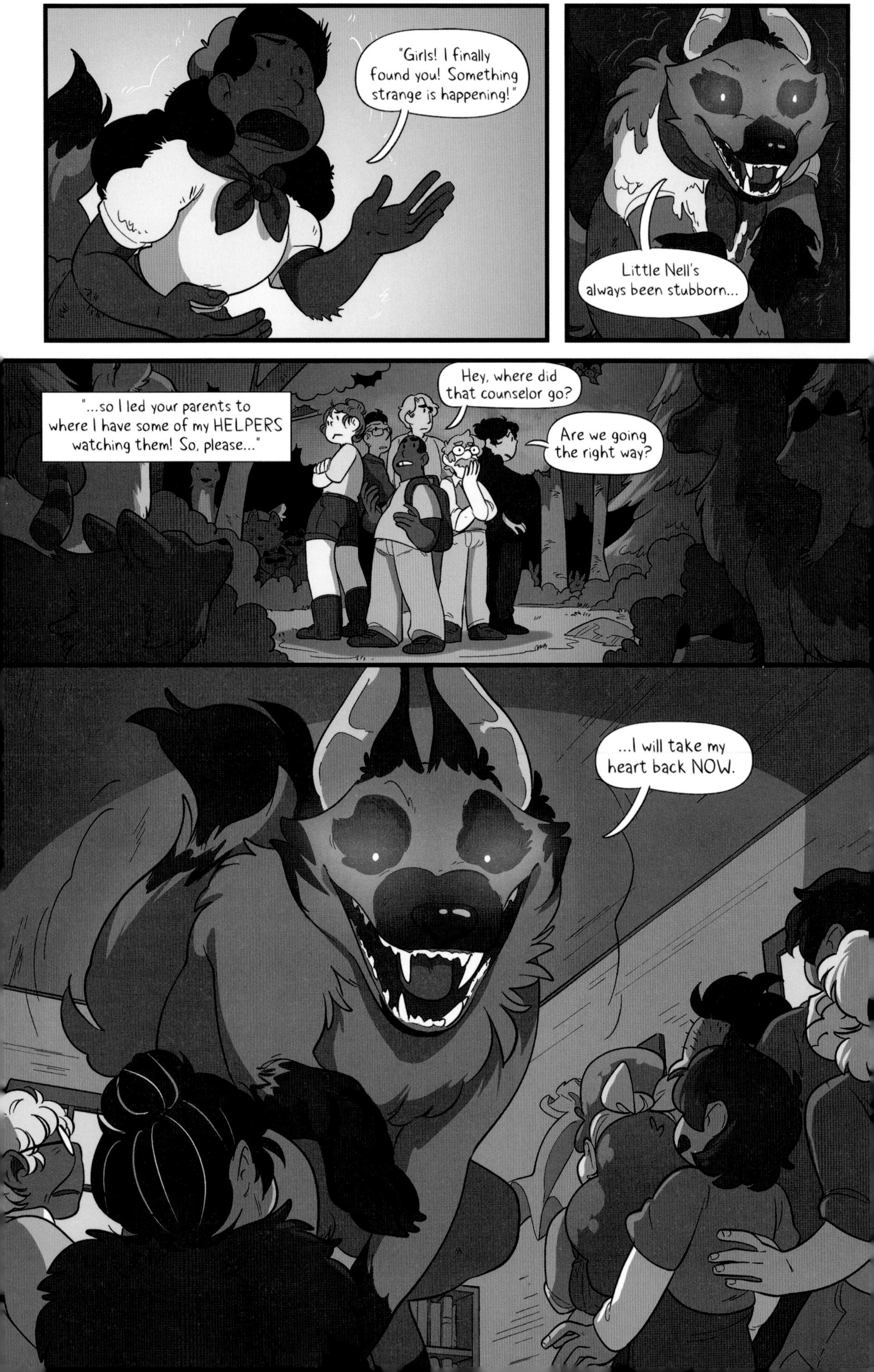
"Girls! I finally found you! Something strange is happening!"
Little Nell's always been stubborn...
"...so I led your parents to where I have some of my HELPERS watching them! So, please..."
Hey, where did that counselor go?
Are we going the right way?
...I will take my heart back NOW.

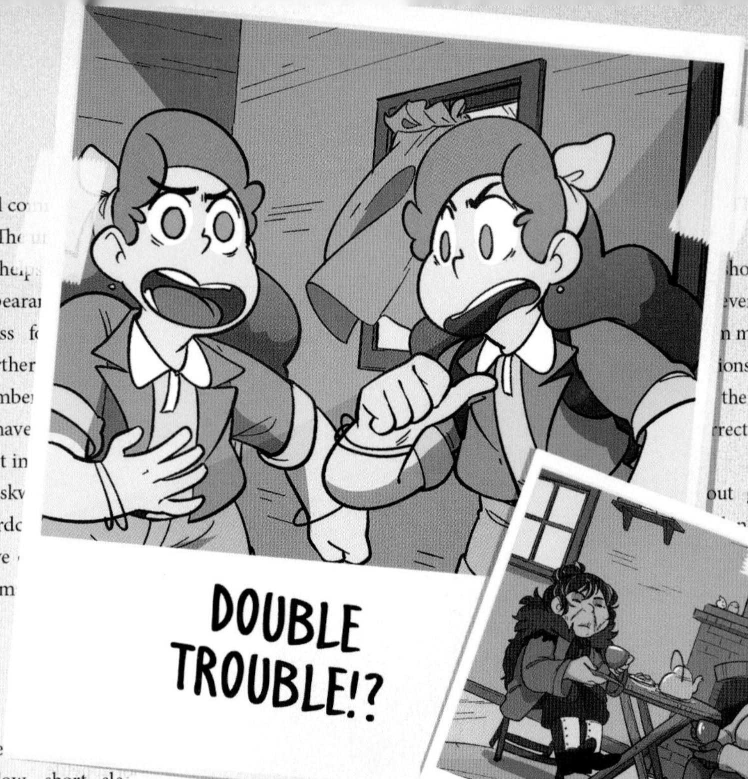
DOUBLE TROUBLE!?

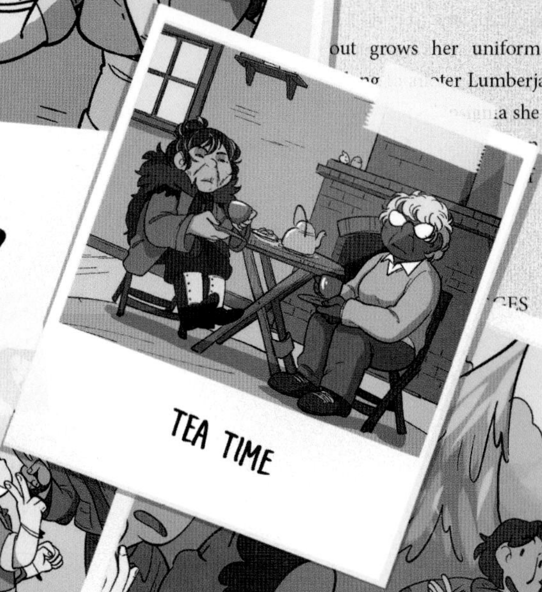
TEA TIME

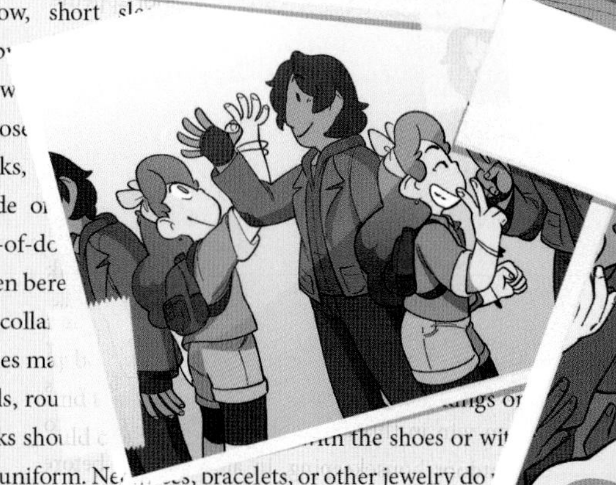

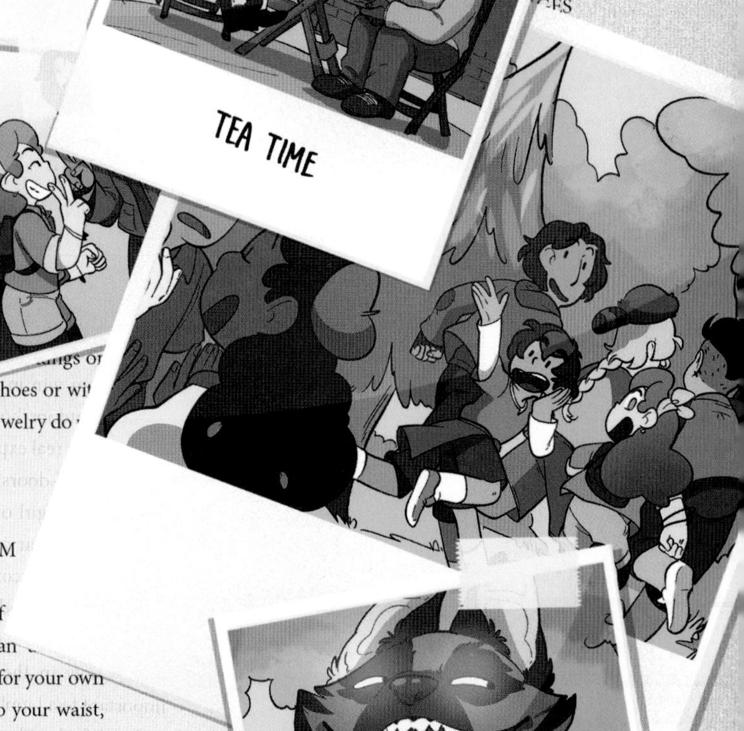

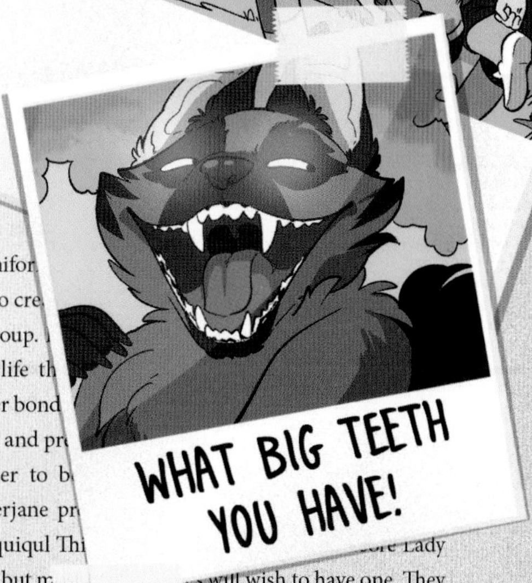
WHAT BIG TEETH YOU HAVE!

will co…

The u… It h… appeara… dress f… Further… Lumbe… to have… part in… Thiskv… Hardc… have… them…

…HE UNIFORM

…hould be worn at camp …vents when Lumberjanes …n may also be worn at other …ions. It should be worn as a … the uniform dress with …rrect shoes, and stocking or … out grows her uniform or …ter Lumberjane. …a she has … her … her

…GES

The … yellow, short sl… emb… the w… choose… slacks,… made o… out-of-do… green bere… the colla… Shoes ma… heels, rou… …ings or socks shou… …with the shoes or wit… the uniform. Ne… …es, bracelets, or other jewelry do… belong with a Lumberjane uniform.

HOW TO WEAR THE UNIFORM

To look well in a uniform demands first of … uniform be kept in good condition—clean … pressed. See that the skirt is the right length for your own height and build, that the belt is adjusted to your waist, that your shoes and stockings are in keeping with the uniform, that you watch your posture and carry yourself with dignity and grace. If the beret is removed indoors, be sure that your hair is neat and kept in place with an insonspicuous clip or ribbon. When you wear a Lumberjane uniform you are identified as a member of this organization and you should be doubly careful to conduct yourself in a way that will show everyone that courtesy and thoughtfullness are part of being a Lumberjane. People are likely to judge a whole nation by the selfishness of a few individuals, to criticize a whole family because of the misconduct of one member, and to feel unkindly toward and organization because of the

The unifor… helps to cre… in a group. … active life th… another bond… future, and pr… in order to b… Lumberjane pr… Penniquiqul Thi… …ore Lady Types, but m… …s will wish to have one. They can either bu… …uniform, or make it themselves from materials available at the trading post.

LUMBERJANES FIELD MANUAL

CHAPTER
FORTY

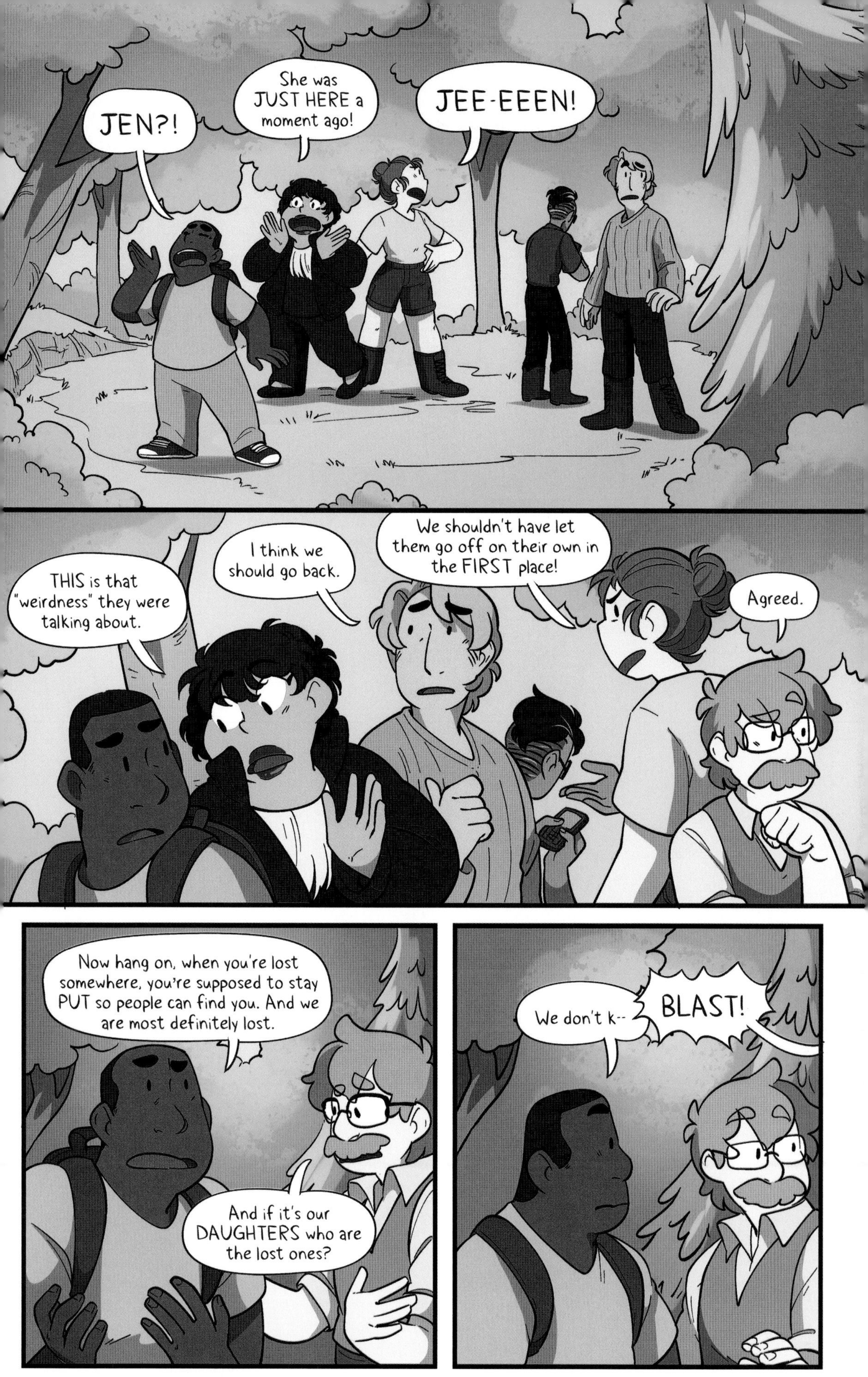
JEN?!
She was JUST HERE a moment ago!
JEE-EEEN!
THIS is that "weirdness" they were talking about.
I think we should go back.
We shouldn't have let them go off on their own in the FIRST place!
Agreed.
Now hang on, when you're lost somewhere, you're supposed to stay PUT so people can find you. And we are most definitely lost.
And if it's our DAUGHTERS who are the lost ones?
We don't k--
BLAST!

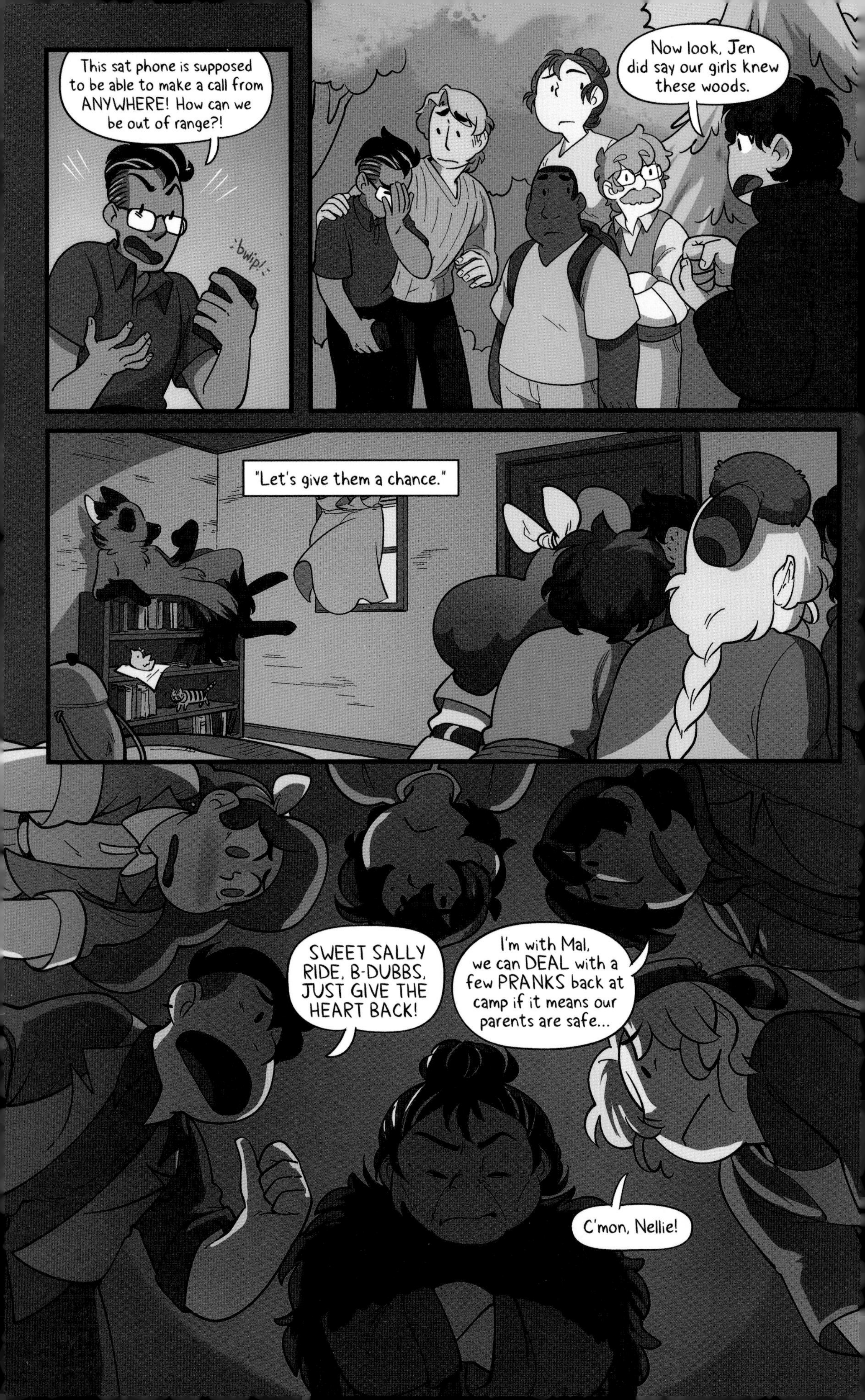
This sat phone is supposed to be able to make a call from ANYWHERE! How can we be out of range?!
bwip!
Now look, Jen did say our girls knew these woods.
"Let's give them a chance."
SWEET SALLY RIDE, B-DUBBS, JUST GIVE THE HEART BACK!
I'm with Mal, we can DEAL with a few PRANKS back at camp if it means our parents are safe...
C'mon, Nellie!

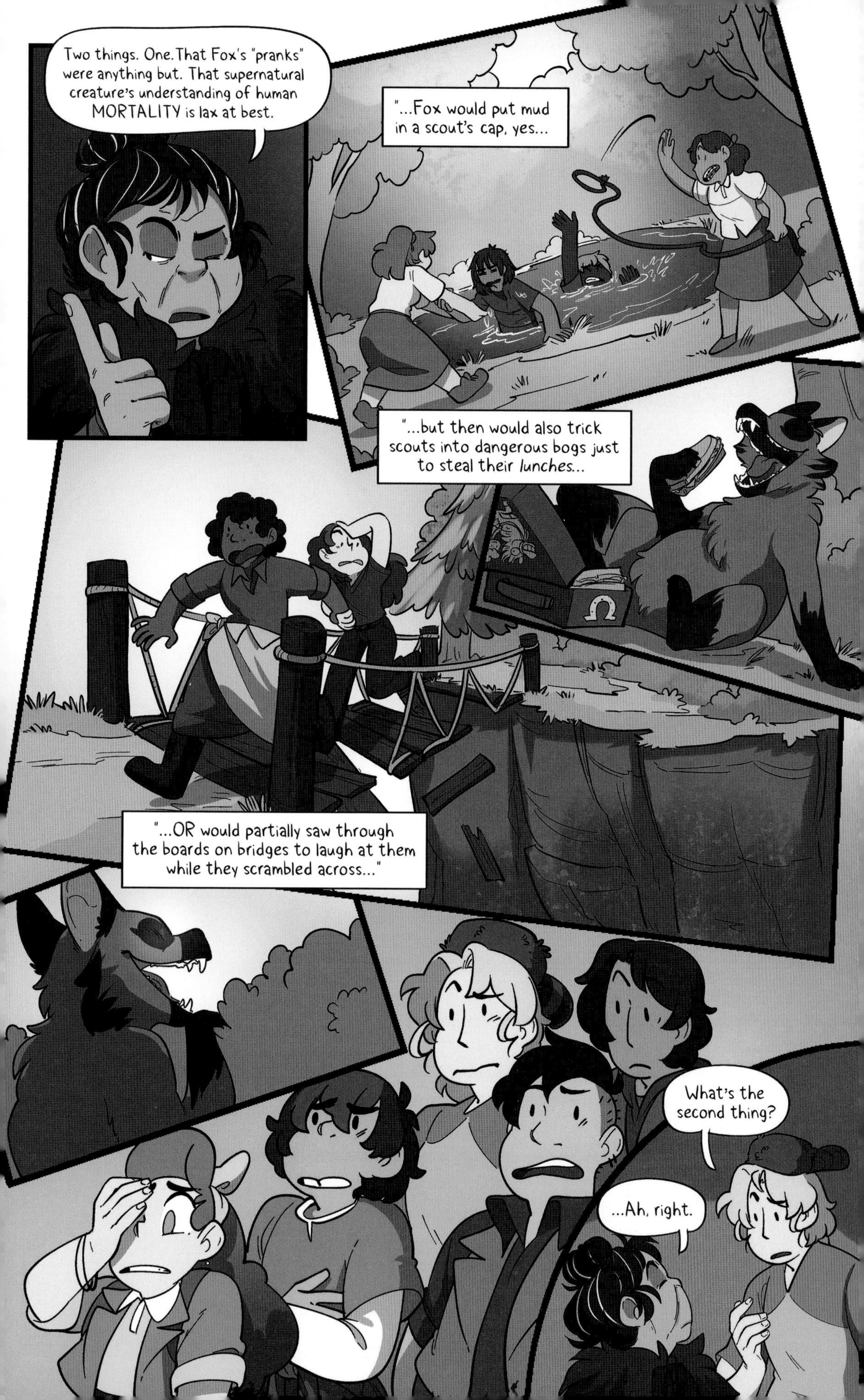

Two things. One. That Fox's "pranks" were anything but. That supernatural creature's understanding of human MORTALITY is lax at best.
"...Fox would put mud in a scout's cap, yes...
"...but then would also trick scouts into dangerous bogs just to steal their *lunches*...
"...OR would partially saw through the boards on bridges to laugh at them while they scrambled across..."
What's the second thing?
...Ah, right.

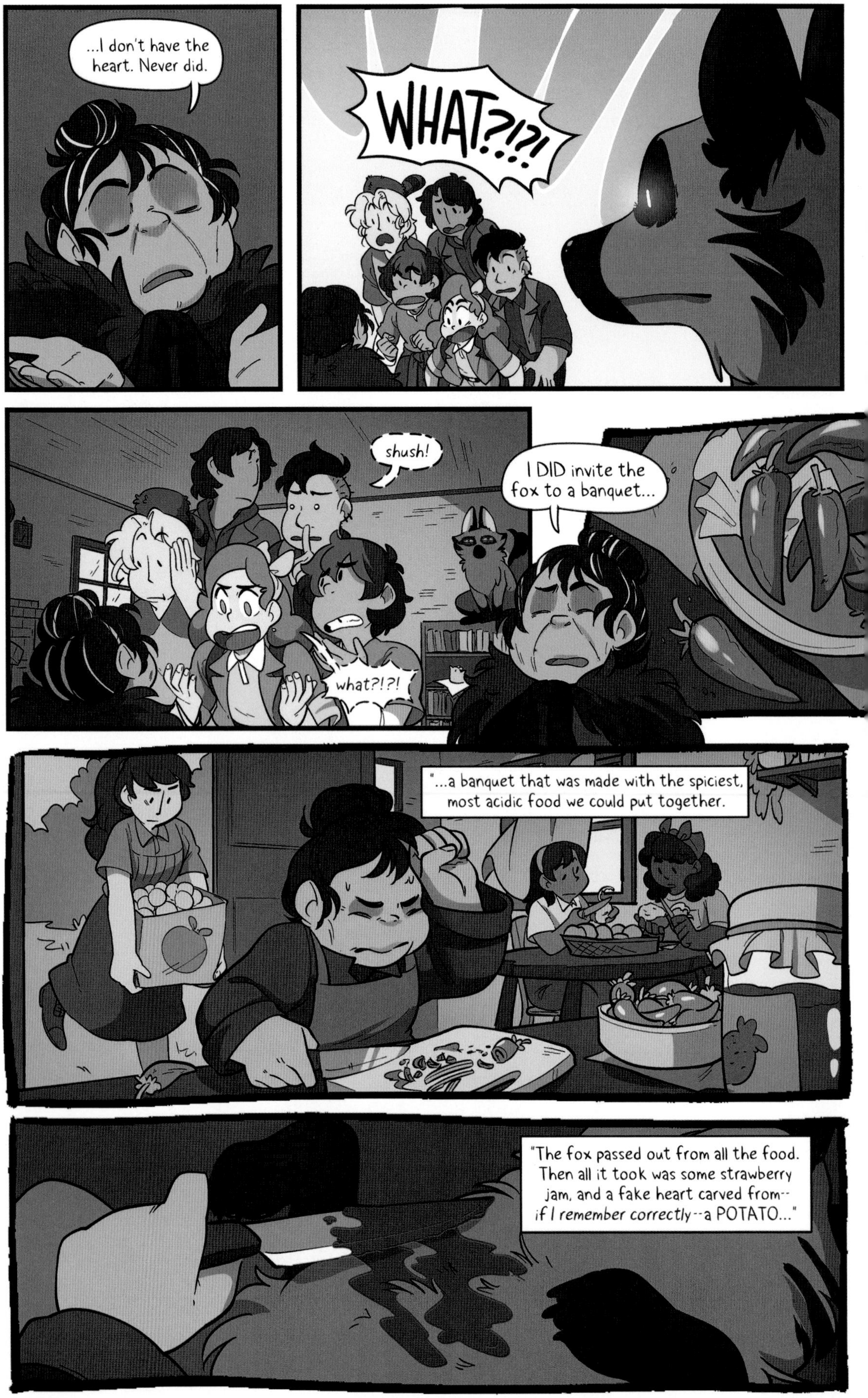
...I don't have the heart. Never did.
WHAT?!?!?!
shush!
what?!?!
I DID invite the fox to a banquet...
"...a banquet that was made with the spiciest, most acidic food we could put together.
"The fox passed out from all the food. Then all it took was some strawberry jam, and a fake heart carved from--if I remember correctly--a POTATO..."

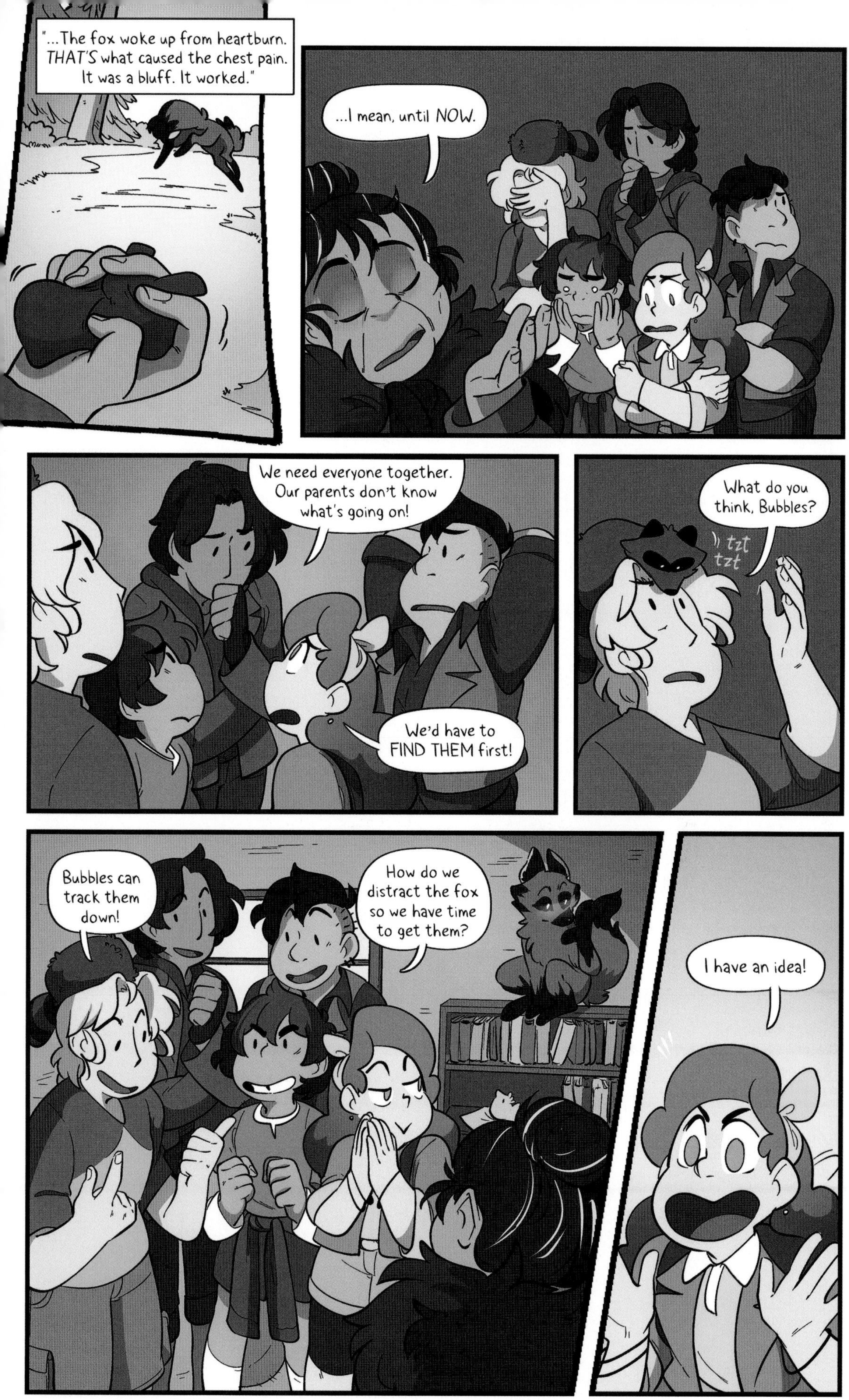
"...The fox woke up from heartburn. THAT'S what caused the chest pain. It was a bluff. It worked."
...I mean, until NOW.
We need everyone together. Our parents don't know what's going on!
We'd have to FIND THEM first!
What do you think, Bubbles?
tzt tzt
Bubbles can track them down!
How do we distract the fox so we have time to get them?
I have an idea!

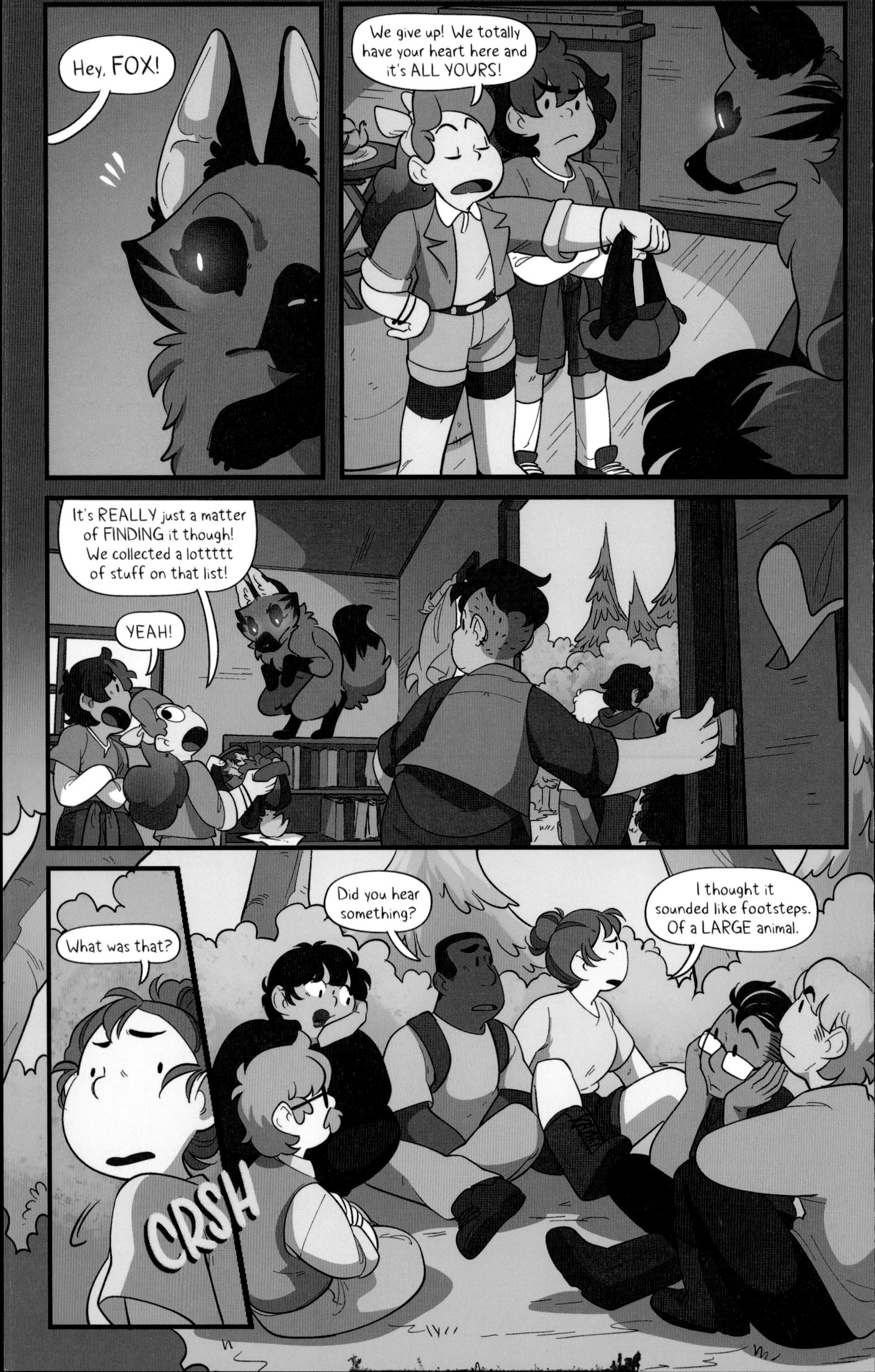
Hey, FOX!
We give up! We totally have your heart here and it's ALL YOURS!
It's REALLY just a matter of FINDING it though! We collected a lotttt of stuff on that list!
YEAH!
What was that?
Did you hear something?
I thought it sounded like footsteps. Of a LARGE animal.
CRSH

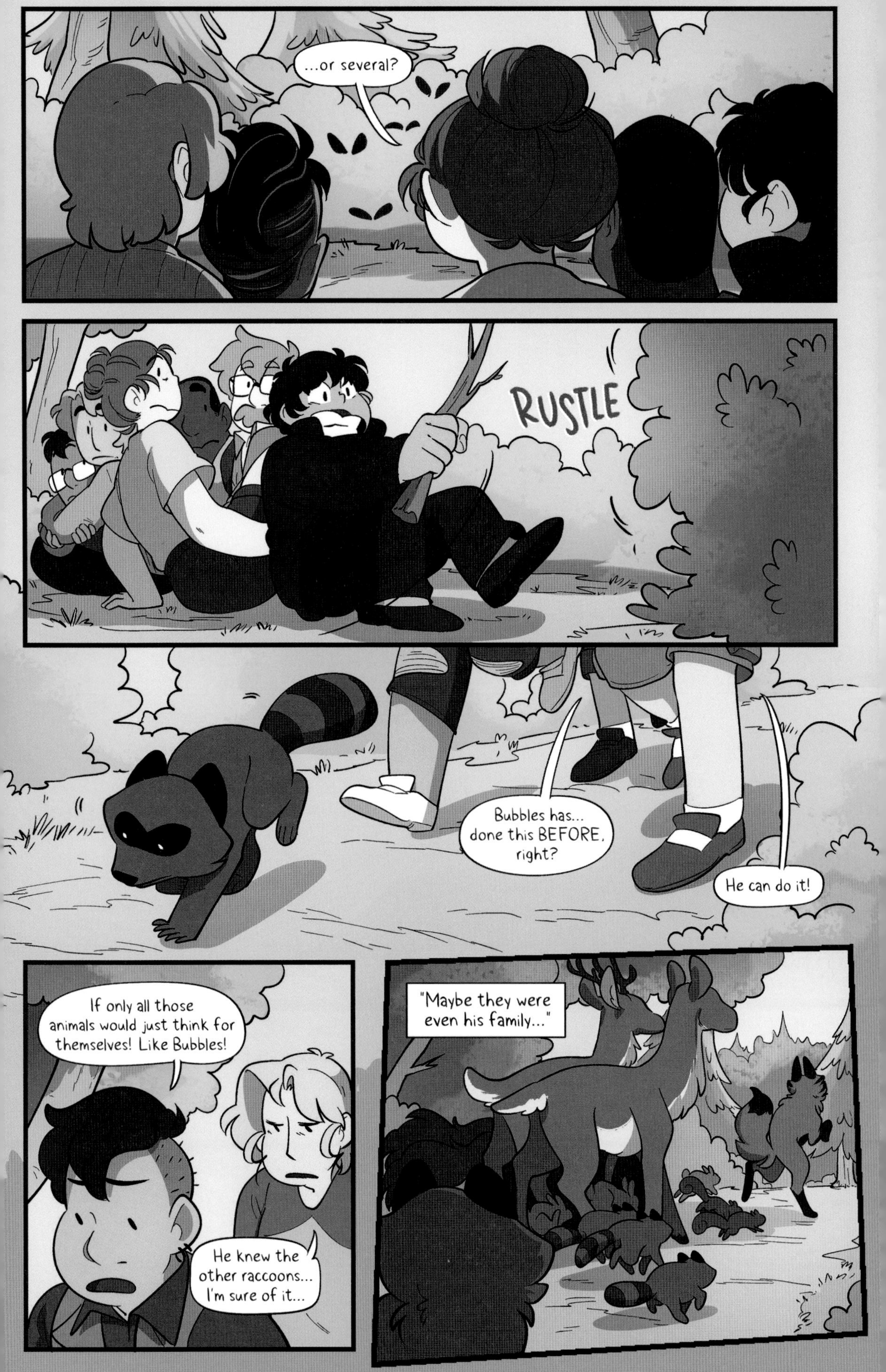
...or several?
RUSTLE
Bubbles has... done this BEFORE, right?
He can do it!
If only all those animals would just think for themselves! Like Bubbles!
He knew the other raccoons... I'm sure of it...
"Maybe they were even his family..."

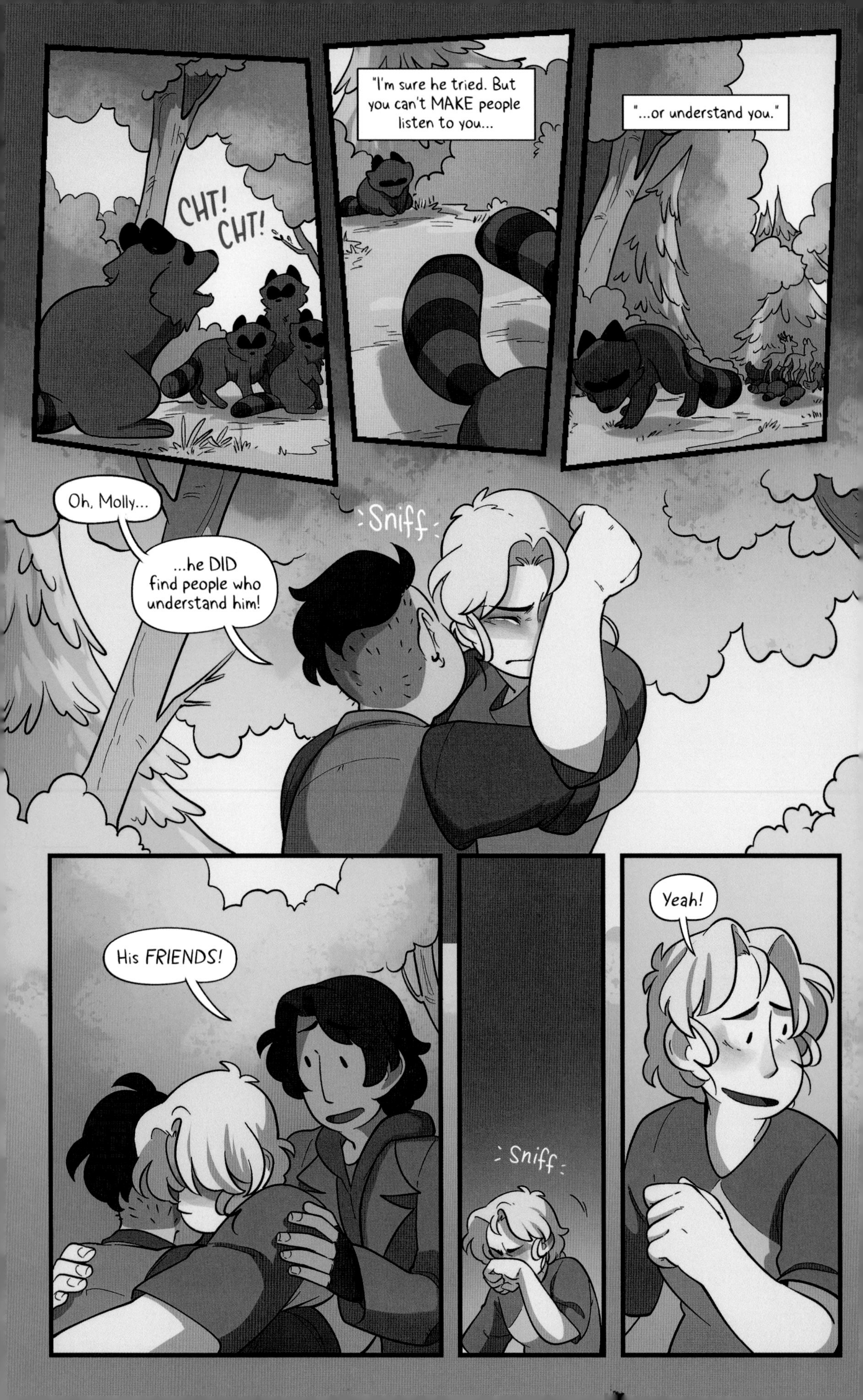
CHT! CHT!
"I'm sure he tried. But you can't MAKE people listen to you...
"...or understand you."
Oh, Molly...
...he DID find people who understand him!
Sniff
His FRIENDS!
Sniff
Yeah!

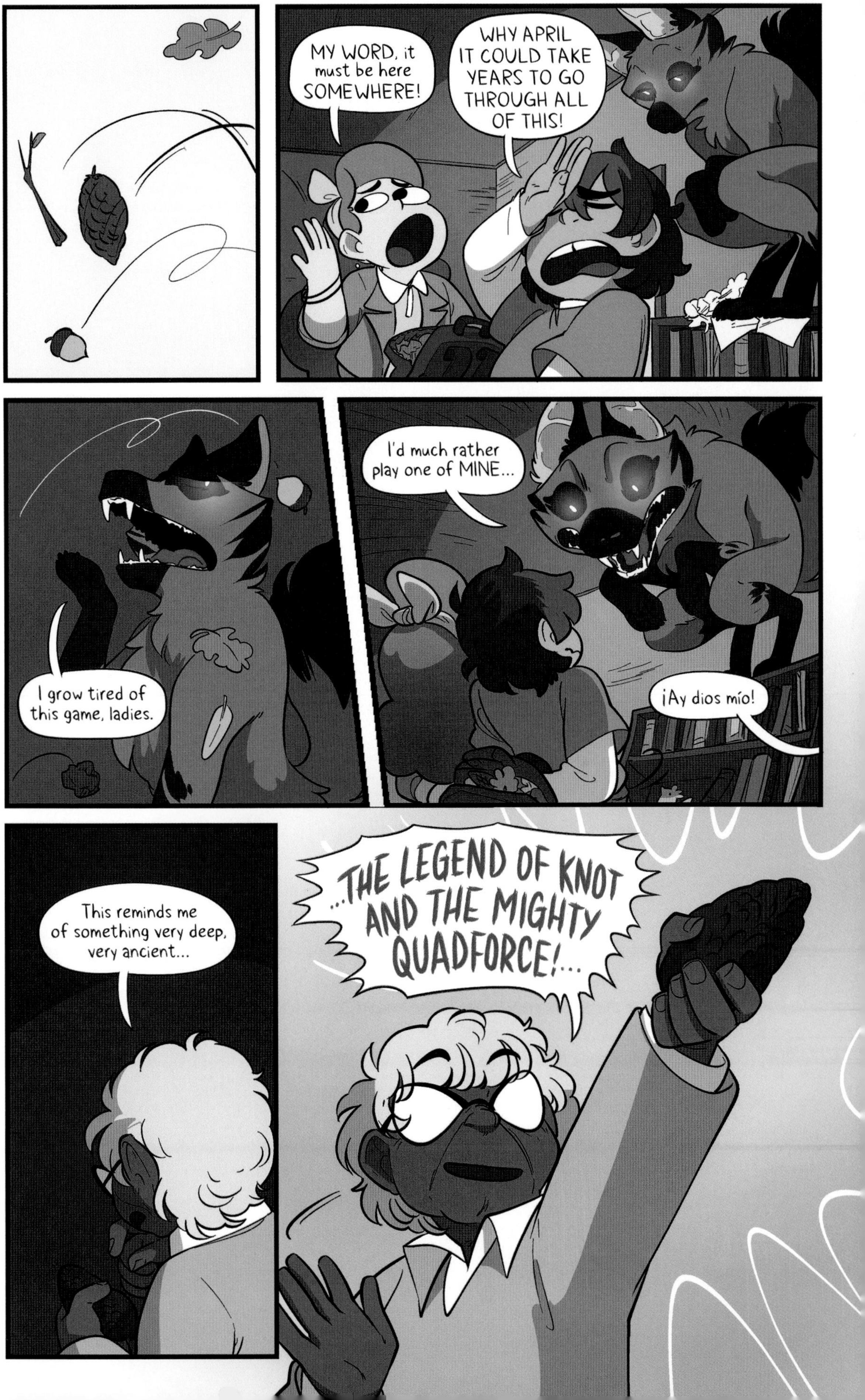
MY WORD, it must be here SOMEWHERE!
WHY APRIL IT COULD TAKE YEARS TO GO THROUGH ALL OF THIS!
I grow tired of this game, ladies.
I'd much rather play one of MINE...
¡Ay dios mío!
This reminds me of something very deep, very ancient...
...THE LEGEND OF KNOT AND THE MIGHTY QUADFORCE!...

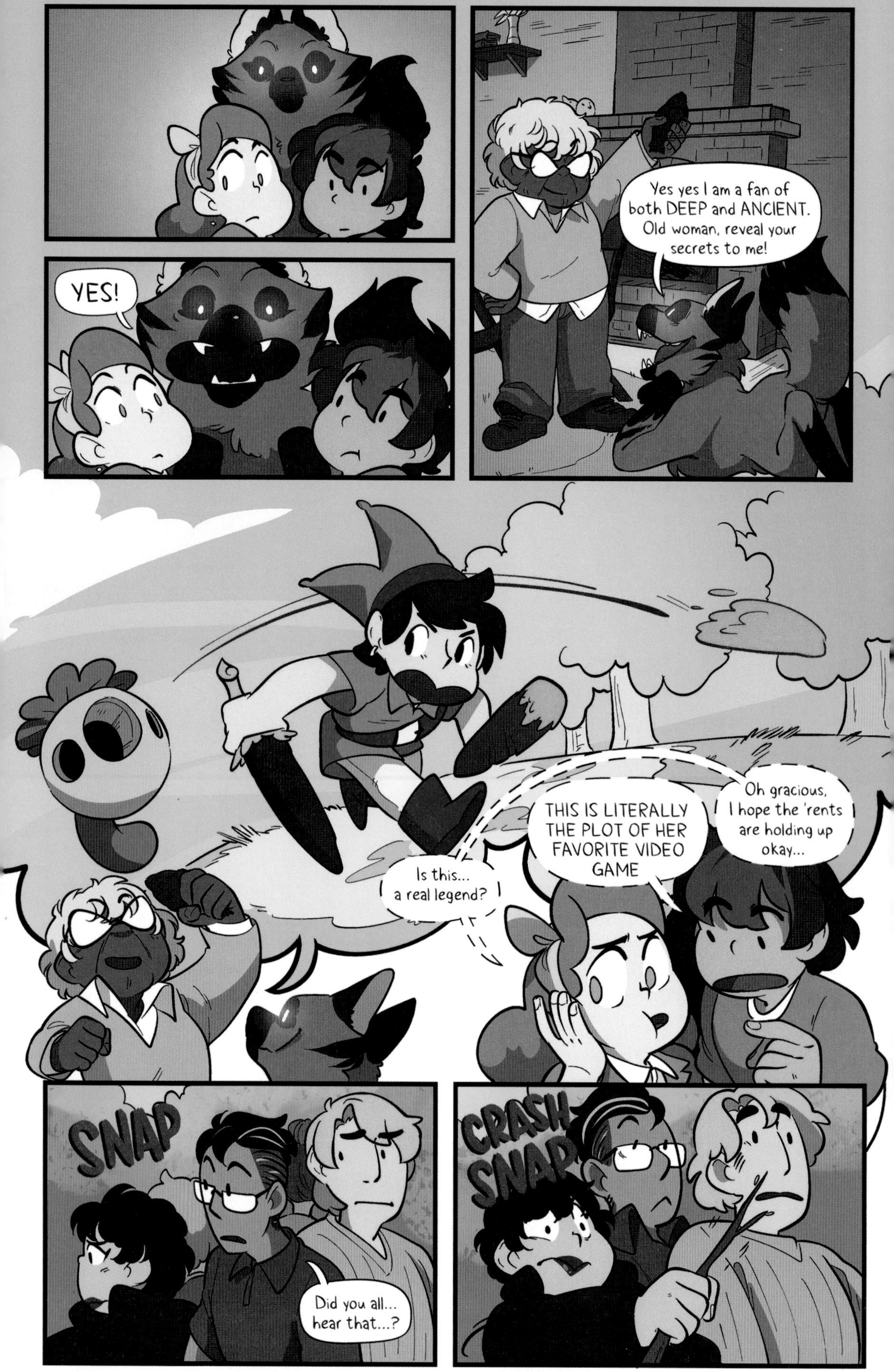

YES!
Yes yes I am a fan of both DEEP and ANCIENT. Old woman, reveal your secrets to me!
Is this... a real legend?
THIS IS LITERALLY THE PLOT OF HER FAVORITE VIDEO GAME
Oh gracious, I hope the 'rents are holding up okay...
SNAP
Did you all... hear that...?
CRASH
SNAP

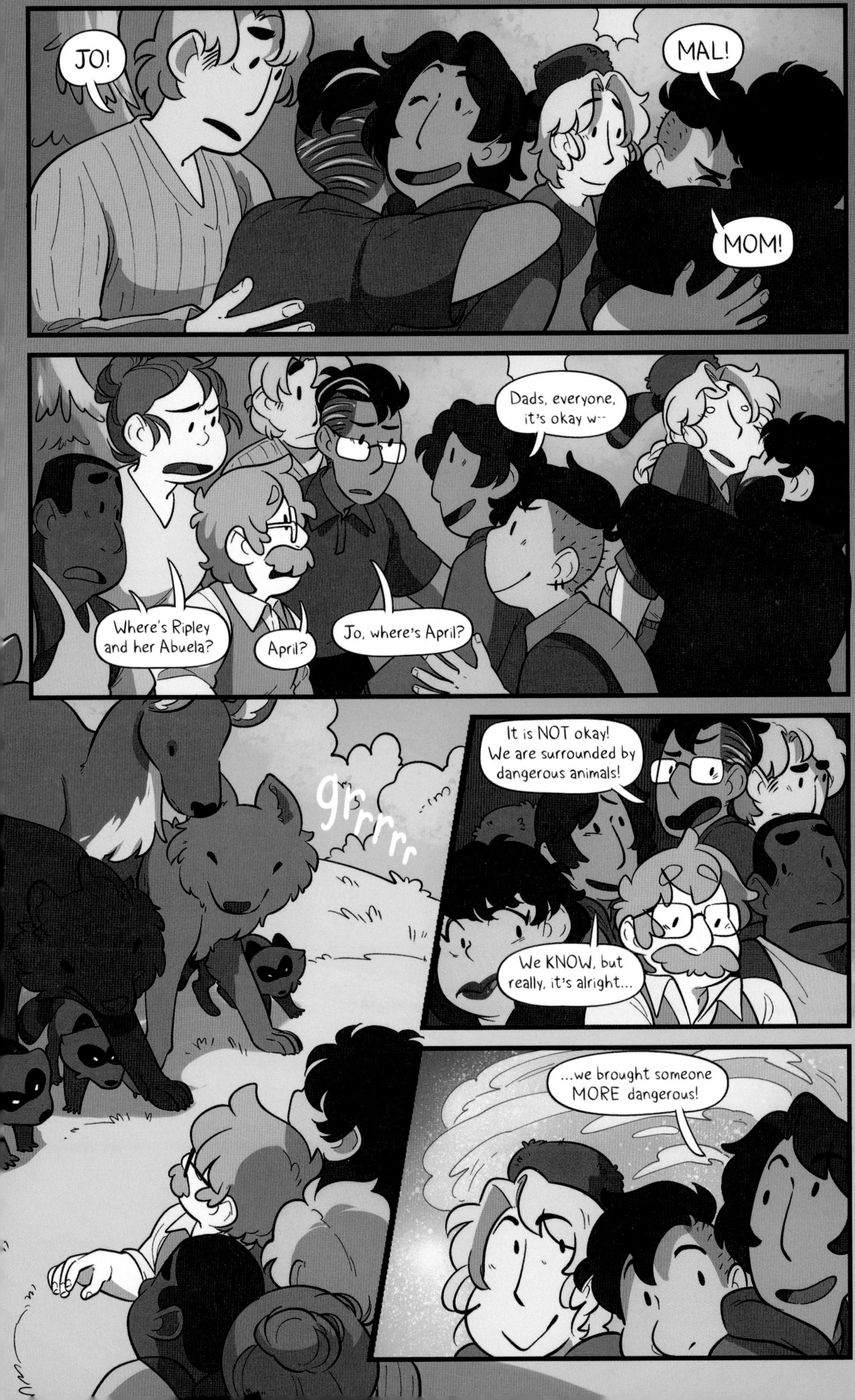
JO!
MAL!
MOM!
Dads, everyone, it's okay w--
Where's Ripley and her Abuela?
April?
Jo, where's April?
grrrrr
It is NOT okay! We are surrounded by dangerous animals!
We KNOW, but really, it's alright...
...we brought someone MORE dangerous!

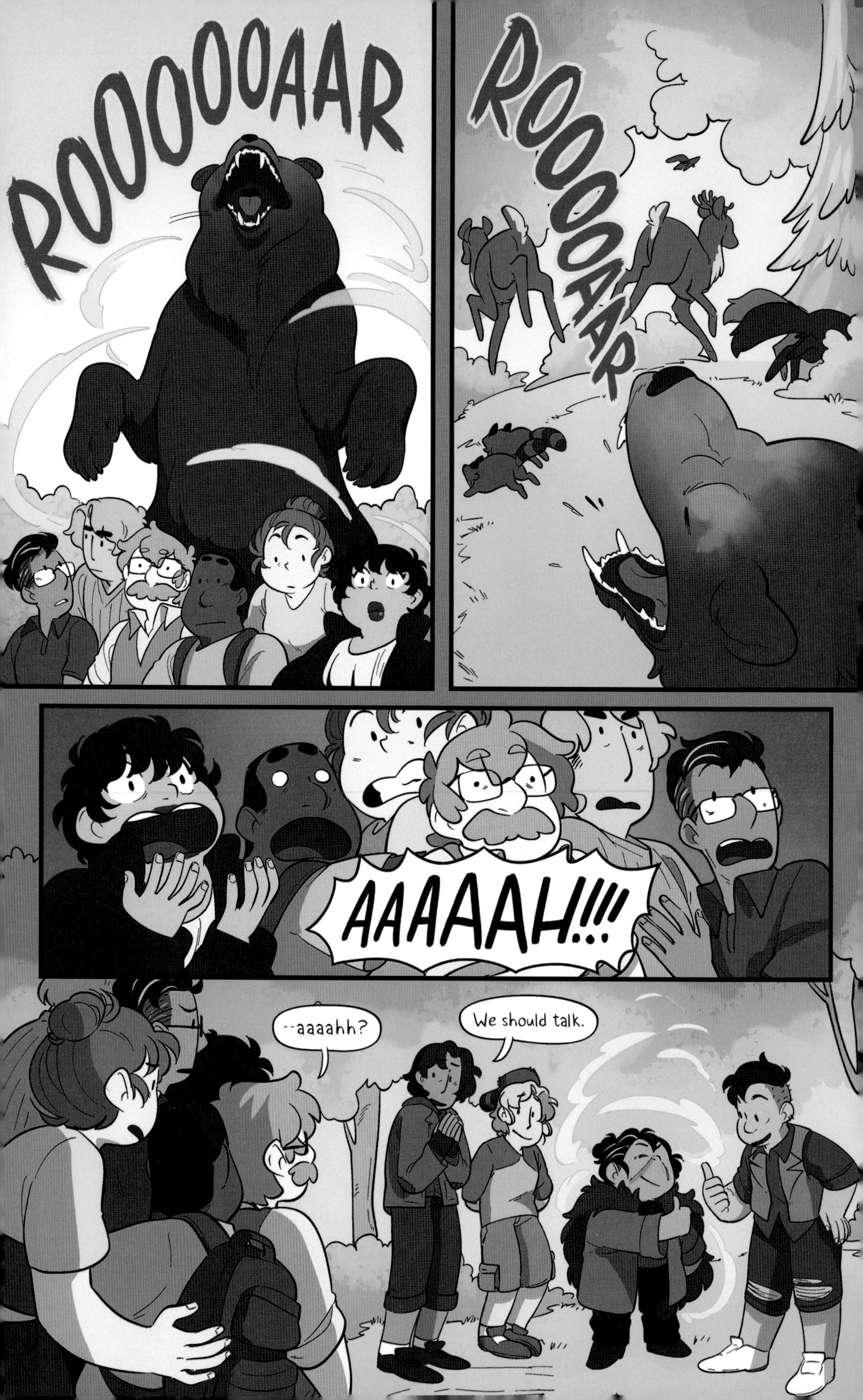
ROOOOOAAR
ROOOOOAAR
AAAAAH!!!
--aaaahh?
We should talk.

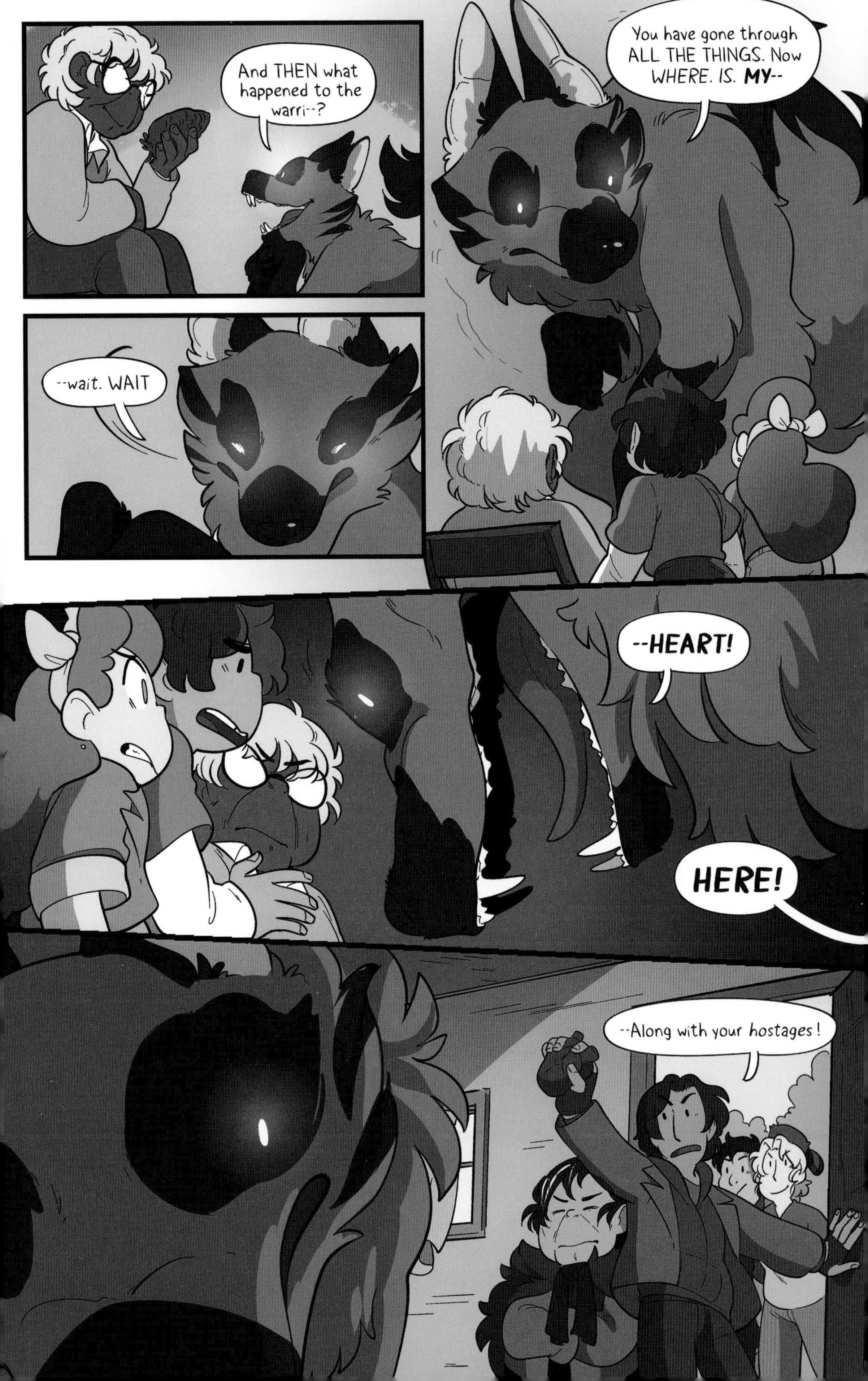
And THEN what happened to the warri--?
You have gone through ALL THE THINGS. Now WHERE. IS. MY--
--wait. WAIT
--HEART!
HERE!
--Along with your hostages!

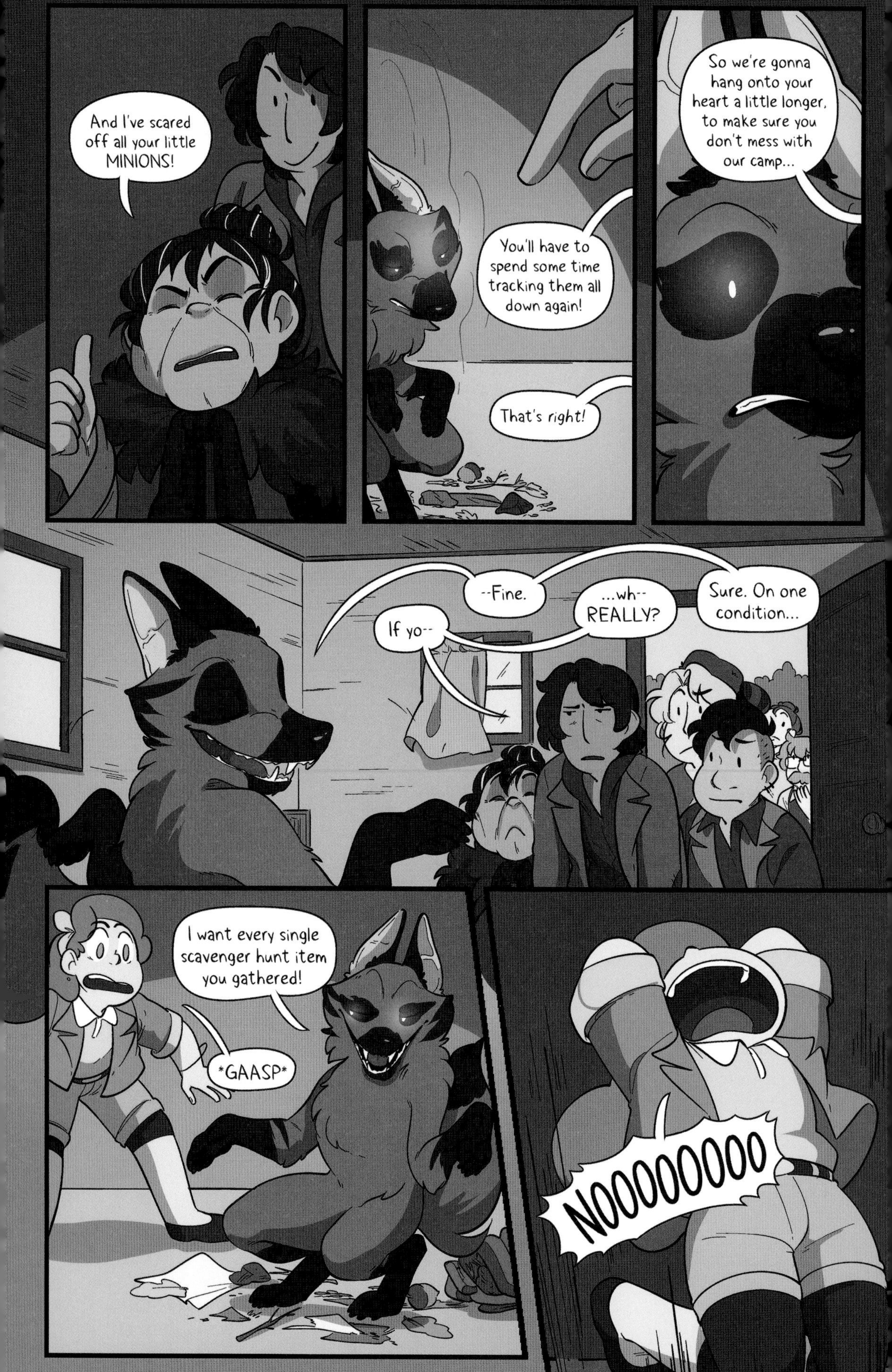
And I've scared off all your little MINIONS!
You'll have to spend some time tracking them all down again!
That's right!
So we're gonna hang onto your heart a little longer, to make sure you don't mess with our camp...
If yo--
--Fine.
...wh-- REALLY?
Sure. On one condition...
I want every single scavenger hunt item you gathered!
GAASP
NOOOOOOOO

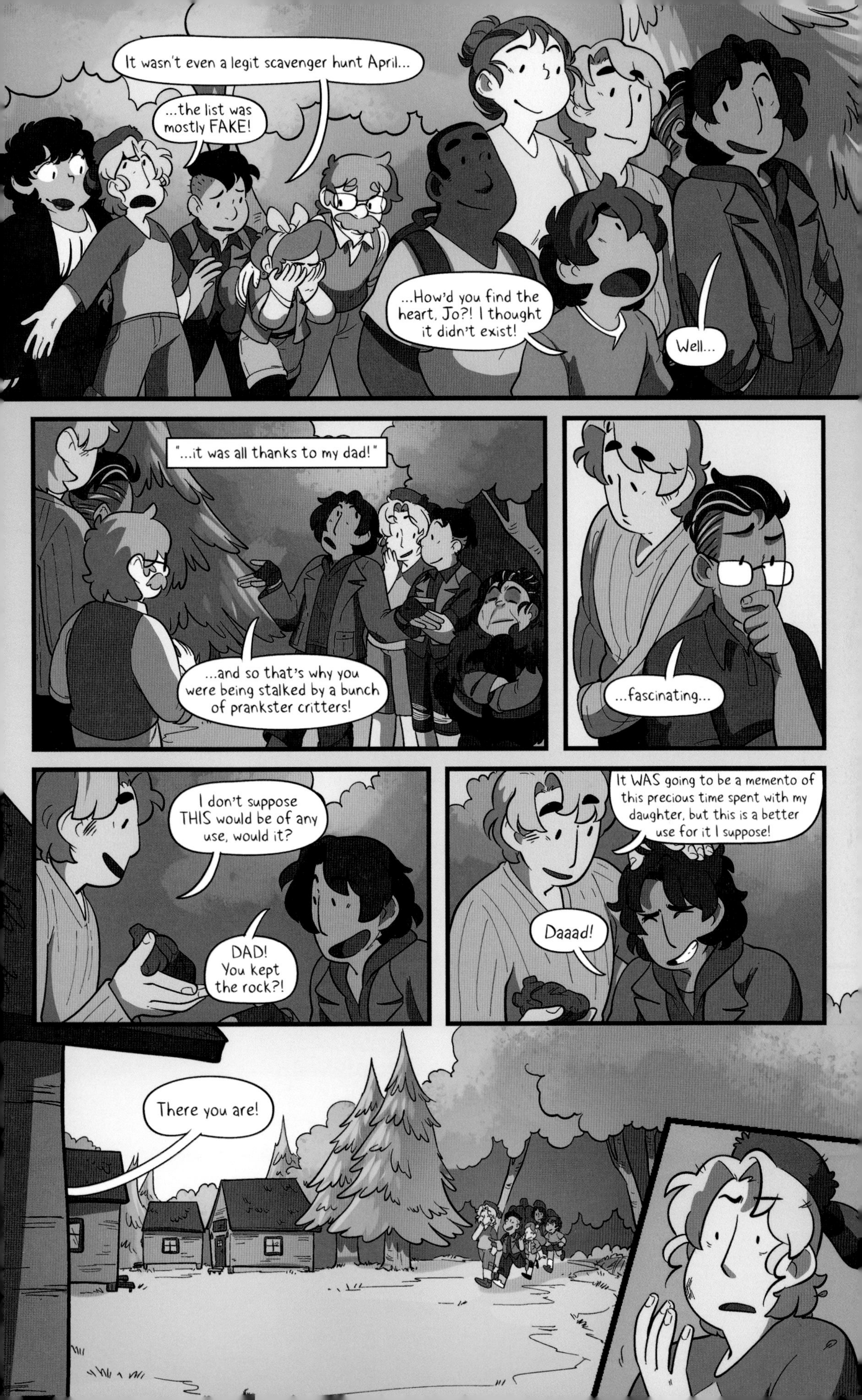
It wasn't even a legit scavenger hunt April...
...the list was mostly FAKE!
...How'd you find the heart, Jo?! I thought it didn't exist!
Well...
"...it was all thanks to my dad!"
...and so that's why you were being stalked by a bunch of prankster critters!
...fascinating...
I don't suppose THIS would be of any use, would it?
DAD! You kept the rock?!
It WAS going to be a memento of this precious time spent with my daughter, but this is a better use for it I suppose!
Daaad!
There you are!

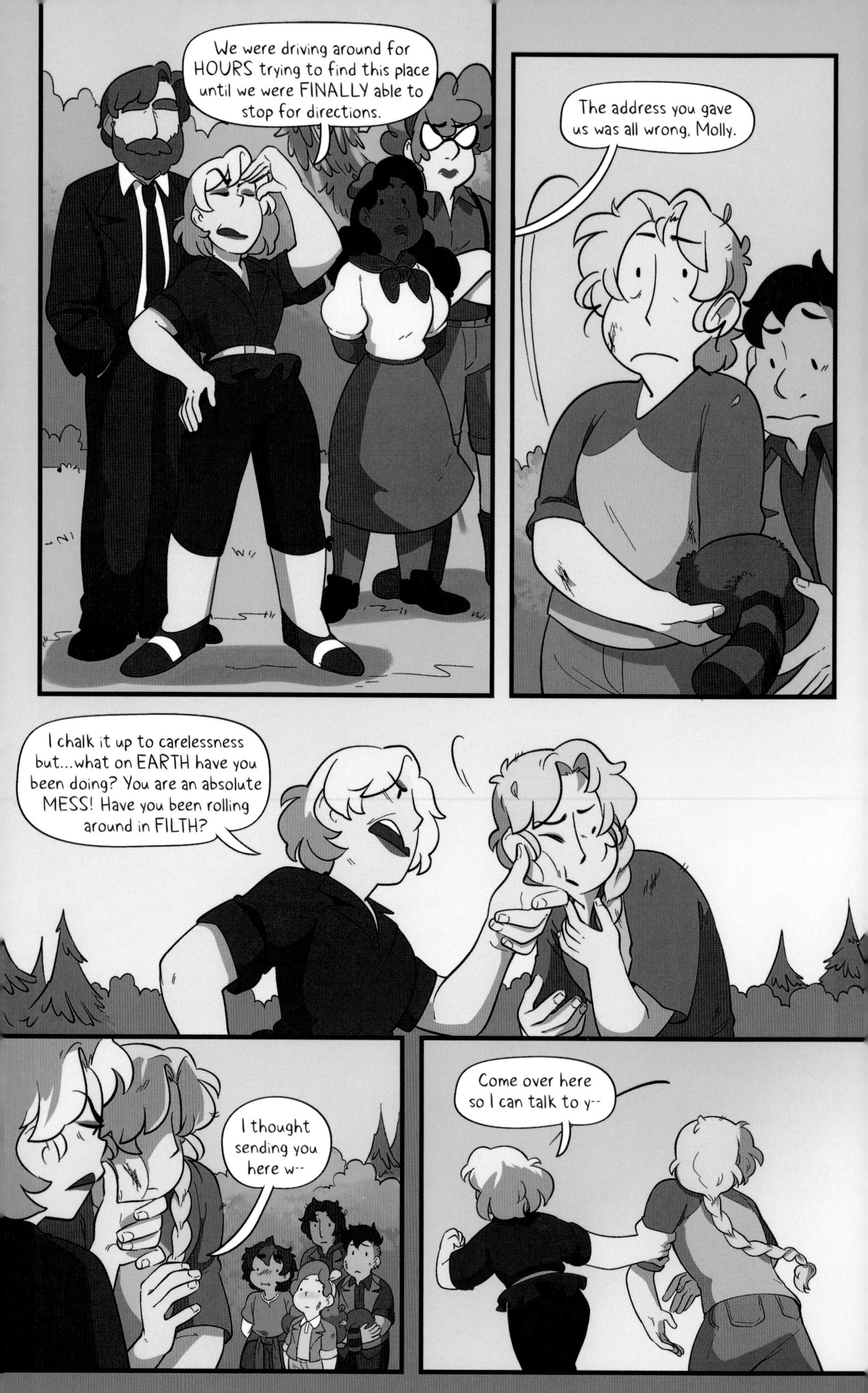
We were driving around for HOURS trying to find this place until we were FINALLY able to stop for directions.
The address you gave us was all wrong, Molly.
I chalk it up to carelessness but...what on EARTH have you been doing? You are an absolute MESS! Have you been rolling around in FILTH?
I thought sending you here w--
Come over here so I can talk to y--

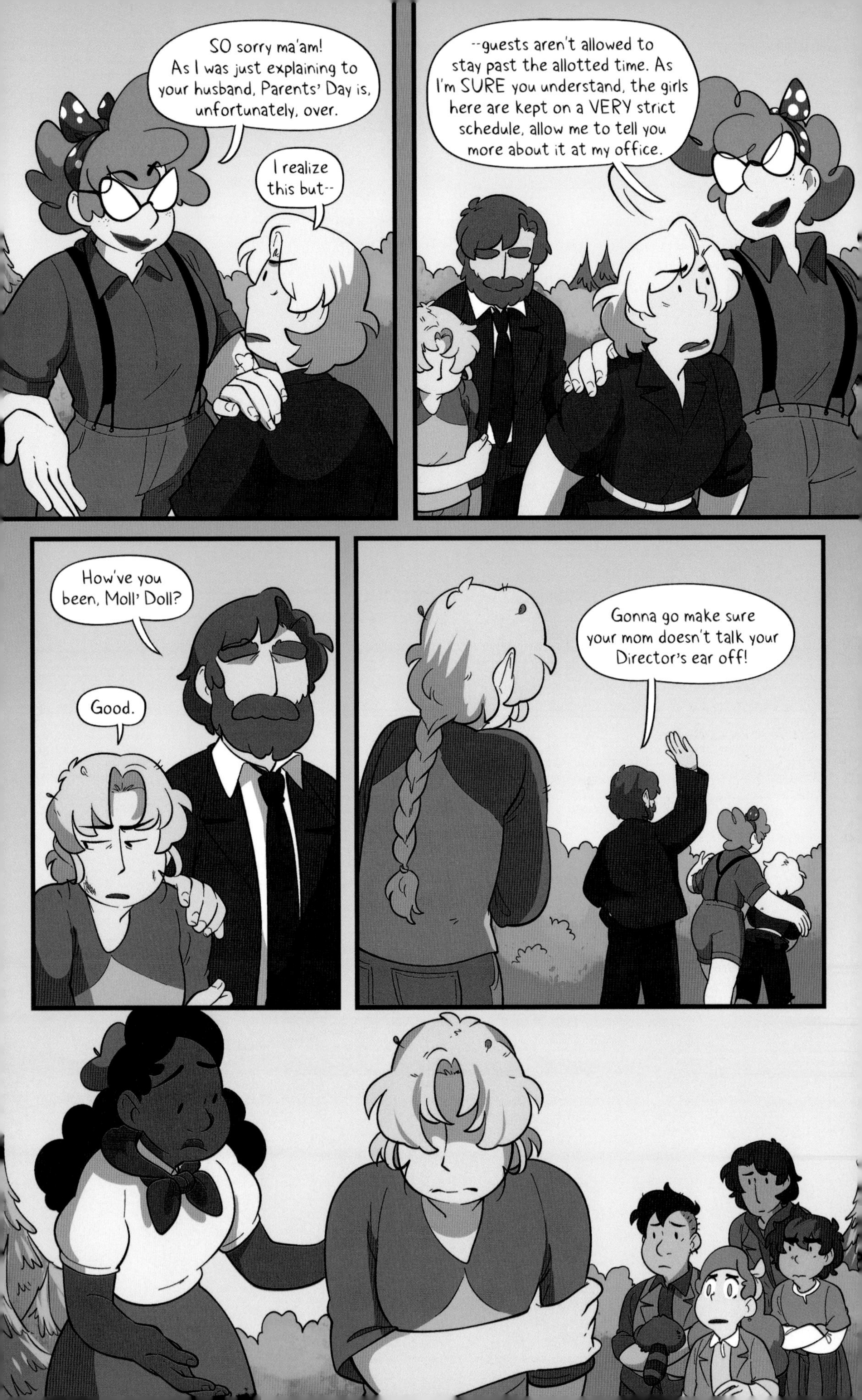
SO sorry ma'am!
As I was just explaining to your husband, Parents' Day is, unfortunately, over.
I realize this but--
--guests aren't allowed to stay past the allotted time. As I'm SURE you understand, the girls here are kept on a VERY strict schedule, allow me to tell you more about it at my office.
How've you been, Moll' Doll?
Good.
Gonna go make sure your mom doesn't talk your Director's ear off!

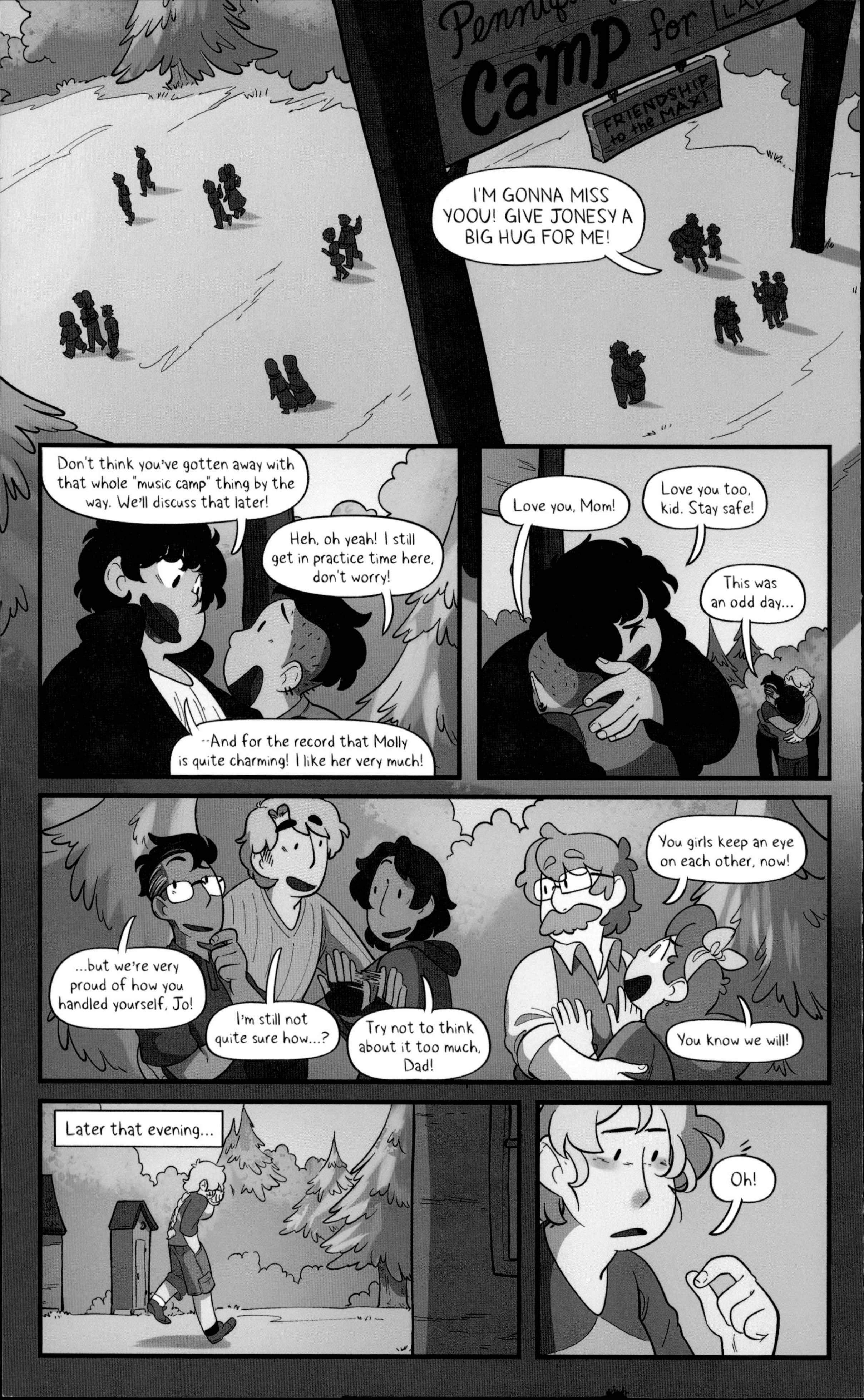
Camp for
FRIENDSHIP to the MAX!
I'M GONNA MISS YOOU! GIVE JONESY A BIG HUG FOR ME!
Don't think you've gotten away with that whole "music camp" thing by the way. We'll discuss that later!
Heh, oh yeah! I still get in practice time here, don't worry!
--And for the record that Molly is quite charming! I like her very much!
Love you, Mom!
Love you too, kid. Stay safe!
This was an odd day...
...but we're very proud of how you handled yourself, Jo!
I'm still not quite sure how...?
Try not to think about it too much, Dad!
You girls keep an eye on each other, now!
You know we will!
Later that evening...
Oh!

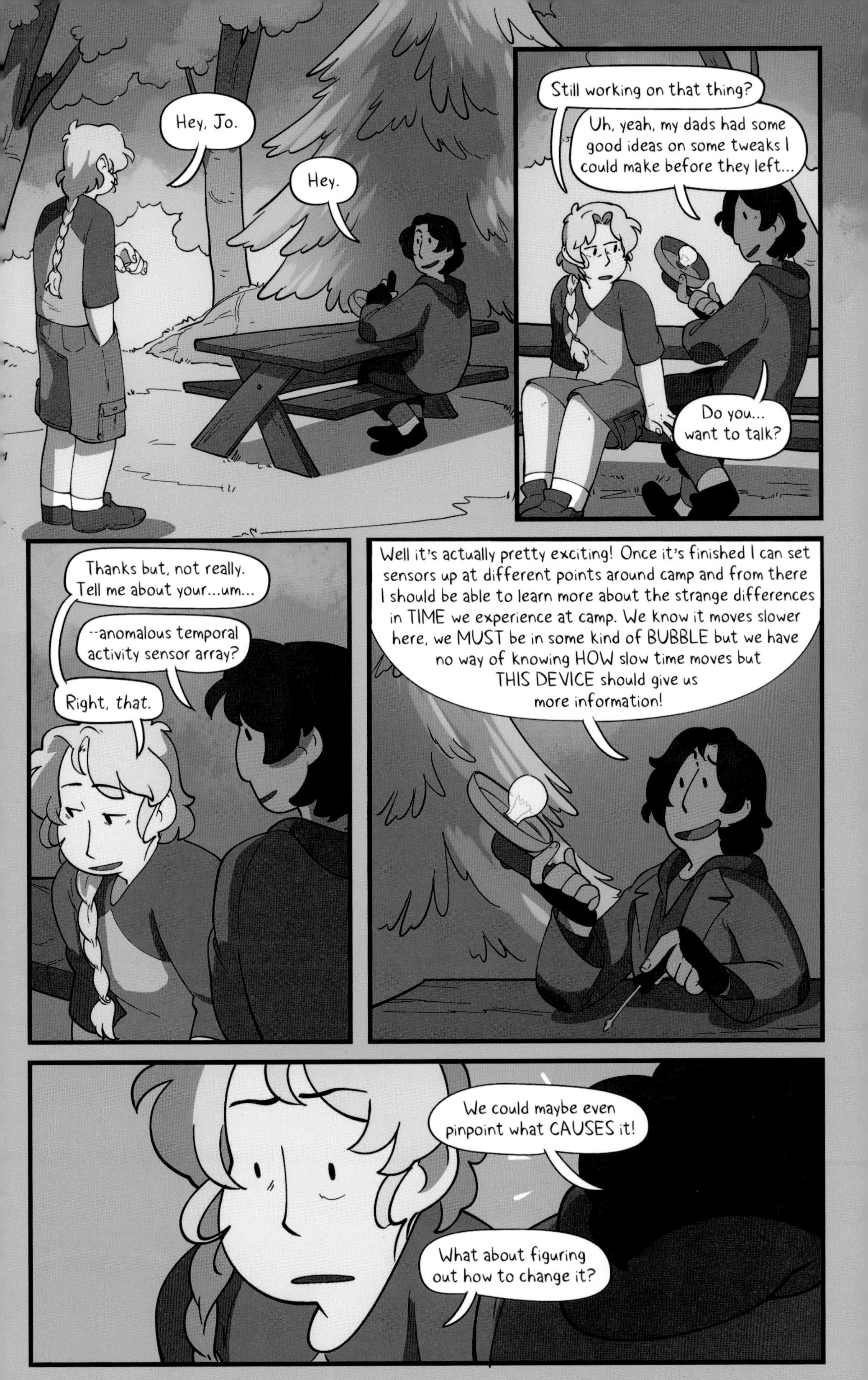
Hey, Jo.
Hey.
Still working on that thing?
Uh, yeah, my dads had some good ideas on some tweaks I could make before they left...
Do you... want to talk?
Thanks but, not really. Tell me about your...um...
--anomalous temporal activity sensor array?
Right, that.
Well it's actually pretty exciting! Once it's finished I can set sensors up at different points around camp and from there I should be able to learn more about the strange differences in TIME we experience at camp. We know it moves slower here, we MUST be in some kind of BUBBLE but we have no way of knowing HOW slow time moves but THIS DEVICE should give us more information!
We could maybe even pinpoint what CAUSES it!
What about figuring out how to change it?

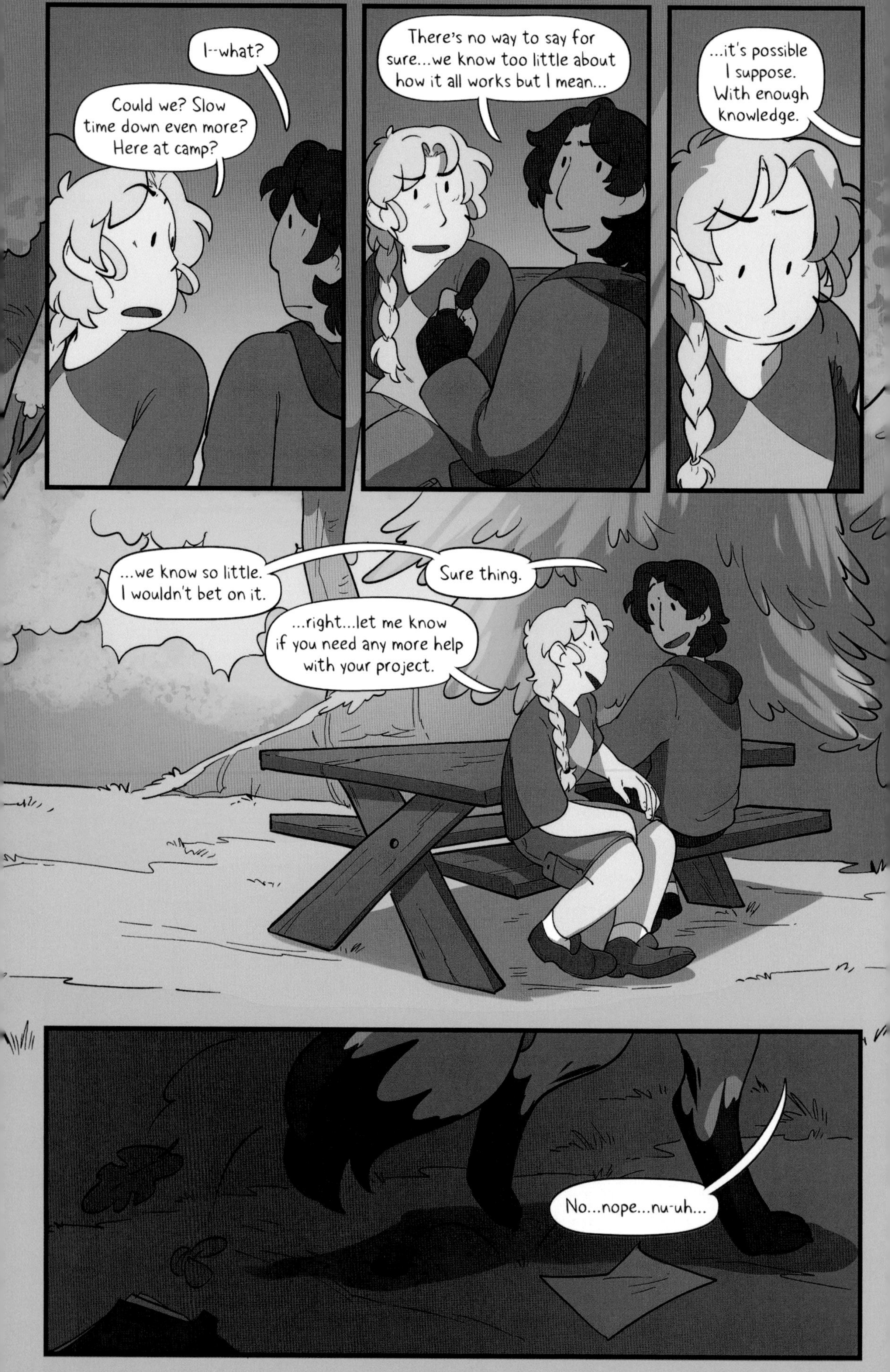
I--what?
Could we? Slow time down even more? Here at camp?
There's no way to say for sure...we know too little about how it all works but I mean...
...it's possible I suppose. With enough knowledge.
...we know so little. I wouldn't bet on it.
Sure thing.
...right...let me know if you need any more help with your project.
No...nope...nu-uh...

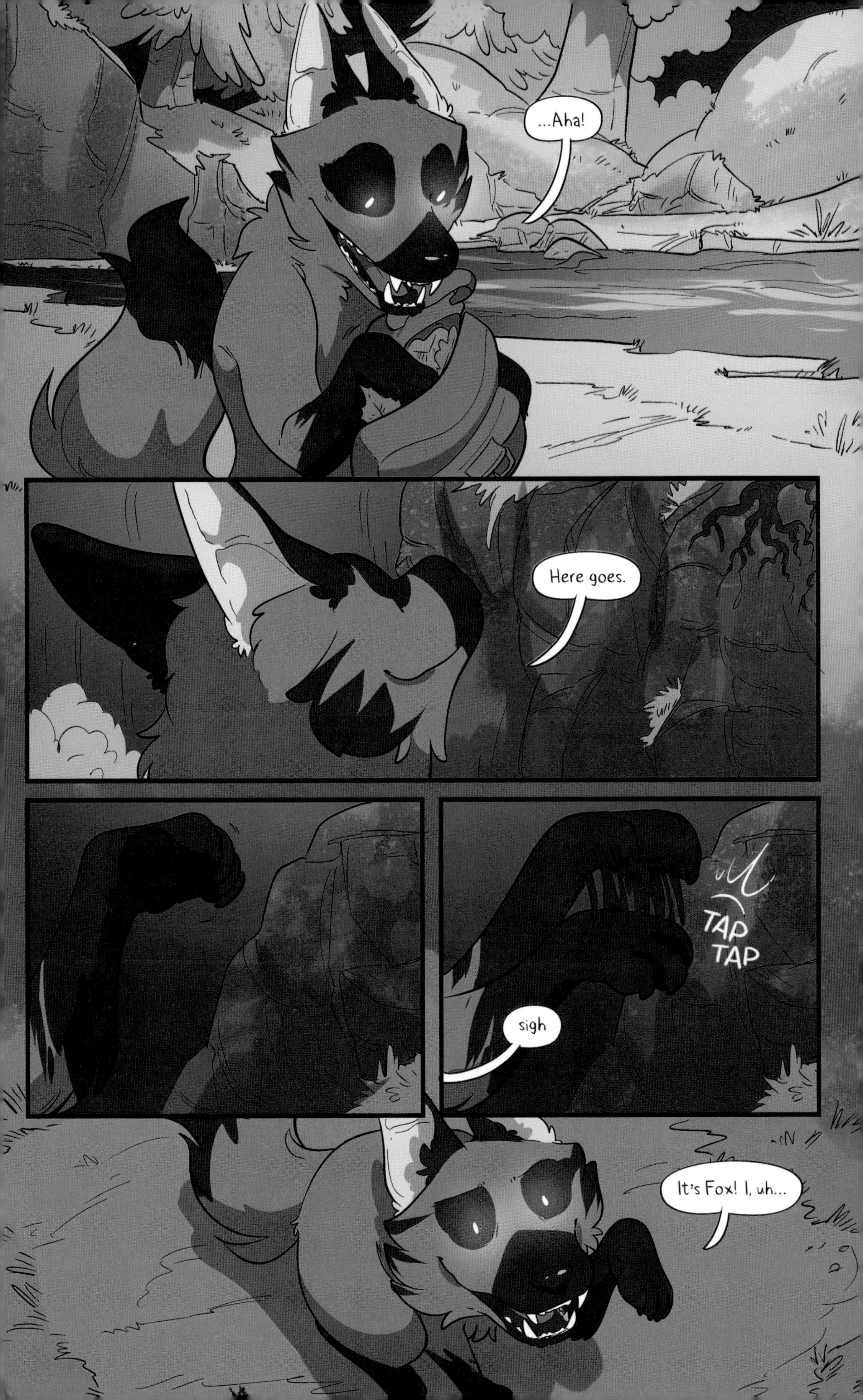
...Aha!
Here goes.
TAP
TAP
sigh
It's Fox! I, uh...

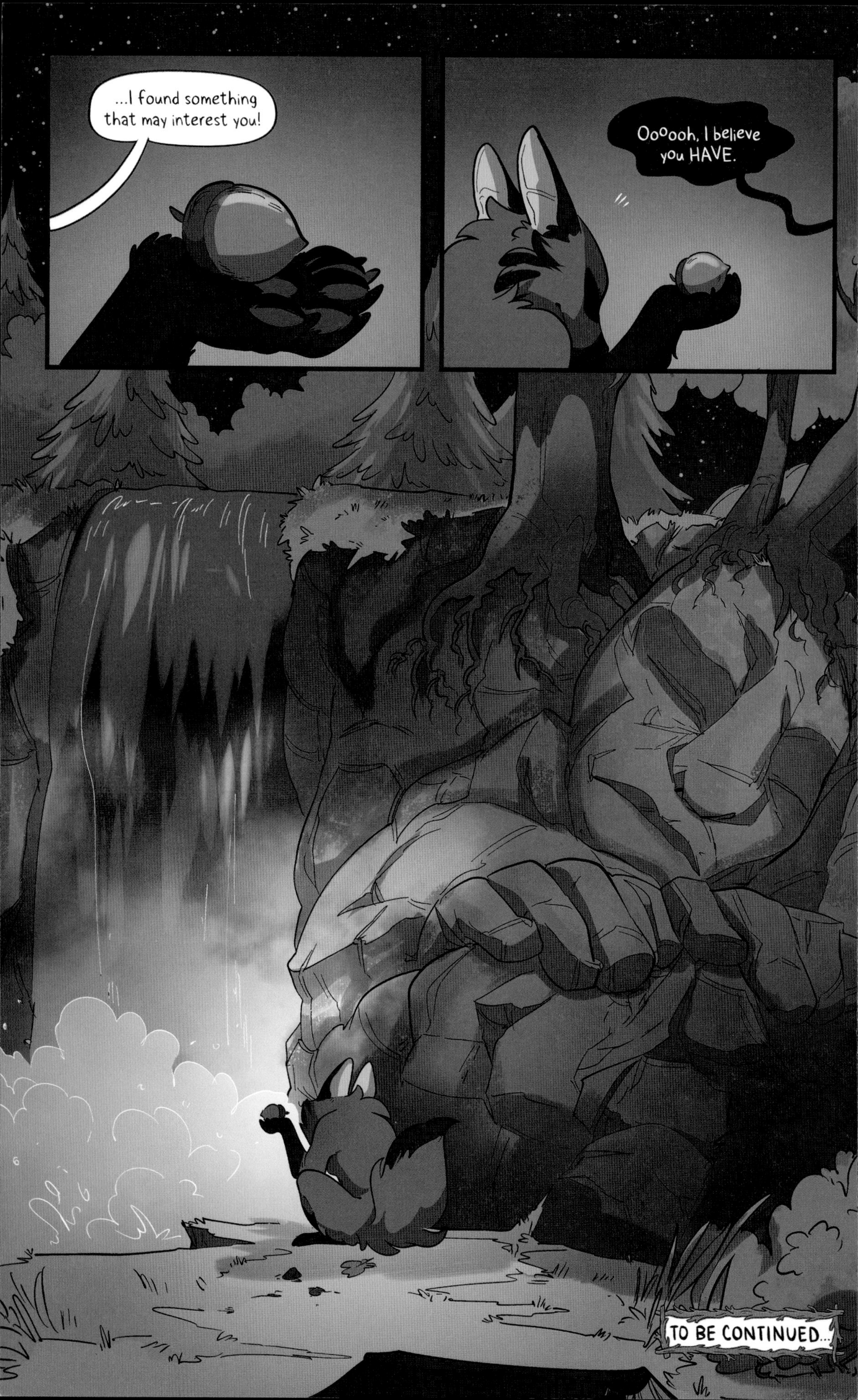
...I found something that may interest you!
Oooooh, I believe you HAVE.
TO BE CONTINUED...

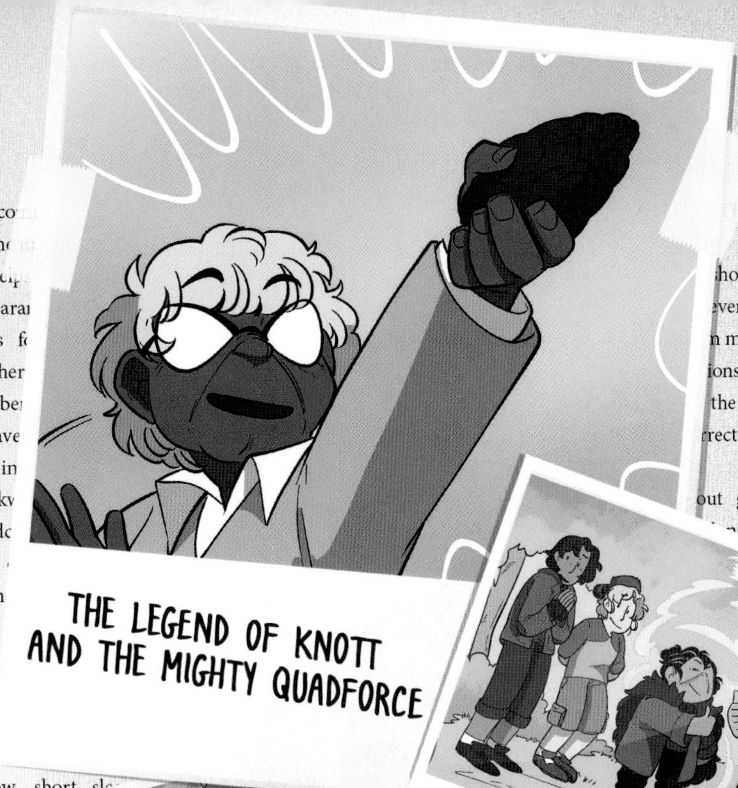
THE LEGEND OF KNOTT
AND THE MIGHTY QUADFORCE

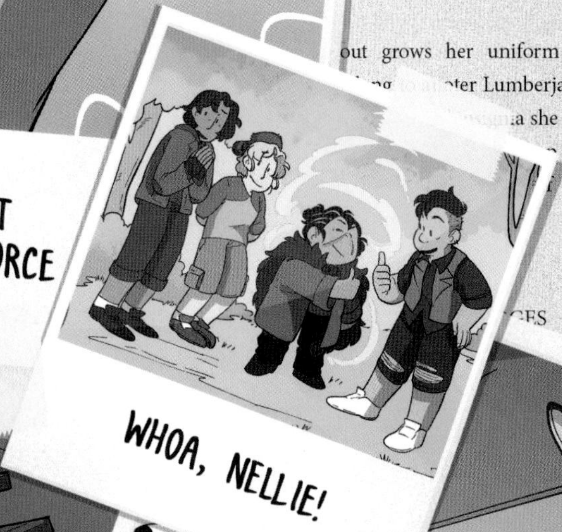
WHOA, NELLIE!

will co
Th
It he
appeara
dress f
Further
Lumbe
to have
part in
Thiskv
Hardc
have
them

...E UNIFORM

...should be worn at camp
...events when Lumberjanes
...n may also be worn at other
...ions. It should be worn as a
... the uniform dress with
...rrect shoes, and stocking or

...out grows her uniform or
...ter Lumberjane.
...a she has
... her
... her

...GES

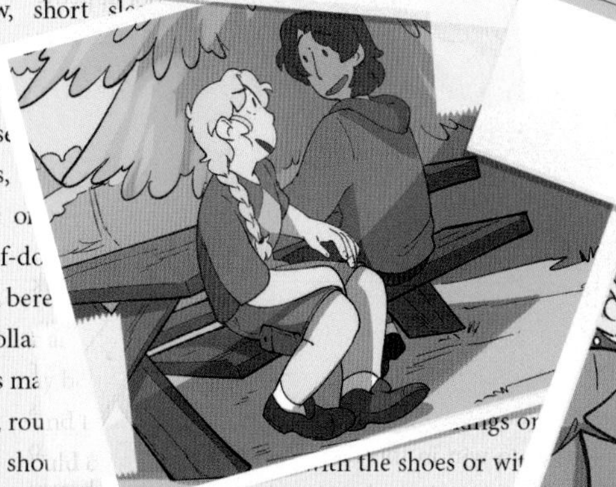

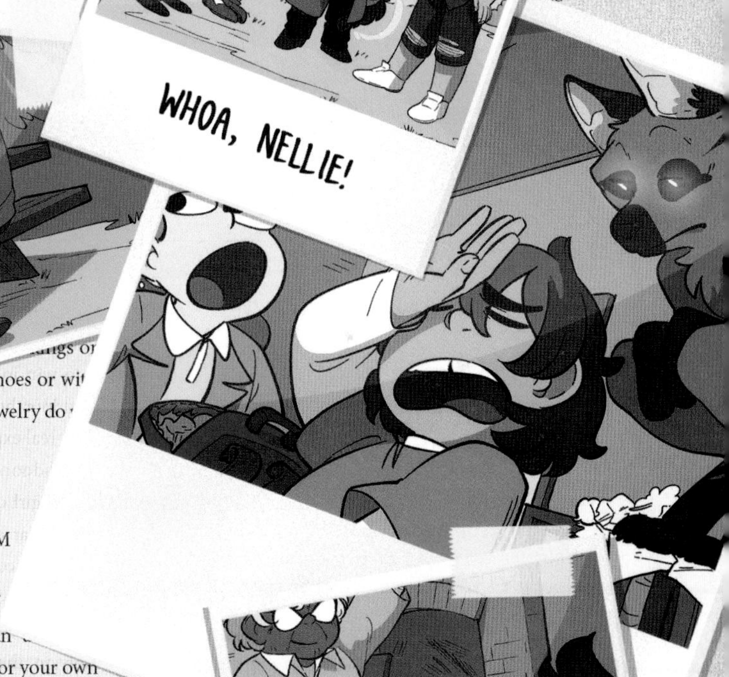

The
yellow, short sl
emb
the w
choose
slacks,
made o
out-of-dc
green bere
the colla
Shoes ma
heels, rou ... ings or
socks shou ... with the shoes or wi
the uniform. Ne...s, bracelets, or other jewelry do
belong with a Lumberjane uniform.

HOW TO WEAR THE UNIFORM

To look well in a uniform demands first of ... uniform be kept in good condition—clean ... pressed. See that the skirt is the right length for your own height and build, that the belt is adjusted to your waist, that your shoes and stockings are in keeping with the uniform, that you watch your posture and carry yourself with dignity and grace. If the beret is removed indoors, be sure that your hair is neat and kept in place with an insonspicuous clip or ribbon. When you wear a Lumberjane uniform you are identified as a member of this organization and you should be doubly careful to conduct yourself in a way that will show everyone that courtesy and thoughtfullness are part of being a Lumberjane. People are likely to judge a whole nation by the selfishness of a few individuals, to criticize a whole family because of the misconduct of one member, and to feel unkindly toward and organization because of the

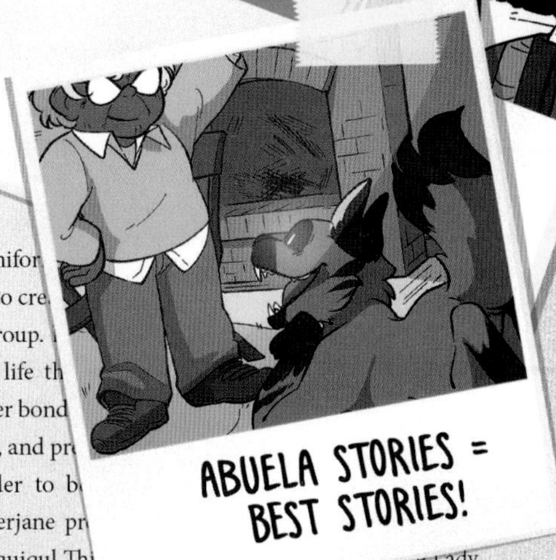
ABUELA STORIES =
BEST STORIES!

The unifor
helps to cre
in a group.
active life th
another bond
future, and pr
in order to b
Lumberjane pr
Penniquiql Thi ... Lady
Types, but m... will wish to have one. They
can either bu... uniform, or make it themselves from
materials available at the trading post.

COVER GALLERY

Lumberjanes "Out-of-Doors" Program Field

LET'S BE PRANK

"The whoopie cushion says it best."

There are quite a few Lumberjanes badges that center around jokes and humor. Whether it's the "lowest form of comedy" (the Pungeon Master Badge), or the "soul of wit" (the Brevity, Briefly Badge) we here in the Lumberjane Scouts believe that girls and women of all sorts are often uniquely and giftedly hilarious, and so we take pride in encouraging this valuable skill set, in all its many forms.

And even if your tight five is more of a loose ten, laughter will always be one of the most important activities we take part in, both at camp and in life. When we share a jape or a goof, we open ourselves up and allow new acquaintances to take the chance to know us better — to laugh with us, and in doing so, to take that first welcoming step toward bridging the gap between us. A joke can help you to find a new friend in a vast crowd of strangers, and it can also help you to remind the people closest to you of all the love and happiness you've shared. And even when you are on your own, laughter can help you both to brighten your good days, and get through the bad ones. So learn to see the humor around

you every day, and to let go and laugh as loud and a long as you like — let your glee echo through the trees, and fly high above the world in your elation.

You might find that what really gets your funny bone is sketch work, or improv. Maybe you'd like to write a comical essay, or create absurdist art, or compose parodic music. Or perhaps you'd like to look into the practical joke. Everyone's senses of humor are different, so explore what makes you laugh and take joy in it!

As with other humor-related badges, the art of the prank requires much work and dedication to master. A good prank should cause surprise and befuddlement. It should take people aback and make them guffaw with delight once the game becomes clear to them, but it should not frighten people or cause undue distress. It is easy to be funny and unkind, sometimes — particularly within the world of the prank — but it is far better to be funny and loving, although it may take more work, and more particular tailoring to the friend who you are trying to play your prank on.

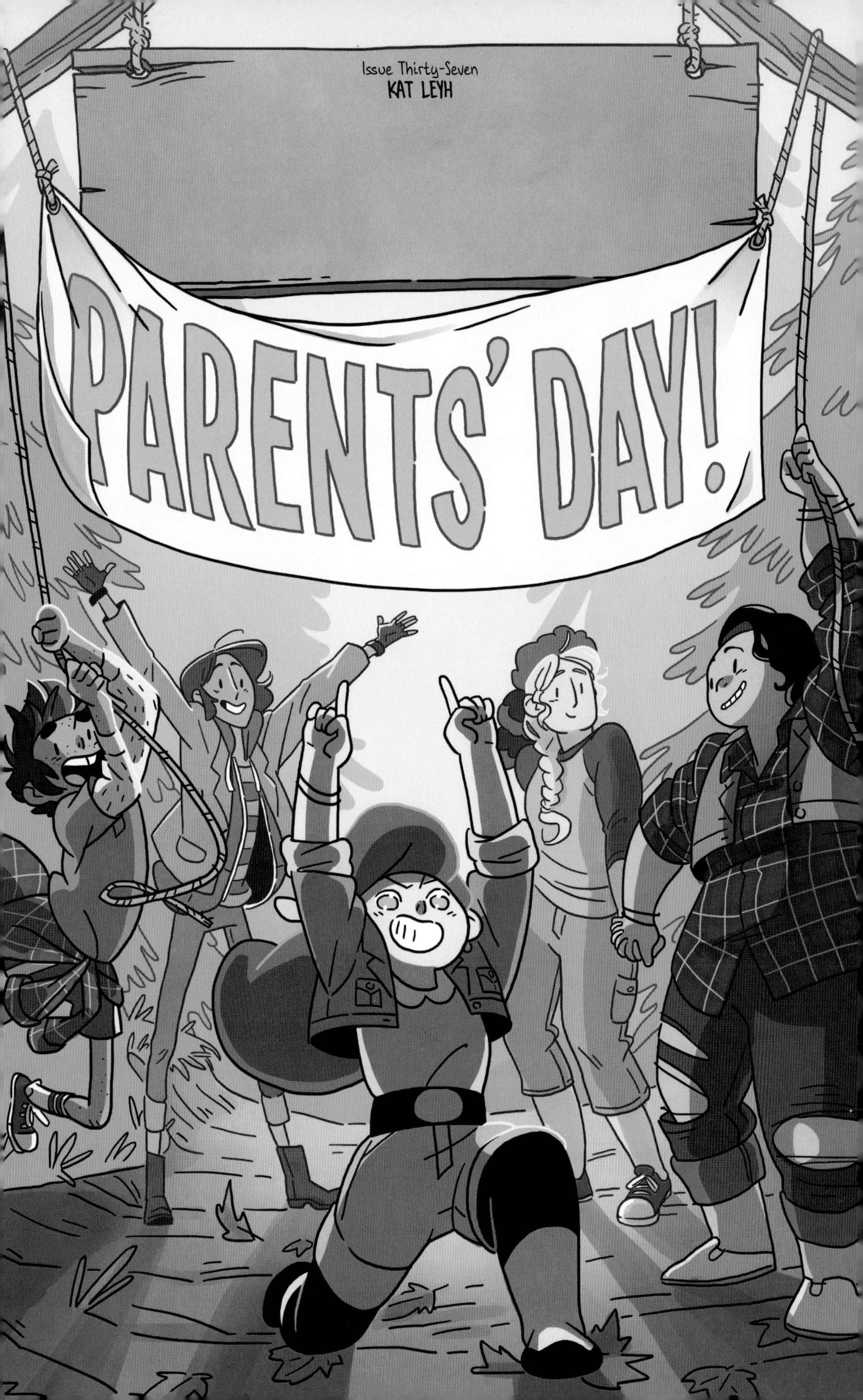
Issue Thirty-Seven
KAT LEYH
PARENTS' DAY!

Issue Thirty-Seven Subscription
AYME SOTUYO

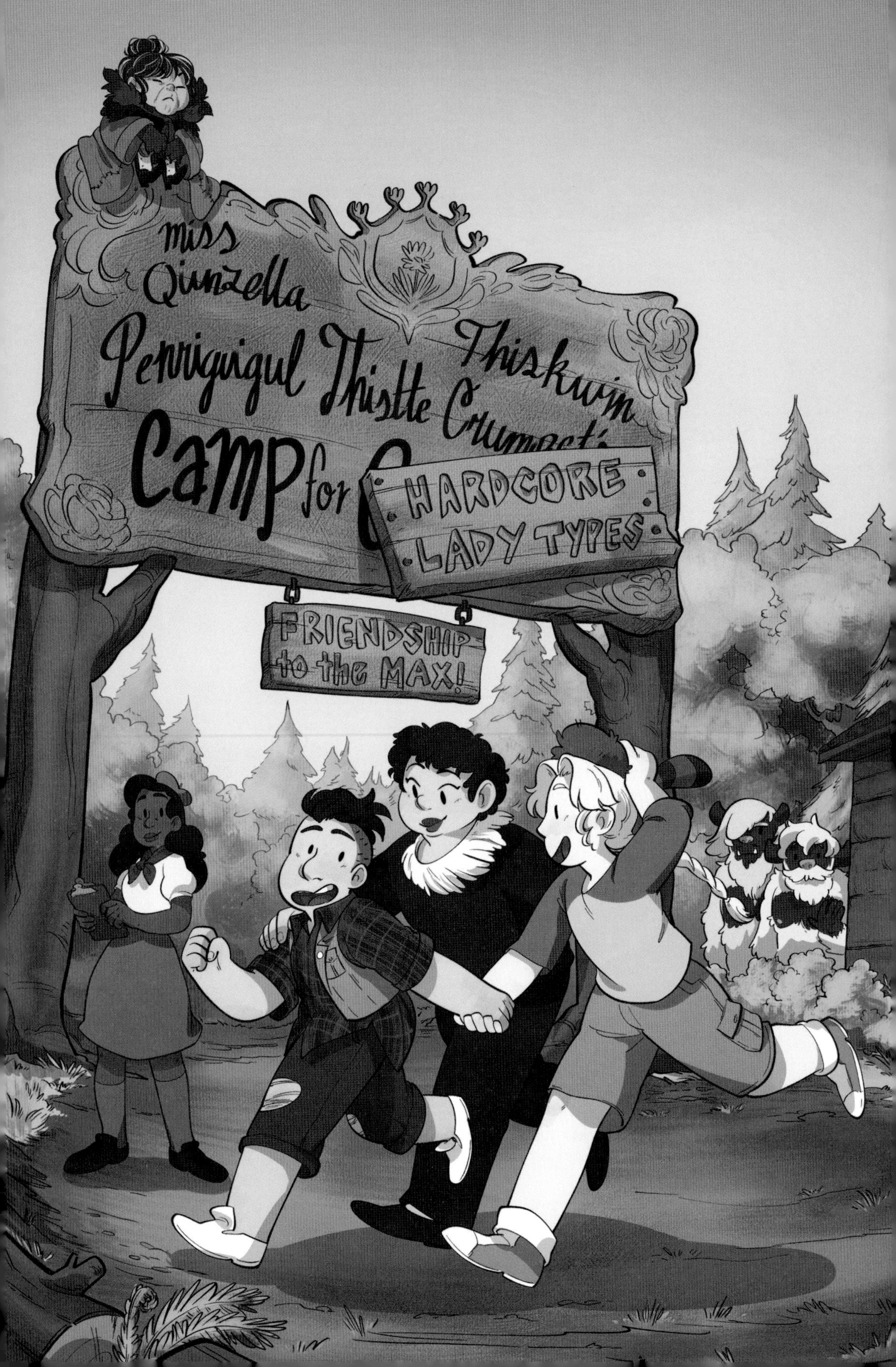

miss Qiunzella
Penniquiqul Thistle
Thiskwin
Crumpet's
Camp for
HARDCORE LADY TYPES
FRIENDSHIP to the MAX!

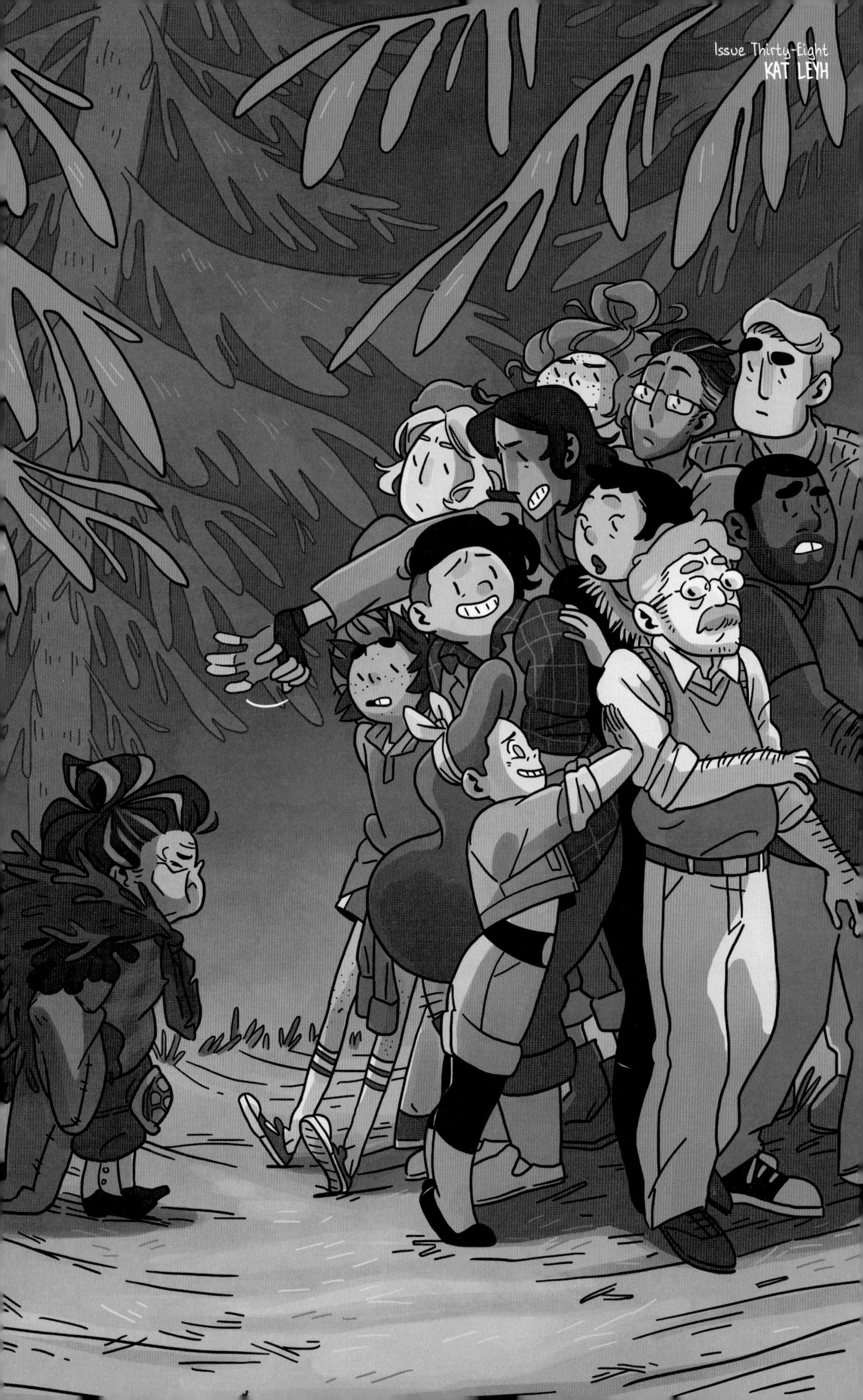
Issue Thirty-Eight
KAT LEYH

Issue Thirty-Eight Subscription
AYME SOTUYO

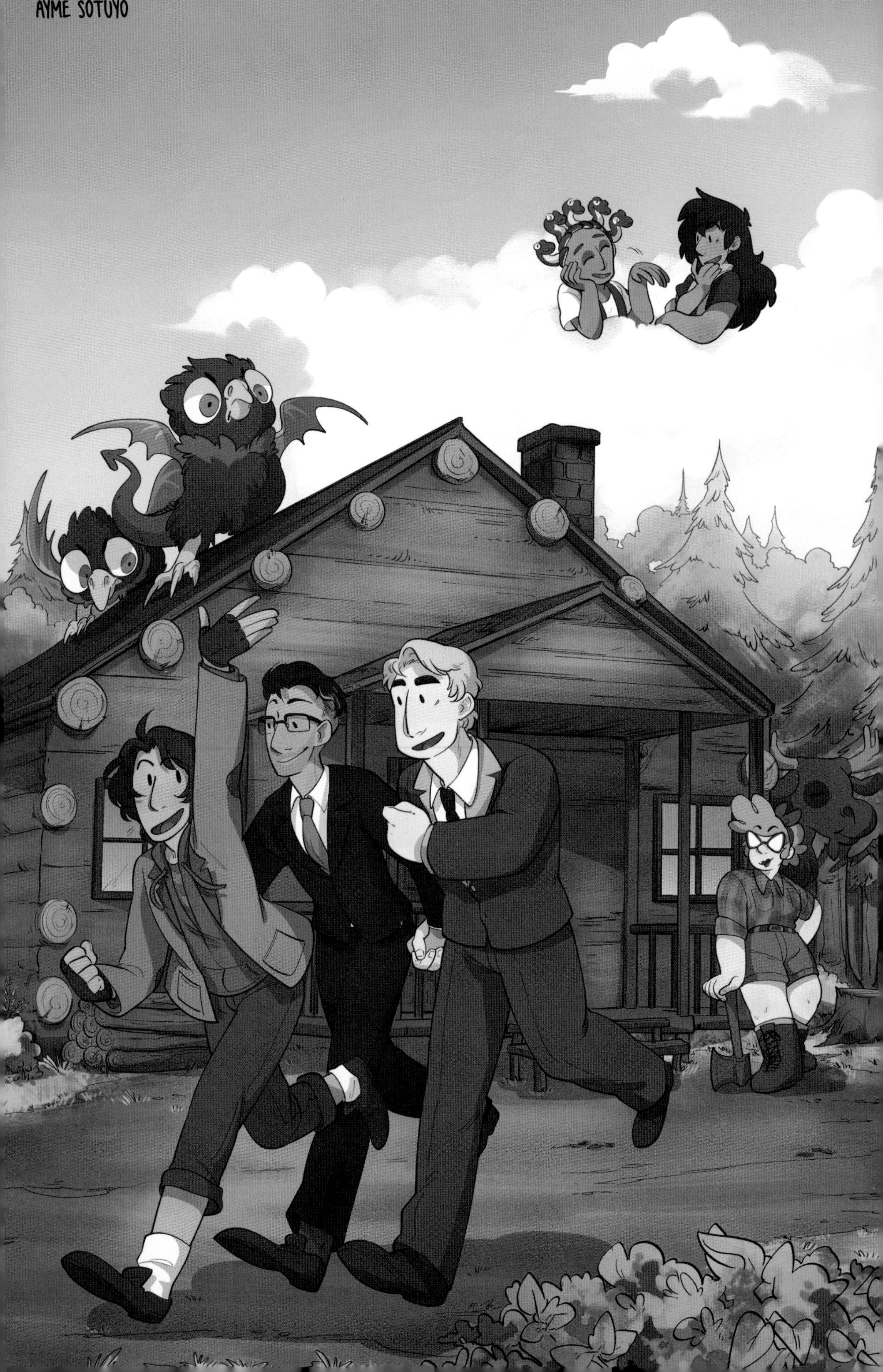

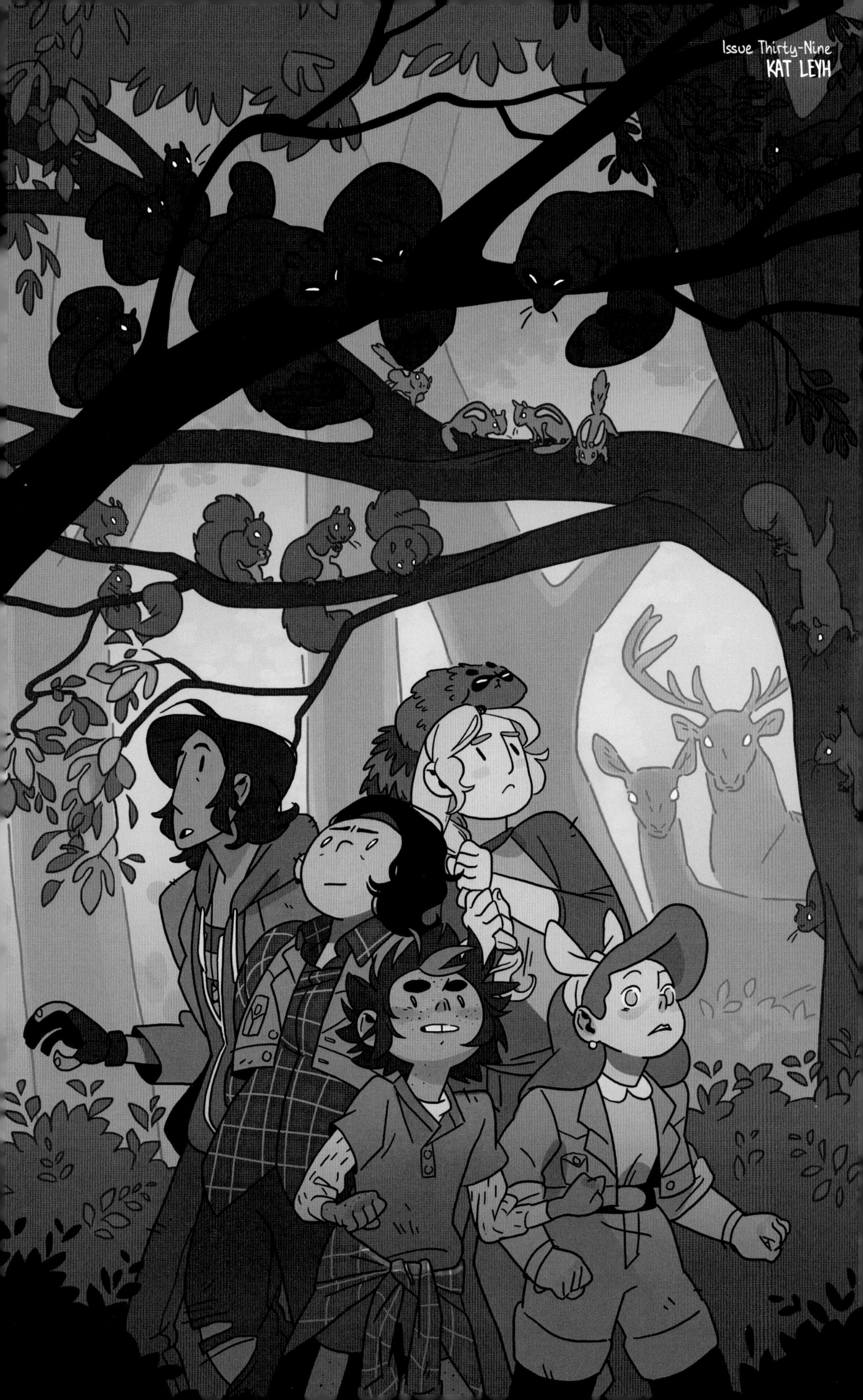
Issue Thirty-Nine
KAT LEYH

Issue Thirty-Nine Subscription
AYME SOTUYO

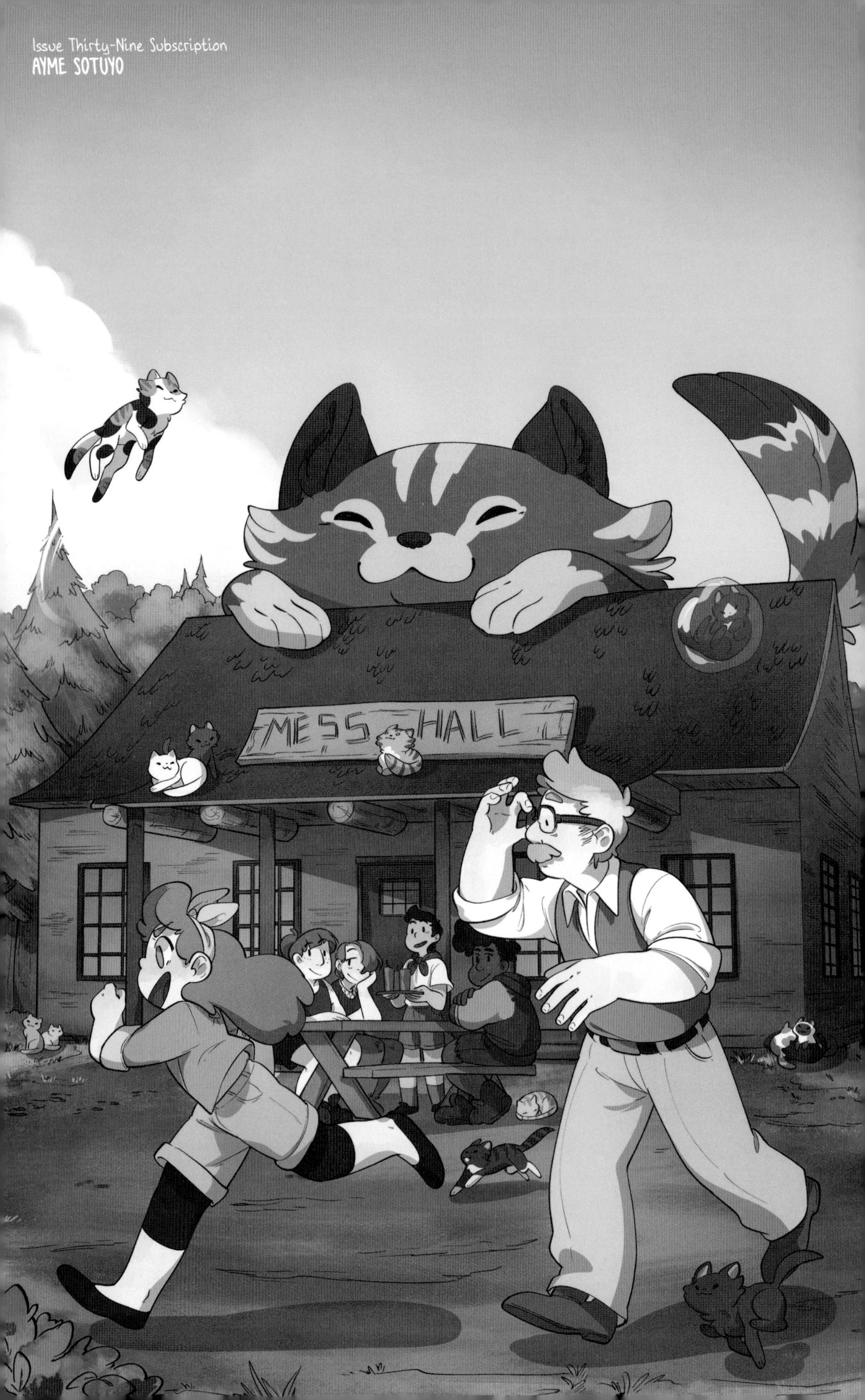
MESS HALL

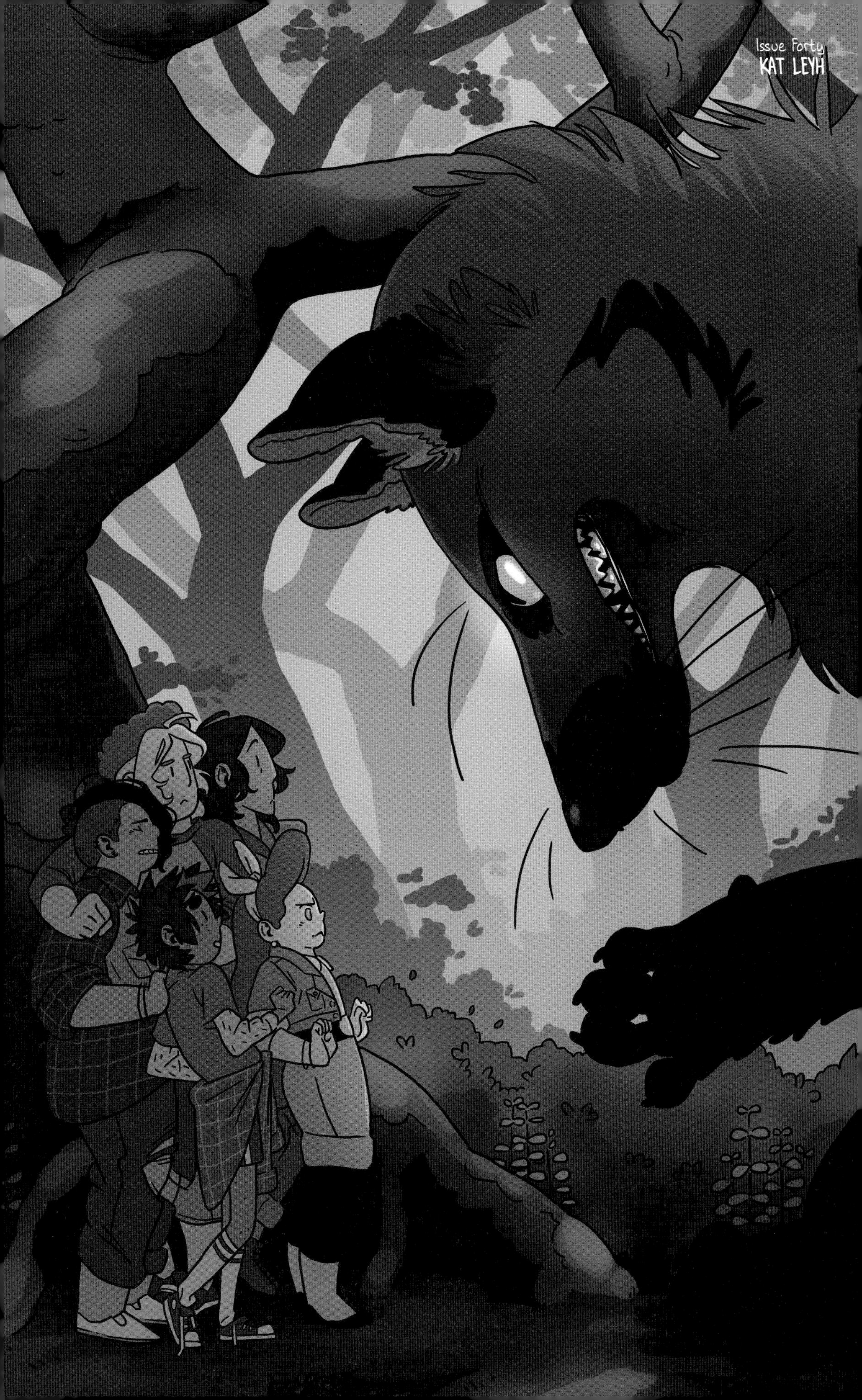
Issue Forty
KAT LEYH

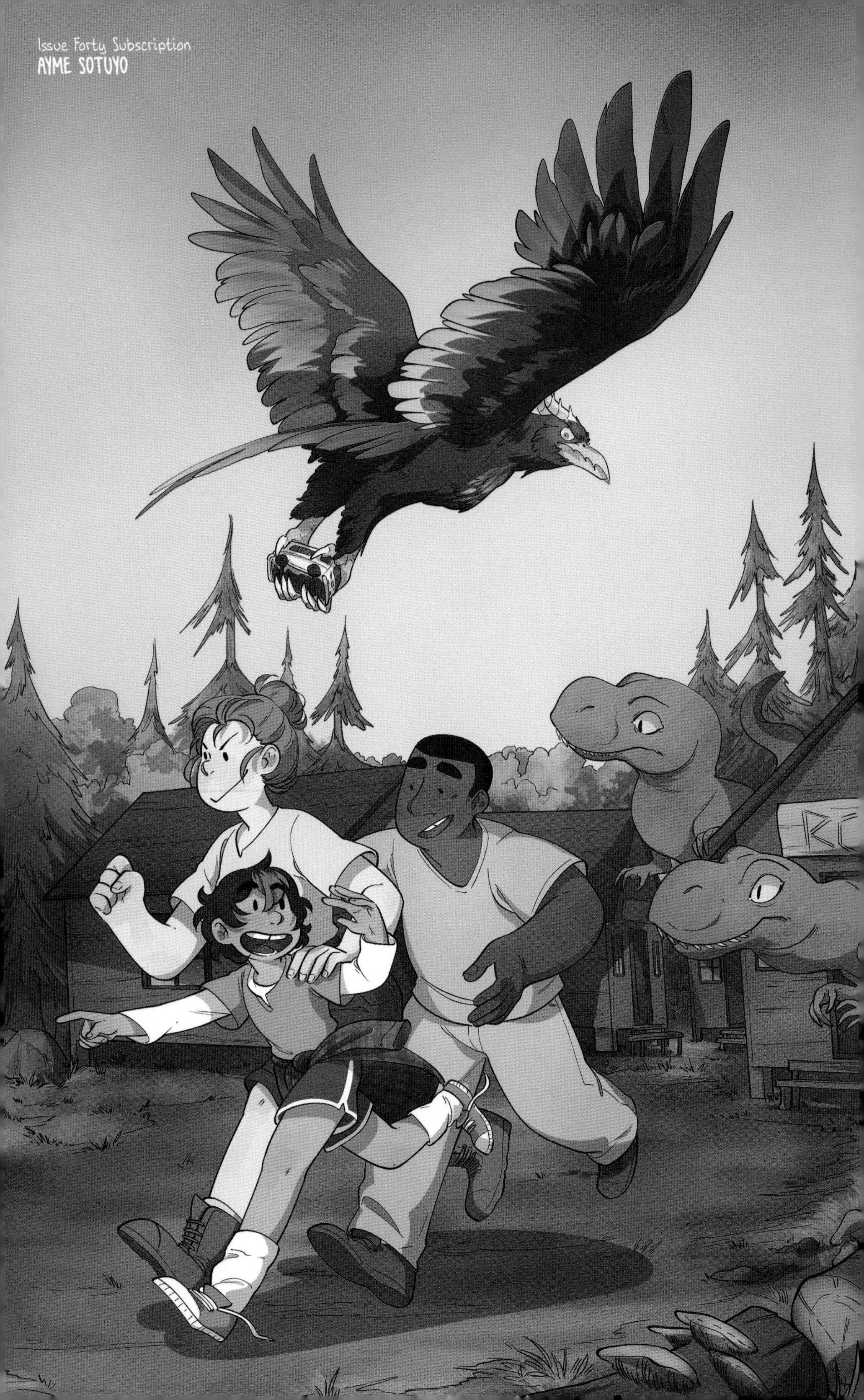

Issue Forty Subscription
AYME SOTUYO